Kathi ♡ **P9-CBJ-834**

1-76

PRAISE FOR SHERYL LYNN

ABOUT THE AUTHOR

Sheryl Lynn lives in a Colorado pine forest with a menagerie that includes a cat, two hairy dogs, two teenagers and a retired sergeant major. When in need of inspiration, she need look no further than the ever-changing views of Pikes Peak, or needs only to smell the butterscotch scent of warm ponderosa pine bark and watch the antics of dozens of resident jays begging for peanuts on her back deck. Nature is a good reminder that all things change and all hurts eventually heal.

Books by Sheryl Lynn

HARLEQUIN INTRIGUE

Bulletproof Heart
Sheryl Lynn

Harlequin Books

TORONTO • NEW YORK • LONDON
AMSTERDAM • PARIS • SYDNEY • HAMBURG
STOCKHOLM • ATHENS • TOKYO • MILAN
MADRID • WARSAW • BUDAPEST • AUCKLAND

This one is for the girls: Maggie, Barbara, Emily, Jane, Ruth, Yvonne and Pamela. Thanks.

ISBN 0-373-22385-4

BULLETPROOF HEART

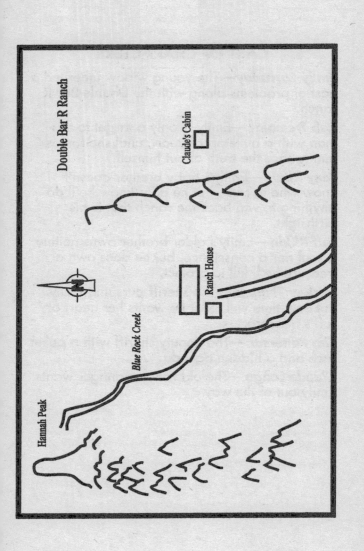

CAST OF CHARACTERS

Emily Farraday—The young widow inherited a host of problems along with the Double Bar R ranch.

Reb Tremaine—Emily is only a target to this man with a bulletproof heart, until she forces him to face the truth about himself.

Joey Rifkin—Emily's baby brother doesn't know who to trust, but he does know he'll do anything to win back the ranch that is his birthright.

Tuff Rifkin—Emily's older brother owns neither a soul nor a conscience, but he does own a treasure he'll kill to protect.

Mickey Thigpen—The sheriff pursuing Emily. But only time will tell if he wants her heart or Tuff's treasure.

Tim Patterson—The deputy sheriff with a poker face and a hidden agenda.

Claude Longo—The old ranch manager wants Emily out of the way.

Chapter One

Emily Farraday held on tightly to the saddle horn as the roan mare picked her way through the forest. Late-day sunlight flirted through the pine trees, forming pockets of heat. She felt tired from a long day of cooking meals in an overheated kitchen, feeding animals in a hot barn, weeding the garden under a blistering sun and riding through the still, dry forest.

She scratched at a bug bite on the back of her neck, and felt a sticky patch on a tendril of hair. She patted upward until she found the source, a big glob of pine sap clinging to her cap, dripping into her hair.

Lifting her gaze, she could see Hannah Peak over the treetops. Hannah Peak was a runt in the midst of the towering Rockies, an outcrop of bald granite sticking out of a thatch of oak tangles like a thumb hitching a ride. Hannah maintained her own brand of majesty, though, including what appeared to be a supercilious smile carved into craggy cliffs. Emily imagined the smirk telling her not only was she sticky and smelly, but she was crazy, too.

Everyone else was right: Tuff hadn't murdered a man, and he hadn't buried the corpse anywhere on the Double Bar R Ranch.

A deerfly landed on her left arm. She swatted at it and missed. The mare gave a little start on the slippery pine straw and flicked her ears. Emily patted the horse's neck.

"It's okay, Strawberry. We're finished for the day. Let's just go on home, nice and easy. Don't kill me or smash me against a tree, okay?"

Finished for the day…Emily knew tomorrow when her chores were done she'd ride out again to poke around the rough terrain in search of a grave. She was sure her older brother had murdered a man and somehow, someway she'd prove it. Even if it meant she searched the entire high-country ranch inch by rocky inch.

The path dropped sharply. Emily gave the mare her head to find a way down the hillside. Ears forward, Strawberry stepped up the pace, eager to reach her corral. Rustling in the scrub oak forewarned Copper's appearance. The mutt bounded into view, his thick coat bristling with bits of leaves, pine needles and bark.

Emily hoped Copper would lead her to the body. He chased squirrels instead, and incited ruckuses among the Steller's jays and crows. He gave Emily a mindlessly happy grin as he trotted past. His jaunty attitude said, *Yep, another fine day romping in the forest. Sure beats hanging around the house. Great fun, old girl.*

Emily managed a smile. Dumb dog.

She left the forest. A scratchy-grass meadow spread lazily across the valley, cut through by the creek and stands of cottonwoods. Yuccas jutted from the ground like bristly candles, brown pods clinging to spikes amid the nests of dagger-shaped leaves. Only the hardy buffalo grass was green; the other alpine grasses had faded to tan and beige and gold under the relentless August sun.

The roan mare's hooves rang dully against the hard pack, and the jarring trot sent needles of fire up Emily's spine. Rear end aching, gritting her teeth, Emily rose in the stirrups and clung to the saddle horn.

She wished she were back in Kansas City, without a horse within ten miles of her.

The house and outbuildings of the Double Bar R sprawling along the banks of Blue Rock Creek were a welcome sight for her tired eyes. The mare broke into a canter, aiming directly for the wide barn doorway. At reaching the shallow pool formed by tractors crossing the creek, she hit the water at a gallop, spraying rooster tails along her sides. Drops splashed Emily's legs, soaking through her jeans.

Emily spotted a Jeep parked near the house. Red road dust clouded its white finish. She jerked the reins, and the mare stumbled, fighting the bit. Hauling the horse to a complete stop, Emily fixed her gaze on the Jeep's rear license plate. She recognized the bright yellow tag as a New Mexico issue.

The ranch was too far into the Colorado Rockies and too far from the main road for casual visitors. She racked her brain for anyone she knew from New Mexico, but she drew a blank. Ever since her grandfather's death, creditors and con artists had come crawling from beneath their rocks. Strange vehicles on the property filled her with dread.

The mare shuffled restlessly and tossed her head, rattling the bridle. Emily tugged the reins and applied her heels to the mare's ribs, but Strawberry balked, straining toward the barn. Emily thrummed her heels, clucked her tongue and hauled the reins. Strawberry finally groaned and turned for the house, plodding as if every step agonized her.

Emily spotted a man on the porch. With one thumb hooked in his jeans pocket, he leaned his shoulder against a post and watched her approach. His attitude befitted a conquering general surveying his newly won domain.

She stopped the horse at the base of the porch steps, and sized up the stranger. He stood well over six feet tall, lean and leggy, with an air of nonchalant grace. His eyes, framed by thick black eyebrows, were a startling bright blue. He met her gaze as boldly as if she were for sale and he was a buyer with cash in his pocket.

A hot pulse thumped low in her midsection. It startled her. Her mouth felt too wet, and she swallowed hard. She gave the bill of her cap a sharp tug, bringing herself back to earth. Her husband had been dead more than a year, but she wasn't ready to finish mourning. She certainly wasn't ready to look at another man as a potential sexual partner.

Trying to mirror his casual air, she looked over his clothes. His grimy blue jeans had seen better days, and the sleeves of a light blue T-shirt strained around muscular arms. No watch or rings, not even a showy belt buckle. His yellow leather work boots appeared to have a few miles on them. Nothing razzle-dazzle or remarkable about him, except for his blue, blue eyes. Her suspiciousness eased. "May I help you?" she asked.

His gaze swept her from head to toe, but it offered no clue as to what he thought. "Depends," he said. "What are you offering?"

His voice was silk and promises. Instinctively her back straightened. Stupid vanity made her regret that she was wearing filthy clothing and that her hair was crammed messily under a pine-sap-stained cap. Strawberry shook her head and stamped a hoof. Emily loosened the reins.

Snappy retorts failed her completely.

Hinges squeaked as her younger brother used his shoulder to push open the screened door. Joey carried two Coors beer bottles by the neck, and held a jar of butterscotch-oatmeal cookies tucked under one arm. At seeing her, he lowered the beer bottles, but as quickly he lifted them. His Adam's apple bobbed, and his face hardened in defiance. As she looked between her baby brother and the stranger, Emily's hackles went up. The stranger was too old to be Joey's buddy.

"I didn't know I had any beer in the house," she said, making no effort to disguise her disapproval.

Like all the Rifkin men, Joey was tall and as tough as Manila rope. Yet the black-haired stranger with his deep chest and mature shoulders dwarfed the boy. Joey's sullenness made him look younger still as he thrust a bottle at the stranger.

"I bought the beer," the stranger said. "My treat."

Looking Joey dead in the eye, she told him with her glower she was sick and tired of him soliciting strangers to break the law in buying him beer. "Maybe you ought to ask for ID next time you go treating boys around here. He isn't yet twenty-one."

Joey slammed down the cookie jar with such force, Emily tensed for shattered glass. The jar remained intact.

"I can drink a beer on my own front porch." The hot color deepened on Joey's face. "You ain't my mama."

She heard how she sounded. An old biddy with nothing better to do than snoop around for ways to spoil his fun. Ever since their grandfather's death, Joey had been lost, unable to climb out of the angry morass of his grief. He drank too much and spent too much time alone. Emily understood how grief turned the days gray and filled a soul with unanswered questions. She also knew how easily Joey could follow their older brother into criminal depravity.

Except he was right. She wasn't his mama.

Emily turned her horse away. The animal trotted out of the small yard to the barn.

By the time Emily had dismounted and stripped the saddle off the horse, a new thought disquieted her. The stranger could be one of Tuff's friends. Emily had steadfastly refused to bail Tuff out of jail, so maybe he'd sent one of his creepy buddies to convince her to cough up the cash. Despite her weariness, she hurried in rubbing down the horse and turning her into the corral. Then Emily strode back to the house, bypassing the back door and going around front.

Joey perched on the porch railing. The stranger sat on the glider, his long legs stretched out and crossed at the ankle. Emily avoided meeting his bright blue eyes. Nothing he said—or did—could convince her to give him a single penny on Tuff's behalf.

"This is Reb Tremaine," Joey finally said. "I hired him on as a hand."

"Pardon?"

"I hired him. What with rounding up steers for the market and all, me and Claude are about tapped. There's too much to do."

Hard times and Tuff's thievery had eroded the Double Bar R's resources. Tuff had finagled away the mineral-rights leases that had sustained the ranch in the lean years; he'd sold off prime bottomland useful for growing hay. They ran a couple hundred head of cattle, but if beef prices dropped again, they wouldn't be able to afford the cost of leasing federal grazing land. Hired hands were a luxury.

She made herself look at Reb Tremaine. His eyes glinted with intelligence and something else, something mysterious and maybe a little bit dangerous. He made her nervous, and she wasn't sure why. Perhaps it was his clothing. The jeans fit like an old friend, but his handsome face seemed better suited for a designer shirt and a hundred-dollar tie. Well-worn clothes, shaggy hair and beard shadow aside, the man had an air of quality.

"I'm sorry, Mr. Tremaine, but my brother stepped out of line. We can't afford another hired hand."

His mild expression never changed. Her uncertainty increased. She felt as if she'd missed something, that he knew something she didn't. His silence left her fumbling for some way to end this encounter in a nice way. "Uh, but you're welcome to stay for supper."

Reb Tremaine merely nodded, and she went inside. The house was hotter inside than it was outside. Once upon a time a giant cottonwood had shaded the kitchen from the afternoon sun. A thunderstorm last spring had finally knocked the old tree down, leaving only a tattered stump now rotting into wood fluff.

Sunshine slanted knives of heat through the window. Boots thudded on the linoleum floor behind her.

"I hired him fair and square," Joey said. "I can't go back on my word."

Emily filled a glass with cold water. "How do you propose I pay him?"

"Claude and I are taking seventy steers to market. We need help."

Simple logic, simple truth. Even running a small ranch was a huge job. Repairing fences and machinery, tending the hay fields, treating cattle—the list of chores was endless. Fall roundup approached, and Joey had only old Claude Longo to help him.

Emily drained the water. "So why this Tremaine fellow?" she asked, keeping her voice down. "He looks as if he's from the city. He probably doesn't know the difference between a cow and a gopher hole."

Joey chuckled without humor. "The way you do? You're as worthless around cows as that stupid dog of yours. Shoot, you can't half stay on a horse, much less drag a steer. Reb knows his stuff. He's got his own gear."

"Okay, okay. But you shouldn't make these decisions without consulting me. The ranch is my responsibility—"

"It shouldn't be!" Anger and hurt shone through Joey's dark eyes. "The ranch is *mine*. You come waltzing in here and rooked Grandpa. If he'd been in his right mind, he'd have left the ranch to me, not you."

"As soon as you're old enough—"

"You're nothing but a quitter. It won't be six months before you find some other rich old fool to run off with."

Joey's words slashed to her heart.

Emily flinched. Echoes of her restless yearnings to be away from this place, away from Joey, tugged at her, but she was trapped. All she could do was grit her teeth, push forward and hope and pray that someday she'd finish paying for her sins.

She doubted if redemption would come easily or soon. Nothing had gone right since her return to the ranch. Grandpa had died, her older brother was a criminal and Joey refused to forgive her for leaving him here ten years ago. Grandpa's will, which bequeathed the entire ranch to Emily, made her look like the worst kind of gold digger. Nobody in the valley cared about her side of the story or gave her the benefit of the doubt. Nobody, especially not Joey, believed her about the promise she'd made to Grandpa. She didn't want the ranch, but she'd promised to keep the place intact until Joey was man enough to own it. Public opinion and Joey's hard heart be damned, she'd keep her promise.

If it didn't kill her first.

She lowered the glass to the counter. She turned slowly to face her brother. "How do you know Tremaine isn't a con artist? A lot of folks think we're rolling in money."

"Just because you're stupid," Joey returned, "doesn't mean I am."

"I'm not stupid," she said through her teeth.

"You married Daniel." Joey's eyes glittered with hard challenge.

"Keep him out of this."

Joey's upper lip curled in a sneer. "If you were so proud of him, how come you never brought him home?"

"This fight isn't about me." Except it was; it always came back to her. Joey would never understand why she'd married Daniel or why Grandpa had left her the ranch. Joey didn't want to understand. All he wanted to do was punish her. Tears gnawed at her throat and scratched her lower eyelids.

"I hired Reb and I'm not going back on my word," Joey said.

The fire drained out of her, replaced by grief. She mourned the boy Joey had once been. The sweetly serious child who listened in wide-eyed wonder while she read him a bedtime story. The boy who came to her with the tears and hurts he didn't dare let Grandpa see. He glared at her now with contempt, his anger a shield against her love, his hatred a constant reminder of her guilt.

"You're right, you need help. I'll figure out a way to pay him."

Joey clamped his lips tight. For a moment he looked like a bronco in midbuck who realized he'd thrown his rider.

He wore a man's body, but inside he was still a boy. He'd loved their grandfather completely. As far as Joey was concerned, Garth Rifkin had walked on water and no man living could hold a candle to him. Losing Grandpa and the ranch was a double blow that still had him reeling. Emily desperately wanted him to understand neither she nor Grandpa had betrayed him.

The telephone rang, and both of them jumped. Emily picked up the handset. A mechanical voice informed her of a collect call; would she accept the charges? Even before the caller spoke his name, Emily knew Tuff was calling from the jail.

"No, absolutely not, I will not accept the charges." She hung up with a bang.

"Tuff's calling me, not you," Joey said.

"And I'm paying for the calls. He can write a letter." She hurried out of the kitchen before they lapsed into another squabble.

Joey called to her back, "He wouldn't be in jail in the first place if you hadn't called the law! It's all your fault. Everyone knows you hate him. You and the sheriff are out to get him."

Sometimes she felt engaged in a struggle for Joey's very soul, with Tuff being the devil tempting the impressionable boy with shiny vice and easy money.

If she could find evidence Tuff was indeed a murderer, then the struggle would end. Joey would realize the truth, and Tuff would go away to prison, out of their lives forever.

A shower did much to cool her body and temper. She combed her hair, leaving it hanging down her back to dry loose. She dressed in a pair of ragged cutoffs and a gray knit halter. Barefoot, she went downstairs to start supper.

Reb Tremaine sat at the kitchen table.

He looked her up and down, making her aware of her bare legs and bare belly. The halter was more modest than a bikini bra and didn't expose any cleavage, but she felt underdressed anyway. Her belly muscles contracted.

She faltered, wanting to run upstairs and throw on a long shirt and blue jeans. Wanted to run away from those bright blue eyes that seemed to strip her naked, exposing her loneliness.

She strode determinedly to the refrigerator. The kitchen belonged to her—her turf, her rules. She'd dress any darn way she pleased. "I guess you're hired, Mr. Tremaine, but in case Joey—"

"Reb," he said, his voice low but strong.

"Pardon?"

"'Mister' doesn't fit. Call me Reb."

She pulled a bowl of chicken marinating in buttermilk from the refrigerator. "Reb. Let's get a few things straight. I own the Double Bar R, not Joey. I'm not rich, so the pay is lousy and there aren't any benefits." She pointed out the window at a ramshackle log cabin nestled in the shade of the cottonwood trees. "That's the bunkhouse. You stay there. It's a mess, so you'll have to clean it up. I don't have time. When you come in my house, your hands and boots best be clean. Other than for meals, you stay out of here unless you're invited. Joey's your boss, and so is Claude Longo. He's the manager." She pointed east. "He lives on the other side of the ridge near the cattle pens. He's an old bear, so if he says jump, don't wonder if he means it."

"Whatever you say, Emily."

"That's 'Mrs. Farraday' to you. And don't you ever mess with me. I have enough problems. If you screw up just once, you'll be out of here so fast you'll think a tornado grabbed you."

"Yes, ma'am."

Her high-handedness should have chased him away. She decided he must be desperate for work. Except he didn't look desperate or even annoyed. His calm acceptance made her aware of taking out her frustration with Joey on him. Shabby behavior, wholly beneath her.

She slid damp curls off her cheeks. "It's been a long day," she said lamely. "I'm not usually so...grouchy."

Reb Tremaine smiled. A closed mouth, lopsided pull of wide, supple lips. A sensual, promising smile full of ancient knowledge. A hot thump hit her low in the belly again, and her chest tightened, making her heartbeat sound against her eardrums. Fleeting images tantalized her: his mouth hot and wet and hungry against her breast; his long-fingered hands hard against her backside, clutching her thighs. She slid her tongue over suddenly dry lips. The temperature seemed to rise twenty degrees, and a thin line of sweat seeped between her breasts. She turned abruptly, focused on the chicken—and felt his gaze searing her back.

"Joey says you cook fine. You ran a restaurant."

A nice voice, low without harshness.

She put a clamp on her wayward thoughts. Heat and worry overtired her, played tricks with her head—that was all, nothing more. Daniel was still her husband in spirit, and she didn't want to let him go. Someday, maybe, but not today, and certainly not with a silky-voiced drifter with heel-shot boots and sexy eyes.

"My husband owned the restaurant. I cooked for him."

"Joey says your fried chicken can make a mime sing."

Emily glanced over her shoulder, wishing Joey would say such nice things to her face. Reb still smiled. She liked his smile. It would be easy to like him. A dangerous cowpoke, she decided, in more ways than one. She kept her smile to herself.

When the meal was on the table, Joey appeared. Head down, gaze fixed on his plate, Joey ate as if it were his last meal, piling in triple helpings of fried chicken and enough fixings to feed four normal people. Reb did her cooking justice, as well.

Later Joey led Reb to the bunkhouse. Emily watched them through the kitchen window. When Joey opened the door and turned on the lights, she grimaced. The roof leaked, the floors were buckled and the bathroom was rusted with cracked fixtures and a stubborn sink. The old cabin should have been torn down long ago.

Joey and Reb emerged, lugging a mattress. They propped it against the porch railing and beat it, raising a cloud of dust. She lifted her gaze to the ceiling. Two bedrooms sat empty upstairs. Even considering having Reb living in the house, separated from her by a thin wall, made her shudder. Weakness settled in her knees.

Absolutely no strangers in her house. Period.

THE NEXT MORNING Reb appeared at the kitchen door at six o'clock sharp. She gestured for him to come inside, but kept her eyes averted. She'd had an interesting dream last night involving a hot tub filled with champagne, a room glowing from a thousand candles and Reb Tremaine.

As he passed near her, she smelled soap. His face looked warm from a fresh shave. His hair was still damp and it gleamed blue black, like the shiny wing of a magpie. He looked more handsome today than he had yesterday. Even handsomer than in her dream.

"Good morning, Mrs. Farraday," he said, taking his seat. As he scooted his chair to the table, his shoulders strained the thin cotton of his long-sleeved shirt.

She bit back the urge to apologize for the old bunkhouse. After all, she had warned him. "Did you sleep okay?"

"Like I had a clean conscience."

Reb's dry, teasing tone made her smile.

From his seat at the table, Joey looked up sharply. She guessed he begrudged her being friendly with the hired hand.

She served up a breakfast of bacon, sausage, fried potatoes, biscuits, gravy and scrambled eggs. Joey drank a quart of milk and half a pot of coffee. Reb drank orange juice and the other half of the coffee. Neither man spoke while he ate, which suited Emily. She had other things on her mind.

Joey finished and stood. He ate like a grizzly bear, but he was lean as a greyhound and his hard-ridden clothing fit like a rumpled old skin.

"We'll be over at the holding pens with Claude," he said. "Have to repair the chutes."

She stacked the plates. "I'll bring you lunch."

"You going out searching again today?"

His question caught her off guard. She'd made no secret about believing Tuff had murdered a man and buried the body on the ranch. This was the first time Joey had brought up the subject, though. He'd steadfastly insisted Tuff was guilty of nothing more than rowdiness and the only reason he ever got into trouble was because the sheriff disliked him. Emily drew her head warily aside. "Why?"

For a moment it looked as if Joey had something to say. He grabbed his broad-brimmed hat off a peg, and jammed the hat on his head. "Just be careful," he muttered as he walked toward the door.

Reb picked up his hat. "Thank you for breakfast, ma'am."

She met his eyes. A mistake. Until he'd shown up on her front porch, she hadn't been aware of missing a man in her life. Now she yearned for the feel of a warm body by her side. She wanted to feel hot skin against skin, to grow giddy with the heady power gained from seeing helpless lust in a man's eyes. She hungered for the taste of desire and the intoxicating scents.

The longer Reb stared into her eyes, the more she felt convinced he recognized her loneliness and her need.

Only after the door had closed behind him did she notice she was holding her breath. Light-headed, she swiped her wrist across her brow. It was only six-thirty in the morning and already far too hot.

Chapter Two

In her bedroom Emily sat at her desk. Morning sun battered the bank of three windows, and oven-dry air seeped through the screens. Colorado summers were blessedly short, but as fierce as they were beautiful. Heat surrounded the house like a blanket and climbed the stairs to fill the bedrooms. Emily shook her head against daydreams of ice blue swimming pools and shimmering waterfalls.

She picked up a bill from the Humbolt hardware store. "Past due" had been scrawled in red ink across the letterhead. "Final notice." It had arrived in yesterday's mail. Emily hadn't a clue as to what had happened to the original bill.

She carried it downstairs, called the hardware store and asked to speak to the owner.

"Hello, Mr. Bollander, Emily Farraday here," she said when he came on the line. "I have a bill for eight hundred and forty-three dollars. It says past due, but I don't know what it's for."

"Tools." His voice held a harsh note she was beginning to accept as a regional patois, at least in regard to her. All her grandfather's old friends treated her as if she'd murdered him in his sleep.

"Mr. Bollander, I'm doing my best to square my grandfather's accounts, but I need to know what I'm paying for. I can't find the original receipts."

"What are you saying, young lady? I'm sending you bills for nothing? I'll have you know, Garth Rifkin and I did business nigh fifty years. He never had no complaints about the way I run my outfit. Do you?"

She had plenty, but ignored the bait. "No, sir," she said, struggling to keep her manner mild. "But I have to keep records for tax purposes. I'm more than willing to pay the bill. That's not the issue. All I'm asking is if you could please send me copies of the receipts so I can reconcile the books."

"Claude signed for most of it. Talk to him."

She supressed a groan. After her grandfather's first stroke, he'd turned over the purchasing and bookkeeping to Claude Longo. Claude considered calculators and computers potentially dangerous contraptions, and his head figuring left much to be desired. When he remembered to give her receipts or bills, they'd usually been residing in his pockets for weeks.

Realizing further attempts to straighten out this matter over the telephone would serve only the store owner's twisted sense of justice, she gave up. "Thank you for your time, Mr. Bollander."

"Don't you be taking no more time, young lady. I want that bill paid in full. I give credit where I think it's due, but you ain't due."

"You'll get your money."

"Darn right I will, one way or t'other." He snorted loudly. "Thieves don't get far in this country. You remember that." He hung up on her.

"Thieves don't get far in this country," she mocked at the dead connection.

When Grandpa died, the ranch had been in debt, behind on its taxes, out of insurance and missing almost a third of the land and assets named in the will. Yet people thought she'd inherited a fortune. Just as they thought her husband had been rich and had left her a wealthy widow. The few people who knew the truth about her finances weren't, unfortunately, the type of people who spent endless hours engaged in gossip.

The unfairness of it all dogged her as she climbed the stairs to her bedroom and wrote out a check to the hardware store. Anticipating the argument she'd have with Claude over the receipts gave her a stomach-ache. She paid the telephone bill, too. It included nearly two hundred dollars in collect calls from the jail. Her stomachache turned into a cramp. Two hundred dollars would buy an automatic dishwasher, and cut down on the hours she spent in the kitchen. Even locked up, Tuff was a menace. She wondered if there was a way to block his calls completely.

After she'd finished paying the bills, she escaped the hot house. Hoeing weeds out of the garden and picking beans and lettuce for supper loosened some of the tension in her neck and shoulders. Anxiety lingered like a quivering, aching little animal low in her chest. Tuff had to stay in jail while awaiting sentencing on a drunk-and-disorderly charge, but he could get probation and be out in a week.

She looked to the forest on the far side of the creek. Ponderosa pines towered over stands of oak and mountain ash. A few stately spruces gleamed slate blue under the harsh sunlight, and aspen groves made patches of cool white and bright green. Treacherous beauty. The forest was full of small caves and rock formations where Tuff could have hidden a body.

When the chores were done, she caught Strawberry and led her into the barn. While she saddled the horse, Copper joined her. He sat, wagging his tail, his eyes bright with anticipation. Being of a lazier temperament, the roan mare grunted pitifully while Emily tightened the cinch.

"Oh, Strawberry," Emily said, kneeing the mare in the ribs to make her stop holding her breath. "Maybe you're right. There are a million places where Tuff could have buried a body. It's useless trying to find it."

Except Tuff knew she knew. The first thing he'd do when he got out of jail would be kill her. He'd bury her up in the mountains so no one would ever find her body.

Something was missing from inside her older brother. Whether from an accident of birth, or some secret terror twisting his psyche, he lacked whatever it was that made a normal person realize actions had consequences. Tuff didn't care about whom or what he hurt. No, he certainly wouldn't think twice about hurting her. Even worse, Emily doubted if anyone would spare two minutes looking for her.

TUFF RIFKIN WANTED Emily dead. "Disappear her. Make it look like she ran off."

The way Tuff had said those words—with a broad smile and his black eyes as flat and soulless as daubs of paint—played over and over in Reb's head.

Seated in the old-fashioned kitchen, surrounded by the savory smell of roast beef and garlic, Reb watched Emily stir gravy. Each movement of her arm caused an accompanying little twitch in her left hip, as if she moved to some inner music.

Disappear her. The phrase had been spoken with a smile that belonged in Hollywood. Tuff Rifkin was a good-looking man with a lean, sculpted face, expensively barbered brown curls and large white teeth. He had an easy charm about him, as personable as a politician on a campaign and as quick-witted as a con artist. He appeared to be enjoying his stay in jail, treating the county lockup like a five-star hotel while lording it over the stone-faced deputy as if maître d' were part of the deputy's job description. Remembering the way the deputy had wordlessly brought the canned sodas Tuff requested made Reb want to laugh in amazement.

Emily glanced over her shoulder, her face solemn.

Her drop-dead gorgeousness was an unexpected twist. Reb had never taken a job before where the target owned the ability to steal his breath and muddy his thinking.

She turned back to the stove, and he lowered his gaze to her suntanned legs. Muscles made alluring curves in her calves before tapering sharply to sculpted ankles. Her thighs were long and smooth, firmly feminine.

Tuff had crudely stated, "Got a body you hate to waste on a relative, you know?" As if a hit man needed the added incentive of wasting a beautiful body.

She carefully brought the pan of gravy to the table. She set it on a trivet in front of her brother, and urged him to begin serving himself.

Her face matched her body. Framed by a cascade of dark brown curls, it was the winsome, full-mouthed, doe-eyed face of an angel.

Even angels could fall. No sense getting personal when the chances were good he'd have no choice except to take her down. Reb made himself look at his hands resting folded atop the table.

As she slid onto her chair, she gave him a sideways glance and a smile. She handed him a bowl of mashed potatoes. "Dig in, Reb." She'd put food on her plate only after he and Joey had taken what they wanted.

Her hospitality shamed him. The rise of conscience surprised him as much as it disturbed him. *Targets,* he flung harshly at the small, insistent inner voice, *nothing but targets who deserve what they get.*

"Do you have gloves?" she asked. She looked pointedly at his right hand.

Reb turned his hand palm up, revealing an angry red blister on the web between his thumb and forefinger. He'd spent most of the day hammering nails into hard, resisting wood. "I forgot them."

She gave her brother a reproachful glance. Joey shoveled carrots and onions onto his plate. *She's got sad eyes,* Reb thought, and immediately tried to squash it. He didn't want his thinking traveling in that direction, didn't want to imagine what might make her smile or laugh. Or what might make her eyes sparkle with joy—or desire.

"I bet you won't forget them again," she said. "I'll bandage that for you after supper."

After she finished eating, she fetched a first-aid kit. "The rule is," she said softly, "don't let wounds go unattended. No matter how small. You hold fast to it for the cattle and horses, do the same for yourselves.''

Joey glared at her. "What's the matter? Scared you might have to use some of your *hard-earned* money for a doctor?''

Reb found the interplay between Joey and Emily interesting. The kid had a chip the size of a California redwood on his shoulder, and Emily's rigid posture failed to hide how often the kid's remarks hit home. In Emily's place Reb would have put Joey on the street a long time ago.

Joey stomped out of the kitchen, slamming the door behind him. He claimed Emily had deserted the family to marry a wealthy restaurant tycoon, then murdered him for the insurance money. She'd returned to the ranch, pulled a snow job on their grandfather so he'd change his will and then murdered him to inherit the ranch. To hear Joey tell it, Emily was the Wicked Witch of the West.

She stared for a moment at the door, then sighed wistfully. "I never say the right things to him," she said, her tone apologetic. "Maybe I should keep my mouth shut." She flashed a grin. "The way you do.''

She opened the first-aid kit. She was twenty-six years old, but long, unruly curls and smooth skin dotted by pale freckles made her look younger. As she examined the kit contents, her lowered eyelashes cast alluring shadows over her eyes. Looking at her, it was impossible to imagine her swatting a fly, much less playing black widow.

Something about Emily Farraday touched a soft spot he hadn't been aware of. Like her older brother, she had distracting good looks. That, he supposed, made her especially dangerous.

She poked gently around the edges of the inflammation. Her fingers were cool. "Wash your hand. Use the detergent and scrub as hard as you can stand it."

He did as she told him. She joined him at the sink. She dressed the blister with antibiotic and a gauze bandage, taking care not to wrap the wound too tightly. Her slender hands roused fantasies of how they'd feel against his chest and back.

He wanted to ease the thick strands of hair away from her face and test the softness of her cheek and the fullness of her lip. Fill his nose with sweet woman scent. Vanquish the fey woundedness in her eyes. When hot blood flooded his groin and fired his veins, he jerked his hand out of her grasp.

She looked up, her eyes wide and startled.

"Tender," he said, and shook his hand as if she'd hurt him. "I won't forget my gloves again."

"I'm sure you won't. Make sure to tell me if it looks like it's getting infected." She replaced supplies in the kit, closed the lid and glanced at the door again. Pain flickered across her features. "If you need antibiotics, you'll get them."

Reb retook his seat at the table. "May I bother you for another glass of lemonade, ma'am?"

Her lips parted and her forehead tightened. She did not want him in her kitchen, but he pretended not to notice. She waited a beat; he smiled blandly. She refilled his glass.

He sipped the tart-sweet drink. It was freshly made and pulpy. "Joey says you're looking for a body in the hills."

She stilled with her hand on the faucet handle. Water rushed into the sink. Her eyes became remote. "That's right."

"Whose body?"

She lifted her shoulders in a quick shrug. "I don't know."

"So why are you looking for it?"

She shut off the water and began lowering dirty dishes into the suds. "Somebody has to."

He tried to get a read on her. She glanced at him, furtive...scared. Hungry, perhaps, for a sympathetic ear, but unwilling to trust him.

Gaining her trust was his number-one priority. "You make it sound like it's no big deal."

"It is to me, but nobody else cares." She tackled the dishwashing as if dirt were the enemy and she stood on the front line of defense. "Pardon me, but you need to take your lemonade outside. I've got work to do."

"Whatever's going on sounds like a big deal to me. Why doesn't anybody believe you?"

"It's not your problem. Now, I've got a lot to do. Go on."

Suspiciousness, distrust, loneliness—her vibes washed over him. He focused on the loneliness. "You look like you could use a friend. I'll listen."

Her entire body went rigid. In the window he could see a ghostly reflection of her troubled, perfect face. A funny pain arced across his ribs and centered on his heart. The nagging voice of conscience echoed stridently inside his head. *Don't hurt her,* it told him, *walk away from this one. Far, far away.*

"Look, Reb, I get my fill of arguments from my brother. Don't make me waste my time arguing with you. Go on outside."

He'd pushed as far as he dared for now. A corpse buried on the Double Bar R could be fact or fiction. Time would prove which one. For now Reb had other things on his mind—including a cache containing crisp bundles of twenties, fifties and hundreds. With three million dollars at stake, it made sense to play Emily Farraday the way rattlesnakes kissed: very carefully.

EMILY STEPPED onto the back porch. Though the sun had reached the tops of the highest mountain peaks, the heat lingered. Since they were at an altitude of seven thousand feet, the nights were cool and the mornings were bearable, but from around nine o'clock until sunset the thin air wavered with the heat. Two weeks had passed since they'd had rain. The air tasted dry, alkaline.

Slathering lotion onto her hands, she watched Joey and Reb. Under the shade of a cottonwood, they worked on the engine of Joey's pickup truck. The truck radio played a wailing tune about lost love.

Balanced on one foot, one boot waving lazily in the air, Joey stretched far into the engine compartment. Reb sat on the driver's seat, prepared to start the engine when necessary.

Around thirty, Reb was young enough to relate to the nineteen-year-old, but old enough to be a role model. A good role model, she thought in bemused gratitude. Since Reb's arrival, Joey had stopped picking at her, insulting her or starting arguments. He didn't display warmth or brotherly love, but he was polite.

Better, Joey didn't hurry through his evening chores so he could head into town in search of someone to buy beer for him. He stayed home, doing odd jobs around the house. Reb and Joey had repaired the front-porch roof, rehung a warped door and replaced torn screens on the house. They'd cleaned the barn and repaired the gate on the corral.

At supper this evening Joey had made a passing comment about Emily buying some paint for the house. The easy nonchalance of his words, lacking belligerence, had stunned her into speechlessness.

Reb was good for Joey, she thought. Her baby brother needed a friend, someone strong and mannerly and stable to look up to.

She'd begun to like and trust Reb, too. He possessed an air of confidence as if yesterday didn't matter and he could handle whatever might happen tomorrow. He never said much, but she liked his company at mealtimes. His dry sense of humor gave her reasons to smile. His handsome face and gorgeous body gave her something other than problems to think about. She shouldn't flirt with him, she knew, but she caught herself doing it anyway. She didn't talk to him about Tuff—or her fears that he'd murdered a man—but she wanted to do that, too. Only the risk of yet one more person calling her crazy kept her from spilling out her heart.

The stove timer buzzed. She braced herself to meet the heat indoors before she left the relative coolness of the porch, entered the kitchen and pulled a cobbler from the oven. Sweet-cherry-and-cinnamon scent rose in mouth-watering clouds. She went outside again and approached the pickup.

Joey had taken off his shirt to work. His ribs stood out like ladder rungs, and lean muscle roped across his concave belly. A pale scar from a bull-riding injury arced like a lightning bolt on his shoulder, flashing down across his biceps. He had a big smudge of grease on his cheek. When he was a baby, she'd never guessed he'd someday outgrow her by eight inches and fifty pounds. Nor had she ever guessed such a charming little boy could grow up to contain such a vast amount of prickly, hurt pride.

"I've got cherry cobbler and ice cream if you fellows are interested."

"Sure. We'll be there in a minute," Joey said. He nodded toward Reb. "Try her now."

Reb turned the key, and the engine roared to life. The roar mellowed to a purring idle. Reb gave Joey a thumbs-up. "You've got the touch, boy."

Joey's entire face lit with a broad smile. Emily's heart skipped a beat. He was so beautiful when he smiled.

"Now, if I can figure out where to get some tires," Joey said, "she'll be set."

"What's wrong with the tires?" Emily asked, peering at the front wheel.

"Nothing, except they're about a hundred years old and balder than Hannah Peak."

When Reb turned off the engine, Emily heard a vehicle approaching the house. She looked down the long driveway. As soon as the white car came into view, she knew who it was. Not in the mood for a visit from the sheriff, she sighed.

Sheriff Mickey Thigpen pulled his cruiser next to the house and parked. Emily folded her arms over her chest as she approached the driver's side. Mickey's busy eyes flicked over her body. Deputy Tim Patterson sat on the passenger side. He propped a clipboard against the dashboard and wrote on it.

"Hi, Mickey," she said. "Tim."

Tim nodded in reply, his gaze fixed on whatever he wrote. She knew the deputy from high school, and couldn't recall him ever saying much of anything.

"Hi, honey," the sheriff said. "Haven't seen you in a while. Aren't you ever coming into town again?"

"I was there this morning," she said. "I bought groceries."

"You mean I missed you?" He widened his eyes in mock dismay. He got out of the car and leaned an arm on the roof. Pale hairs glinted silver on his forearms. He pointed with his chin at Joey's pickup. "Your brother isn't out running the streets, huh?"

She looked behind her. Reb and Joey had disappeared. "There's some hope for him." She wondered if the sheriff had good news concerning Tuff. "So what have you found out?"

The corners of the sheriff's mouth tipped in a smug grin. "About you and me, honey? Not much, but I'm hopeful. How about dinner tomorrow night? I'll treat you to a steak. Then we'll go dancing."

Emily lowered her face. She tapped her fingers against her upper arms. Mickey Thigpen's wife had divorced him a few years back, and local ladies considered him the most eligible bachelor in the valley. He owned a house on a nice piece of property. He sported a handsome mane of salt-and-pepper hair, and his rangy leanness and deep voice reminded her of the actor Sam Elliott.

She suspected he enjoyed his most-favored single-guy status and had no intention of ever changing it. She had no intention of becoming another notch on his bedpost.

"I'm talking about the man Tuff killed. You promised to check missing persons."

"And I did. I ran the description through state and federal computers." Impatience edged his voice. "Nothing turned up." He didn't add, *And nothing ever will because you made him up,* but the patronizing cant of his eyebrows spoke it for him.

"He killed a man, Mickey. Somebody has to be missing him. Did you talk to Tuff?"

"Sure. He says you're crazy."

"You know I'm not."

He lifted his brown Stetson hat and smoothed back his hair. "There's been bad blood between you and Tuff all your lives."

"I'm not on some kind of vendetta. I know what I saw, what I heard. There's a body out there."

"Now, darn it, don't go getting all hot and bothered, Emily. What exactly am I supposed to do? You say you saw a man, but you don't know his name or where he comes from. His description doesn't match anybody. There's no gun, no body, no blood."

"If you'd gotten here when I called you instead of fiddling around for hours, you'd have seen the blood before rain washed it away."

"Tuff is as rowdy as they come, but that doesn't make him a killer. That's a hell of an accusation to make against your own brother."

She raked her bare toe through the dirt.

"My patience with you two is wearing thin, honey. Got you on one side calling him a cold-blooded killer, and him on the other saying you're a thief."

"I'm a thief? Me?"

He showed his palms and grimaced sheepishly. "Have to admit it is peculiar the way things worked out between you and your grandfather."

"I cannot believe you, of all people, would say such a thing. I thought we were friends."

He flinched, ducking his head. "I said it's peculiar, that's all. I don't mean it in a bad way."

Anger crept up her spine and tightened her scalp. She glanced at the deputy, catching him looking at her. He dropped his gaze to the clipboard. Embarrassment tangled with her anger. One of these days people in the valley might stop talking about her, but she doubted it would happen soon.

"Tuff's the thief, not me. He stole from Grandpa and Joey." She pointed at the house. "Do you know what Tuff did while Joey and I were at the funeral? He stole Grandpa's pocket watch and gold cuff links."

Mickey fiddled with his wristwatch. "What proof do you have?"

An incredulous little laugh huffed from her throat. "What kind of proof do you need?"

"If you want to discuss criminal investigations, let's do it over dinner. Saturday?"

"I'm busy," she said through her teeth. "I've got a body to look for. Since your britches are too big to help with something as piddly as a murder, then I guess I'll just have to do it all by myself."

His eyes narrowed, and he fingered his gun belt.

He pointed a thick finger at her. "This county gives me just enough money for two deputies. I should have twice that even to run the jail right. I don't have the manpower to search the mountains for something that might not exist. I don't have enough evidence to call in the state police. If I asked for an investigator based on what you say, they'd laugh right in my face. You find me some proof. Blood, or something belonging to the victim."

"I see, you'd rather let Tuff get away with murder than risk being laughed at. You wait and see, Mickey Thigpen. I will find proof. Only I'm not calling you. I'm calling every newspaper and television reporter in the state of Colorado."

He jerked down the front brim of his hat. "You do that, honey, you just go right on ahead and do that. I'll be glad to eat crow." He slid behind the wheel of his cruiser and pulled the door shut.

The deputy leaned over and spoke softly to the sheriff.

Mickey snorted. "Yeah, yeah. By the way, Tuff got himself sixty days on the drunk-and-disorderly. Thought you might want to know."

"Only sixty—?"

The sheriff gunned the engine and roared backward away from the house. He wheeled in a tight circle, turning to face the road, and drove away in a cloud of dust.

"Jerk," she muttered, and trudged to the back porch. "Bet if I went to bed with you, you'd be more than happy to help me find evidence of murder on my property. Stupid, pigheaded, chauvinistic—"

In the shadows next to the door, Reb sat on the porch. Seeing him cut her off in midgrumble.

He was too darn quiet, she decided. He was taller than Joey, at least six foot three, and probably weighed two hundred pounds, but he moved as quietly as a cat on the prowl. He'd spooked her too many times, and she was tired of it. Right at the moment she was sick to death of all things male.

She raked hair off her face. "What are you doing here?"

"Cherry cobbler." He grinned, showing white teeth and a glint of mischief in his jewel-bright eyes.

His smile stripped some of the fight out of her. She didn't know what kind of cowboy he was, but he sure had a gift for making a woman feel pretty.

"What did the sheriff want?"

She looked from him to the corner of the porch. A chuckle rose. "Don't even try pretending you don't know. You can hear every word from here. You were eavesdropping."

His eyelids lowered in silent acknowledgment. "Innocent bystander, ma'am, I assure you."

She rested her back against the house, and the siding was relatively cool through the thin fabric of her T-shirt. She watched chickens wandering toward the henhouse. The lone rooster, a tall white Rock with a rose comb and evil, reptilian eyes, paced in front of the narrow door like an anxious father waiting for his daughters to come home from a dance.

"You think your older brother killed a man," Reb said.

"I don't think it, I know it."

Sixty days... in sixty days the cattle would be sold, the last summer hay would be harvested and stored, and the pickling and canning would be finished for the year. In sixty days Tuff would get out of jail, come back to the ranch and break her neck to shut her mouth.

"You're scared of him."

Reb's simple statement touched her. He sounded as if he sympathized. As if he understood. As if he cared. Weariness hit her like a rock dropping onto her shoulders. The vast landscape surrounding her with towering peaks and forbidding rocks and dark, shaded

forests was too empty, too alone. Missing Daniel and
the bustling restaurant and constant stream of people
who loved and cared about her struck her square in the
throat.

She pushed away from the house and caught a
porch post in a loose hand. She sank to the top step
and stretched out her legs. "Yes, I'm scared."

"Because you witnessed a murder. That's the body
you're looking for."

She nodded absently. "I'm surprised Joey hasn't
told you all about it." She turned her head just enough
to see him. "Whenever I see you two, you're talking."

"He's a bit . . . lost."

"You don't have to sugarcoat it, Reb. I know how
Joey feels about me. Trouble is, he doesn't know how
Tuff feels about him. Joey doesn't believe Tuff is capable of murder. Or he doesn't want to believe it. Tuff
talks a good line, and Joey always falls for it, hook,
line and sinker."

"Tuff has bad feelings toward Joey?"

His neutral tone gave away nothing of what he felt.
She smoothed her hand back over her forehead, gathering hair, tugging her scalp. "Not bad feelings. Not
good feelings, either. Tuff doesn't feel anything at all."
She caught her lower lip in her teeth, angry all over
again at Mickey. He'd been in law enforcement for as
long as she could remember. Surely he could see
through Tuff's lies.

"Do you think he'll hurt Joey?"

"If it suits him. He hates me, but as far as he's
concerned, Joey is nothing but a toy."

Chapter Three

Reb slipped a spoon into the warm cobbler. Steam curled around the scoop of vanilla ice cream, carrying the scent of cinnamon to his nose. The amount of food he'd been packing away lately embarrassed him. He'd always enjoyed exercise and working up a good sweat. Keeping up with Joey and Claude Longo, however, felt like training for a triathlon, and he stayed ravenous all the time.

He kept his head down, but watched Emily as she settled onto the top porch step. Remaining sunlight formed a golden halo where it sparked against her hair. Her long, elegant legs gave him a hunger no amount of juicy cobbler could satisfy.

Target, he reminded himself harshly, *she's a target.* He had to keep operating on the premise that she was greedy, dishonest and murderous, unworthy of his respect or regrets. He survived by keeping his emotions under control, by never acknowledging the humanity of targets. They made their own messes; he was the cleanup man.

Still, he liked her. Even if she weren't so beautiful that he had to keep checking to make sure he wasn't imagining the exquisite line of her throat or the depth of her eyes, he'd like her. He recognized in her a fellow survivor.

"So what did Joey tell you?" she asked, looking toward the barn. Yellow lights gleamed through the open doorway. Joey was working inside. "About me and Tuff?"

Plenty.

According to Joey, Emily had run away from home because she was spoiled and greedy. Their grandfather had refused to cave in to her endless demands, so she'd run off with a rich older man and never once bothered to let their grieving grandfather know she was alive. When she returned, she'd coerced their grandfather into leaving her the ranch. Tuff knew her dirty little secrets, so she convinced her good friend, the sheriff, to bust him on trumped-up charges.

Reb felt positive Joey didn't know about the three million dollars.

But did Emily? If she suspected Tuff had killed a man and buried the body on this property, she might well know about the missing money. If so, she was a conspirator and a double-crosser, as willing to rat out her brother as he was willing to kill.

"Joey says you called the law on Tuff because—" Reb kept his voice carefully neutral "—you'll do anything to get him out of the way."

Emily surprised him with a laugh. "I wish I had the guts to do anything." Her smile faded.

Reb mourned the loss of her smile. "So who did Tuff kill?"

Her brow wrinkled in a puzzled frown. "I haven't the faintest idea. I've never seen him before."

"A visitor? A lost hiker?"

"Let's talk about something else. Like Mickey says, I don't have evidence of anything."

She was dying to talk about it. All she needed was a nudge. "How do you know?"

She swung her head around, frowning at him. Such an expressive face—a hell of a liability for a crook.

"Maybe you have evidence, but don't know it. Murderers always leave clues. That's what I've heard. Talk it out. See if you missed something."

"You don't think it's weird I suspect my own brother?"

Reb shrugged. "Nothing weird about a murderer having a family. So what happened?"

For a long moment she sat quietly, staring into space. He kept a lid on further comments. Either she'd open up or she wouldn't.

"Tuff disappeared for a few days. I don't know where. He's always taking off. I always hope he'll stay away for good."

Reb ate a spoonful of cobbler. The cherries popped sweetly against his teeth, and the buttery crust made his eyelids lower in pleasure. Dangerous, greedy, dishonest or not, Emily sure knew how to cook. He liked that about her, too.

"Tuff came home in the middle of the night. A man was with him. They were in the kitchen, arguing. They woke me up."

"Did you talk to him?"

Her eyes widened incredulously. "If you knew Tuff, you wouldn't ask."

"What were they arguing about?" He watched her face. Looking for twitchy lies in her eyes and listening for cracks in her voice proved difficult in light of marveling over the clear texture of her skin and the rich color of her full lips. Sunset agreed with her, heightening the contrast between her dark hair and fair skin, and playing golden with the slim, strong lines of her legs.

"Tuff was telling the other man they had to split up, and the other man was saying Tuff didn't trust him." She lowered her voice as if Joey could by some chance hear. "It sounded like they didn't want to get caught together. Tuff never works, but he always has money. I don't know how he gets it. I went back upstairs and heard them leave the house."

A thin line deepened between her brows. "They kept arguing. I tried to hear what they were saying, but a storm was coming up and I had closed the windows earlier because of the wind. I didn't want to open one in case Tuff heard me. Then the other man pulled a duffel bag out of the car. Tuff got a shovel and pickax from the barn."

"You're sure it was a duffel bag?"

She nodded. "I couldn't help but think that maybe Tuff was dealing drugs or something. They headed off that way." She pointed west at the forest. "They had flashlights, so I could see them cross the creek and go into the trees."

A duffel bag, Reb mused. He considered the possibility she didn't know the duffel bag contained three million dollars.

Only a possibility. "So you think they may have buried a stash of drugs. Did you call the law?"

"Uh-huh. But there was a rock slide on the highway, so I had to wait until somebody was available." Her dark eyes glittered, and one bare foot waved in a furious circle. "The dispatcher said I didn't have an emergency."

"So what did you do?"

"They left a huge mess in the kitchen. They ate all the leftovers in the refrigerator. I got mad. It was just like Tuff, trash everything then walk away as if a good fairy is waiting to clean up after him. So I cleaned the kitchen. By then I was mad enough to wait up for Tuff and his buddy to give them a piece of my mind—or to keep them here until the police came."

A shudder shook her from head to toe. Her gaze went distant and afraid. "Tuff came back alone."

"And you think he murdered the other man out there in the trees."

Eyes wide and solemn, she nodded. She gestured with her spoon at the security light mounted atop a tall pole. It illuminated the house and driveway, a shining beacon that could be seen from miles away. "I was furious, but nervous, too. When I realized he was alone, I got really scared. I watched him from the doorway. He put the shovel and pickax in the trunk of his car. When he turned around, I could see his T-shirt was covered with . . . blood."

"You're sure it was blood? Not dirt?"

"I'm sure. He used the faucet by the side of the house to wash up. When he came back around here, he was soaking wet. He'd even washed down his hair. His hair, he washed blood out of his hair." She drew in a long, anguished-sounding breath. "I slammed the door and turned the bolt."

"Did he try to get in?"

"No, thank goodness. He ran to his car. I must have spooked him as much as he spooked me, and he took off. I called the sheriff again, but they were still working on the highway. So I got the big flashlight and checked the faucet. There was blood on the ground."

She closed her eyes, sighed and set the bowl aside. The ice cream had melted into a pebbled lake atop the bumpy cobbler. "And then it rained. What my grandfather used to call a frog strangler."

"And washed away the blood," Reb said. His credulous tone shocked him. He was falling for her story word for word.

"Stupid me, I had cleaned. If I had a dishwasher, it would be different. I'd have fingerprints on cups and plates. But no, I have to do everything by hand in that antique kitchen. There isn't a single bit of evidence anyone was with Tuff that night. Or that I even saw Tuff. The sheriff went to talk to Tuff the next morning. He tried to outrun them in his car, but he'd been drinking and he wrecked. Then he got into a fight with Tim, the deputy. So they arrested him for being drunk and disorderly. He'd gotten rid of the tools. He had blood on him, but Mickey says it's Tuff's blood. I don't have any proof. Tuff denies he was even home."

"Where was Joey?"

"The rodeo. Joey competes in the bull-riding events. He was gone all weekend and didn't get home until Sunday night."

"Did Tuff know Joey wouldn't be here?"

"I have no idea. Not that it makes any difference. Tuff could tell Joey that Martians had landed, and Joey would believe it."

"Sounds like the sheriff believes Tuff, too."

The comment earned him a glare.

"Sorry." He concentrated on another bite of cobbler.

"I'm not mad at you. It's—it's . . . I have zero credibility around here. I get so frustrated. I make one little mistake, and nobody lets me forget it. But Tuff flashes a smile, and all is forgiven. It's sickening." She drew up her knees and hugged them. "I've been all over the forest, and I can't find anything suspicious."

"You're sure you never saw the other man before?"

"Positive."

"What did he look like?"

"What difference does it make?" She gave him a mischievous sideways glance. "Most likely he's the only dead guy out there."

Reb chuckled. "Don't do this to me, ma'am. Get me all interested in the story, then leave out details. Did he look like a drug dealer?"

"Like I know what a drug dealer looks like. Shoot, if you met Tuff, you'd think he was a movie star or something. Girls go gaga over him." Her easy smile faded, turned troubled. "By the time they figure out how mean he is, it's too late."

He was beginning to wonder if Emily realized how beautiful she was or what kind of effect she had on him. "So was the other guy good-looking?"

"I suppose he looked like a thug. My height maybe. Light hair, worn in a ponytail. Real muscular, like he worked out a lot in a gym. I didn't see his face very well, but he had a tattoo." She patted her left shoulder. "I saw it underneath his shirtsleeve. It looked like a mountain lion or panther."

His heart lurched, pounding hard against his chest wall. Up until now only suspicions and rumor told him he was on the right track. Her description fit Jimmy Mullow, former small-time hood who'd promoted himself to big-time murderer and thief. Excitement rippled through Reb's muscles, along with dismay. If

Emily spoke the truth, then Mullow was dead and Tuff wasn't about to let slip where he'd stashed the cash.

"What about the duffel bag? Found it?"

She gave him a gee-you're-dumb look. "That's the least of my worries. I have exactly sixty days to either find the body or get my practice in on the target range. I'd prefer not to shoot my own brother even if he did kill a man."

"I'm surprised the sheriff won't help you out. He sounds like he likes you."

Her entire body stilled. Reb realized his comment sounded as if he cared about her love life. When she lifted her eyes to him, the softly amused gleam in their dark depths said that was exactly how she took it.

She picked up her cobbler bowl and rested it on her knee, then scooped out a small amount onto her spoon and nibbled it. A fat drop of melted ice cream clung to her upper lip. She licked it away with a kittenish flick of her tongue. "Mickey's always asking me out, but I don't take it personally. He thinks because I'm a widow, I'm desperate for... company."

"Are you?"

She dropped her gaze, her eyelashes sweeping down like a curtain. "No."

Joey said Emily's husband had died a little more than a year ago, leaving her a wealthy merry widow.

Reb suspected the wealthy part was true. If she had her hands on the three million, then finding Mullow's body would ensure her older brother couldn't hunt her down, and she could skip with the loot without spending the rest of her life looking over her shoulder. But merry? Emily Farraday owned the saddest eyes Reb had ever seen.

"Mind a personal question?" he asked.

Color rose on her cheeks. The sight struck him square in the diaphragm, stealing his breath, firing his blood. For a moment he didn't care about the money. All that mattered was finding out what caused her blush. Low-key anxiousness made him squirm on the seat, bringing him back to earth.

"Ask what you want, but I probably won't answer," she said. She fixed her stare on the barn.

"Why don't you leave?"

"Pardon?"

"Vamoose. Get while the gettin's good. You don't appear overly enchanted with living here."

Lights winked out inside the barn. Joey pulled the big barn door along the tracks. Metal screeched in protest, and the door rumbled like far-off thunder. Head down, his cowboy hat hiding his face, he ambled to the henhouse and shooed a stray chicken inside. He closed the door after her. For a long moment he stood still, facing north, staring at the craggy finger of Hannah Peak.

"Joey scattered Grandpa's ashes up there," Emily said. "The rock was their private place." She dashed the back of a hand surreptitiously at her eyes. "I have to stay for Joey. I made a promise."

"To him?"

She didn't answer. She watched Joey cross the driveway and yard. He climbed onto the porch, careful not to hit Emily with his feet, but not acknowledging her, either.

Reb hoisted his bowl. "You're missing out. Best cobbler I ever ate."

"I'm on my way," Joey said absently, and entered the house. He rattled around the kitchen cupboards.

A few minutes later Joey's footsteps faded down the hallway toward the stairs.

"He'll never forgive me," she said.

"For what?"

"For anything." She sighed. "For everything. For living, I suppose."

EMILY SHIFTED on the wooden step to better see Reb. The unmistakably masculine shape of him filled the corner. Shadows hid his face, except for the corner of his mouth illuminated by the thin edge of light coming through the kitchen doorway. If she wanted to, she could touch his boot without stretching and trail her fingers up the length of his leg to his knee.

She told herself he reminded her of Daniel, of how they used to sit outside on nice evenings to discuss the day. Except Daniel had loved the sound of his own voice. Conversations with him had meant looking interested and nodding in the appropriate places while he exclaimed, laughed, gestured, told stories, hashed over problems and gossiped. No thought crossing his mind ever went unsaid.

Reb sat quietly, his thoughts contained. After a few seconds she noticed the rise and fall of his chest and the almost imperceptible tapping of one finger against the bowl he rested on his thigh. Images rose of his fingers playing soft as a sweet dream against her skin. Of how his hair might smell of shampoo and sunshine and a hint of horse. His arms secure around her, holding her close so she could hear the rhythm of his heart and feel his solid strength against her cheek.

Dangerous thinking. She was beginning to sound desperate even to herself. She jumped to her feet. She snatched up her cobbler bowl and held out her hand for Reb's.

He handed over the bowl. "Did I say something wrong?"

"You don't say anything." She laughed uneasily. "And I'm talking way too much."

He rose from the chair. Moving air brought his scent to her nose, and he smelled exactly the way she imagined: sun, soap, horse. His skin would feel tough, she knew, and his tan would be uneven, dark on his forearms and neck and throat, paler where he wore a shirt. His legs were probably untanned, furry with dark hair and steely with muscle and heavy bone.

Daniel is dead, a voice whispered from far back in her mind. *You're not.*

"You could use somebody to talk to, Mrs. Farraday."

He made the formality sound both polite and ludicrous. "Emily," she said. "Call me Emily." She reached for the door. "No offense, Reb, but talking so much to you isn't right. We aren't friends."

"We could be. Emily."

The way he said her name ruffled deliciously over her scalp and left her ears tingling. "I don't think that would be a good idea." She slipped into the house, escaping with her virtue intact and widow's weeds firmly in place.

As she cleaned up, she listened for Reb to leave the porch. Music from Joey's radio filtered down through the ceiling. Given reprieve from the sun, the old wooden house creaked and groaned, its dry timbers seeming to sigh. A cricket chirped, first from near the door, then as if by a feat of ventriloquism from beneath the sink. Outside an owl warbled a mournful *whoo-scree.*

The owl does cry, tonight you die. Goose bumps tickled her arms.

She finished the dishes. Her entire body ached from listening so hard for boot steps on the creaky old porch. She rubbed lotion into her hands and stared at the screened door. The porch was dark except for a crooked rectangle of light shining through the screen onto the boards.

Reb waited for her. She felt him.

To tell for certain she would have to step outside to see if he remained on the chair in the corner. If she did, he'd know she was looking for him.

He wanted to be her friend.

Cowboys tended to be loners, able to withstand long stretches of solitude, but everybody needed a friend. Despite his calm independence, Reb could be lonesome. She liked talking to him. He didn't appear to have a judgmental bone in his body.

Copper barked, loosing a high-pitched yodel wavering one note below a howl. He was silent for a moment, then he began barking in earnest, a steady *hark-hark-hark* rising in tone and frequency.

Emily backed a step and caught the counter for support. Despite Copper's muscular sixty pounds and powerful jaws, he was a gentle, rather cowardly dog who rarely barked, especially the way he barked now, with urgency and alarm. In the four years she'd owned him, the only person she'd ever known him to growl at was Tuff.

Her first thought was Mickey had made a mistake and now Tuff was out of jail and gunning for her.

Joey called from the top of the stairs, "What's that stupid dog of yours yapping at?"

She frowned at the ceiling. Joey liked Copper as much as she did, but would never admit it in a million years. Stupid dog, indeed. "I'll check and see," she called back.

"If it's a bear, holler."

Bears occasionally visited the trash barrels or chicken house. Having never seen a bear face-to-face, Copper might get excited. He might not realize how badly a bear could hurt him. She grabbed a nine-cell flashlight and left the house.

Beside her Reb said, "Sounds like he's behind the barn."

So, he had remained on the porch, waiting for her. She walked to the center of the driveway, fully inside the glow of the security light.

Copper stopped barking.

She cocked her head this way and that. Because of the hilly terrain and rock formations, sound traveled in deceptive directions. "Copper?" She whistled, then paused, listening. Nothing disturbed the chickens, horses or the milk cow. Creepy little fingers crawled up her spine, and she debated fetching Grandpa's shotgun.

Reb strolled to her side. "Barking at shadows."

"He never does that. My husband trained him not to bark. He's worthless as a watchdog." She cupped a hand around the side of her mouth. "Copper! Here, boy, come on. Copper!" She flicked on the flashlight and followed the wobbling beam to the barn. Reb followed her. "It might be a bear," she tossed over her shoulder.

"If it is a bear, all I have to do is run faster than you."

She laughed. At the back of the barn, she flicked the flashlight beam over the trash-burning barrel. She saw no signs of any animal, not even mice or a raccoon. She called a few more times for the dog, but he failed to show.

Worry settled in her chest. "I shouldn't let him run."

"He seems tough."

If Copper was chasing a bear or, heaven forbid, a mountain lion, he'd still be barking. Unless it wasn't an animal and he'd found a person. He might bark if a stranger startled him—until the stranger put out a friendly hand or spoke a soothing word, then they'd be the best of buddies.

The kind of people who slunk around in the dark were not the kind of people she wanted to meet in the dark. Despite the warm night air, she shivered.

She turned off the light, plunging her and Reb into darkness. The security light shone over the barn rooftop, but didn't reach where they stood. She listened intently for a bark or the pounding of paws or the *choo-choo* train huff of Copper's panting.

Reb's touch on her arm startled her. He closed his fingers gently around her elbow. He put his other hand on the flashlight. Against her ear he whispered, "Do you see something due north?"

Urgency colored his soft voice. She barely dared to breathe, moving only her eyes as she searched the darkness. No moon tonight, only billions of stars glittering icy in the inky sky. As the seconds ticked past, her concentration moved inward, focusing on the heat of Reb's hand on her arm and the rise and fall of his chest where he stood against her shoulder. His scent wafted around her, teasing her.

Unable to stand the silence or his physical presence any longer, she said, "Maybe he's on the trail of a deer. No use looking for him in the dark."

"I thought I heard something running." His breath grazed her cheek.

"Nothing out there." Her throat felt filled with hot dough, making her whisper croaky.

"Do you want some help looking around the property for anything...suspicious?"

The unexpected offer gave her pause. "You?"

"Why not?"

"Joey would pitch a fit."

"Technically you're the boss."

"And I don't need you making trouble." Reb believed her story; she had heard it in his voice. The novelty of it filled her with gratitude—and it threatened to make her do something stupid. She turned for the house, but Reb halted her in midstep.

"You need help."

"So does Joey. You've got roundup and then transporting the cattle to auction in Denver."

"What happens if Tuff gets out of jail before you find evidence that he's done something wrong?"

Unhand me, quivered on the tip of her tongue, but she couldn't force out the words. She couldn't recall the last time a man had touched her, and she liked the comfort of it.

"Joey doesn't need me in Denver," Reb continued. "I can do the chores and help you, too."

"Who do you think you are? Some kind of angel who solves problems in your spare time?"

He leaned close enough to fill her head with his man scent. "I'm no angel, Emily."

Okay, fine, she was a little bit desperate. She laid a hand against his cheek and felt scratchy stubble and the hard jut of his cheekbone. He went rigid. She imagined he was shocked by her boldness. She shocked herself. The very air crackled against her skin, making her tingle.

He lowered his mouth to hers. His lips were cool, spiced with cinnamon. She slid her fingers over his cheek and touched his ear and the soft bristles of his sideburns. Her knees trembled. Her heart sounded like a drum, deafening her to the chirping, squeaking, scratching creatures of the night.

The flashlight swung limply in her numb hand. All feeling centered in her mouth, now greedy for the sweet, fresh coolness of his lips and the powerful thrust of his tongue.

He clutched the small of her back, and she pressed her belly against his, shocking herself anew. She slid and slipped her tongue around and over and under his, eagerly absorbing the slippery strength of his tongue and the smooth evenness of his teeth.

He stepped back, breaking away.

Reality returned with a thud. Mouth open, skin tingling, she stared wide-eyed into the darkness, thankful he couldn't see her blush.

"Good night, ma'am," he said. He strode away, disappearing into the night.

Chapter Four

Reb tried hard, but nothing knocked kissing Emily Farraday out of his head. Hot sun beating down on his back, soaking through his clothes, reminded him of her slim hands burning against his face. Wind whispering through the pines roused memories of her slightly husky voice. At night he dreamed of her, feeling the sweet fit of her against his body and tasting the honey of her pliant mouth.

Even exhausted after a long day chasing wild cows through the brush, he was consumed by thoughts of Emily. He wondered what she was doing right now. Cooking, probably, standing in the sweltering kitchen, stirring a pot while sweat made her dark curls cling to her neck while those ragged old denim shorts cupped her round bottom.

The money, he reminded himself. Find the money, figure out Emily's involvement, do his job and get out. Never get personal. Seducing women to get information was for wise guys and amateurs. He knew better.

Kissing her had been a momentary lapse, one he had no intention of repeating.

"Head up, Reb!" Claude Longo shouted.

Reb snapped his attention to the approaching cattle. Under him the big sorrel gelding, Jack, trembled in anticipation, ready for action.

"Shue, shue, girls, easy inside," Claude Longo sang. Swinging a lariat in lazy arcs, the old man urged cows and calves through the gate of the holding pen. A black-and-white border collie darted back and forth behind the herd like a shadow, nipping at hooves and flanks, keeping the cattle moving. Claude whistled sharply, sending the animal racing after a frisky calf.

The old man intrigued Reb. Claude was at least sixty, maybe older, but he was wiry as a rat terrier and as energetic. If there were limits to his stamina, Reb hadn't seen them, but he had seen Claude's hatred toward Emily. At least once a day he groused to Joey about how Emily had hoodwinked Garth Rifkin and stolen the ranch. As far as Claude was concerned, Emily was to blame for everything from outdated ranch vehicles to the price of beef. It hadn't taken Reb long to catch on to what kept Joey so sour about his sister.

Reb leaned over on the saddle and grasped the gate rope. As the last cow and Claude ambled through the opening, Reb nudged his horse and closed the gate behind them.

Joey rode up beside him, his dark eyes mellow with weary satisfaction. They'd spent a hard four days bringing in the Double Bar R cattle. Steers and heifers destined for market milled about in a nearby corral. The cows and calves in this pen would be inspected for disease, inoculated and treated, ear-notched as needed, then released.

"The truck will be here day after tomorrow," Joey said. "Claude and me will be gone three or four days."

Three or four days alone with Emily, Reb thought, then scowled, pushing down his eagerness. He slouched on the saddle, resting his forearm on the saddle horn. Must be the ranch to blame for the strange turns his brain kept taking.

He'd grown up on a cattle ranch in eastern Arizona. Handling cattle was much like riding a bicycle; the body didn't forget the moves. He'd forgotten what a tough, dirty job it was, though. Despite thick chaps, his thighs felt as if someone had beaten them with a baseball bat. His spine ached from riding a horse through the harsh, mountainous country. In the past few days he'd been stomped on by hooves, knocked against trees and he'd smacked himself numerous times with his own rope.

But he liked it. A few times he'd found himself seriously considering a change. Drop out of sight, erase the past, never look back as he settled on a ranch to live a peaceful life.

No lies, no pretenses, no targets.

He shook away the musing as if shaking away flies. Being on the ranch was making him sentimental.

Keeping an eye on Claude, Joey lowered his voice. "While I'm gone, best watch out for Pat Nyles."

"Who's that?"

"He's a loser who lives over other side of Humbolt. He'll do anything for a buck. And I do mean anything." His mouth pulled, straining downward, and he rubbed his hands nervously over the saddle horn. "Him and Tuff run together. Pat is crazy, totally nuts."

Reb's forehead tightened, and the tension spread over his scalp and reached his neck. "What aren't you telling me, Joey? What does this Nyles have to do with anything?''

The kid flinched, looking guilty. "Tuff's antsy. He keeps asking me what you're doing. He thinks you're ripping him off. What am I supposed to tell him? He says it doesn't matter if I have an alibi or not.''

"Nyles. What about Nyles?''

"He sort of mentioned Pat in passing. I—I didn't think he was, you know, serious.''

Reb itched to land a hard one on Joey's chin, knock him clean off the saddle. "You think this is a game, kid?''

"No!'' He stared blankly at his gloved hands.

Reb glanced across the pen. Claude had dismounted, and now fiddled with the pump on the water trough. "You don't get it,'' he said. "You hope Tuff is kidding. Hell, you hope I'm kidding. But he's not and I'm not. This is dead serious, and if you want to save your skin and this ranch, you better get serious, too.''

"I don't want anybody hurt,'' Joey muttered weakly. He peeked at Reb. "Tuff'll come around. He can't be meaning it. He doesn't want Emily dead, not really. He's just mad 'cause she got him locked up. He'll get over it.''

Reb could have groaned. Joey worked like a man and looked like a man, but he was a confused kid blind to the facts of life. Fact one—Tuff Rifkin wanted Emily dead. Fact two—as soon as Reb got his hands on the money, Tuff and Emily were going down. Fact three—Joey lost all say-so in the script the minute he'd picked up the telephone and said Tuff needed a hit man. No turning back, no changing his mind, no regrets.

"Did he," Reb said slowly, "put Nyles on to Emily?"

"I don't know. Maybe. I don't know."

"Will you see Tuff before you head off for Denver?"

"Yeah. Tonight."

"Two things. Tell Tuff he must be talking in his sleep, because the sheriff heard a rumor about him hiring a hitter."

Joey scowled, shaking his head. "That'll blow it."

"It'll make him cautious, trust me. Drop Nyles's name into the conversation, let him think his buddy is the bigmouth. Second thing, tell him Emily invited some friends to visit. That'll buy some time. Can you do that much, Joey?"

"Why don't you get it over with, Reb? What do you need time for?"

"Trust me. Tell your brother another thing. I want another grand up front."

"You're crazy! I can't ask him that. He'll take my head off."

Reb suspected Tuff had a partner, someone besides Emily, who knew where the money was hidden. Someone who might fetch another thousand bucks and lead Reb straight to the stash.

Joey licked his dry lips. "You believe her, don't you? That's why you're fixing up things around the ranch. Snooping. You think Tuff killed a guy."

The way he looked at Reb said he suffered from doubt. He was finally wising up and realizing his older brother wasn't soliciting murder for hire because he was ticked about spending sixty days in jail for a drunk-and-disorderly charge.

"What do you think?" Reb asked.

Joey shook his head. "I wish both Tuff and Emily would just disappear and leave me alone." With that, he hauled the reins, spurred his horse and the animal carried him away from the holding pen.

EMILY LUGGED STRAW down the center aisle in the barn. The clumsy bale bumped against her knees with every step. Straw dust floated around her head, irritating her nose.

Leave now, she thought. Forget ranching and lousy weather and living in the broken-down old house with its sixty-year-old kitchen and an ungrateful brother who acted like a spoiled-rotten little brat.

This morning at breakfast all she'd asked was for him to make checks from the cattle sale out to her. Checks to Claude Longo meant a hassle with the bank, *after* she'd cleaned up the messes he always caused with his head figuring. Joey had shouted at her, saying Claude would take care of business the way he always did. He'd accused her of being greedy and a cheat.

He'd looked and sounded just like Grandpa.

If she had an ounce of self-respect, she'd sign the ranch over to Joey and walk away. Staying on at the Double Bar R was futile. She didn't belong here, and she owed Joey nothing. Not a single, blasted thing. She had enough money to start a new life. She could open a catering service or attend the culinary institute the way she once dreamed of doing. Grandpa would never know about her broken promise. He had no right to make her promise to do anything in the first place. *He's the one who ran me off the ranch and refused to forgive me for marrying Daniel. Grandpa should have felt guilty, not me.*

Suddenly she realized Reb was watching her. Standing partially inside a stall, he leaned a shoulder against a post. He'd pushed his hat to the back of his head, and its whiteness emphasized the sooty blackness of his hair. Heat flooded her face and throat. It had been easy to avoid him since that dangerous kiss. He'd been busy, working roundup, but now Joey was gone to Denver. That left her and Reb, alone.

"Something wrong, ma'am?" he asked, revealing nothing of what he felt.

"No."

"You look mad about something."

She compressed her lips. Reb had eaten breakfast this morning as if her argument with Joey was no more interesting than a television show. She wondered how Reb had managed to acquire the skill of ignoring crazy goings-on. "I'm not mad about anything," she lied.

"I'm not trying to interfere or anything, but slapping a big wooden spoon upside Joey's head might do you both some good."

She envisioned herself chasing Joey with a spoon and laughed in spite of her mood. "A rolling pin might work. Or a frying pan."

She dropped the straw bale in front of the milk cow's stall, then flexed her gloved fingers to bring back feeling where the baling twine had cut off the circulation. "I'm sorry you have to see us squabbling all the time."

"Family," he said as if it explained everything. "I finished my chores. Need some help?"

What I need, she thought, *is to have my head examined. Why do I keep torturing myself trying to hold this ranch together?* "You can fetch the wheelbarrow." She tried to think of some chore to send him out of the barn and away from her, but nothing came to mind.

He brought the wheelbarrow and two pitchforks. Seeing his intention to help increased her discomfort. He'd walked away from kissing her without any explanation. Most likely Joey had told him some juicy stories about her bad reputation. The way she'd practically offered herself to him in the darkness must have convinced him Joey was telling the truth. She wanted to explain herself, but didn't know how to do so without humiliating herself completely. She grabbed a pitchfork and dug into the task of mucking the stall.

Blossom, the jersey milk cow, ambled across the pasture and peered over the half door into the stall. Emily gave the cow's wet nose a pat. As if realizing somebody received a petting and it wasn't him, Copper trotted into the stall and nudged Emily's leg.

"Get out of here, you big baby," she said fondly. She caught Reb grinning at her.

He wielded the pitchfork as if it had no weight. Within a few minutes they'd filled the wheelbarrow with old straw.

"Are you going out to ride over the property today?" he asked.

"Yes." It was only a matter of time until Tuff was out of jail—and she was in danger. She *had* to find evidence of his wrongdoing on the ranch. She grasped the barrow handles. "Are you serious about helping me, Reb?"

"Sure." He stepped in, easing her aside and taking the handles from her.

She started to protest, but bit it back. She paid him to work, not watch her work. She watched his back muscles working under his thin cotton shirt as he wheeled the barrow out of the barn. She lowered her gaze and admired the fit of his blue jeans and the easy swing of his stride.

She'd never been a flirt or a hunk watcher. So why all of a sudden was it so hard keeping her eyes and wayward thoughts off Reb Tremaine? It was as if a shell had been holding in her exuberance and feelings and needs. Reb with his sexy smile and beautiful eyes had broken the shell, and she fooled only herself in thinking she could fit the pieces back together.

The capriciousness of her soul bemused her. She began flaking apart the straw bale to spread a fresh bed inside the stall. If she needed a man, she should turn her sights on Mickey Thigpen. At least he had a steady job. Reb never said a word about himself, so he remained a mystery.

She'd finished strewing fresh straw and had filled Blossom's water bucket with clean water when Reb returned.

"So, how are you searching?" he asked.

She blinked in puzzlement. "What do you mean, how?"

"Your method. You aren't riding around just hoping to spot something suspicious."

Sheepishly she nodded.

He tsked his disapproval.

"How else am I supposed to do it?" She pointed with her chin at Copper. "I take him along." The dog opened his mouth in a grin, and his tail thumped against the floor, raising dust. "I've been concentrating on one patch of woods, though," Emily continued. "See . . . here, let me show you."

She hunkered into a crouch and smoothed a spot on the barn floor. She used her finger to draw in the dirt. "The forest is diamond shaped. It peters out at the base of Hannah Peak, and there's a deep ravine on the west side. To the south it's all winter pasture and mostly open. Maybe in the daytime Tuff would have chanced climbing down the ravine or up the peak, but not in the dark. Besides, we're talking about a lot of acreage. Rough, rocky ground with plenty of hiding places."

"What about the ravine?"

"I checked. I've been up and down it a couple times. But I didn't see anything unusual." She shook her head. She poked her crudely drawn map. "We should be looking in the woods."

"Searching from horseback is a mistake. Hard rain would have washed away signs of digging or footprints. We'll search on foot and use probes." He scratched underneath his hat and clucked his tongue. "Is there a trail?"

"Several. Deer and cattle wander through there." She touched her map again. "I'm pretty sure Tuff took this main trail that starts almost due west of the house."

"How long was Tuff out there?"

She had to give it some thought. Some details, such as the traces of blood surrounding the outdoor water faucet, haunted her with distressing clarity. Other details, such as the exact time Tuff's arguing had awakened her, were fuzzy. She dredged through her memory and recalled looking at the clock while she cleaned the kitchen. She'd noted it had been an hour since she called the sheriff's department. Tuff had returned about an hour later. "At least two hours," she said. "Certainly no more than three."

"Hmm, then you're right, he couldn't have gotten far." He rose gracefully from a crouch and extended a hand.

She took his hand automatically, and he pulled her upright. His grip remained firm a fraction too long. His touch affected her despite her heavy work gloves. She pulled her hand free.

"We'll use something for markers and conduct a search section by section."

His matter-of-factness caused a funny sort of pain in her heart. He wasn't humoring her or patronizing her or treating her like a crazy woman. He believed in her conviction Tuff was a killer. Having someone treat her like a reasonable human being was almost more than her battered psyche could take. Gratitude made her want to kiss him again.

At least, she told herself it was gratitude.

When she started walking, he swung into step beside her. Her boots thudded dully against the dirt floor, but his made no sound she could detect. "Do you mind me asking where you're from?" She glanced at him. "Originally?"

"Here and there. I grew up in Arizona, near Winslow."

She walked a few paces, awaiting elaboration. It was a rare man who didn't like carrying on about himself. His silence amused her.

"Ah," he said, "she smiles."

She shrugged. "I've always been the quiet one. But around you, I feel downright chatty."

"I don't think you're chatty. I like talking to you."

In a storage shed they scrounged through the decades-old clutter for broom handles to use as probes, and also found a package of red automotive rags to use as markers. Emily filled canteens with water. They headed for the forest. Copper bounded after them, his curly tail waving like a flag.

At Blue Rock Creek, Copper leapt into the pool of water at the tractor crossing, his paws lapping noisily as he paddled across to the other side. He hit the opposite bank running. Reb jumped lithely from a boulder, over the water and onto a flat rock. His easy strength and agility made her nervous all of a sudden. Her brother would be gone for days. No one she knew realized a stranger was working on the ranch. And now she'd accompanied Reb into the forest.

"Hey, little Red Riding Hood," said the handsome wolf, *"come walk with me into the big bad woods."*

Reb held out a hand, urging her to jump the creek. "You can make it."

She glanced at the house. If Reb meant to do her harm, he could easily have entered her house at any time. She grasped the canteen slung over her shoulder to keep it from swinging and jumped the creek.

Reb caught her upper arm to steady her, and time froze as she looked up into his crystal blue eyes. Fearful thoughts wisped away like water vapor. His grin faded, and his mouth softened. His hand tightened on her arm. He was going to kiss her again. She felt it all the way to her toes. She wanted to kiss him.

He turned her loose. "Let's go, ma'am." He hopped off the rock and strode toward the forest.

Disappointment dropped into her belly with a reality-jarring thump. Imagining he liked her was just that—imagination. She huffed in self-disgust. She didn't want a man anyway. She hurried to catch up to him.

"So you suspect your older brother is a drug dealer," he said.

"I know he gets his money from somewhere. When he was a kid, he held wild parties whenever Grandpa was gone."

"So he flashes a lot of cash."

"All I know is, he always has money for booze and parties. And he doesn't believe in holding a job. He hasn't even worked on the ranch since Grandpa died. He gives money to Joey, too, and that scares me. I'm afraid he'll get Joey involved in whatever he's doing."

"What about the sheriff?"

"Mickey basically says he has more important things to do than worry about Tuff. And Tuff is too smart to get caught."

"You've been trying to find evidence against him a long time."

The mildly spoken comment stung. "It's not that way at all. Joey thinks I have a score to settle with Tuff, but it isn't true. I've tried to make peace with him. Live and let live. You don't know what it's like."

"Sorry. I shouldn't have spoken out of turn."

She kicked a rock on the path, and it struck a yucca, sending up a cloud of dark butterflies. She watched their erratic flight path across the meadow to another plant. "I've always been afraid of Tuff, even when we were little. The scariest thing is how good he is at fooling people. He lies for the fun of it. He turns on the charm and gets away with ... murder."

Reb made an encouraging noise.

"He never fooled Grandpa. Brute strength is the only thing Tuff really respects, and Grandpa had plenty of that. Until he got sick. Then Tuff turned on him. He's like a coyote. Once he spots a weakness, there's no stopping him from getting what he wants." She looked up at Reb, sharing her dismay. "The saddest thing is, Grandpa wouldn't ask Joey for help or even let him know what Tuff was doing. He was such an arrogant old man. I'm sure he wanted to protect Joey, or maybe he couldn't admit how Tuff took advantage of him. He was ashamed or something."

She stopped at the edge of the forest. Pounded rock-hard by the passage of countless hooves, the path meandered through the widely spaced Ponderosa pines. Tiny gray-and-black nuthatches hopped around the tree trunks, searching for bugs. Patches of kinnikinnick formed brilliant green carpets dotted by red berries. A jay screamed at them. Crunching wood, rustling and flashes of golden red fur marked Copper's progress through the oak tangles.

"How far is it to the ravine?" Reb asked. He used the broomstick probe as if it were a walking stick.

"As the crow flies?" She made a mental calculation. "Quarter of a mile maybe. The trail goes all over the place, though."

"I take it Tuff is familiar with this forest."

"Very much. When we were kids, this was his forest. Trespassers beware." Seeing him dappled with the cool green light gave Emily the idea Reb was at home in a forest, too. A wild man, as one with Nature.

"Let's start with the obvious. We'll follow the trail and search ten feet along each side."

"Inch by inch."

Reb gave a single nod. He paced off ten steps to the south of the trail and tied a piece of red rag to a twig. "Start here. Keep your head down, assume nothing and use your probe. I'll mark out your search area."

Emily began a zigzag course along the trail. Eyes focused on the ground, she poked the broomstick into piles of leaves and pine straw, beneath fallen logs, under every rock and into every crevice. Except for the occasional scrape of his boots on rocks or the crunch of a pine cone, Reb made no sound while he searched along the opposite side of the trail. The trail followed the hills and valleys, and wound around piles of boulders and massive old trees. Poking and prodding, Emily made slow progress marked by little red flags to show where she'd been. By the time they finally reached the ravine, the sun was skimming the mountain peaks.

Emily drank deeply from the canteen. She poured some water in her cupped hand and rubbed its soothing coolness over her hot face and throat.

Reb swept his gaze up and down the ravine. The other side rose sharply in a chalky gray cliff. Stubborn aspen trees grew at impossible angles near the top, wherever a bit of dirt collected between the rocks. He tested the wire fence erected to keep cattle from wandering over the edge and getting trapped in the ravine. The barbed-wire strands sagged, rusty with age.

"You searched the ravine?"

"I went down into it and followed it from top to bottom. Nothing." She leaned her head far back to get a read on the sun's position. "It'll be dark soon. We best get back."

"We'll look again tomorrow. I'll see about getting the chores done quick—"

His abrupt silence made the short hairs snap to attention on her nape. She followed his line of sight where he stared into the ravine.

"What is it?" she asked.

"I'm not sure." He used one hand to push down the second strand of wire, and he eased through the fence. The top strand knocked off his hat, but he ignored it, his attention fixed on something at the edge of the ravine. Gravel broke and went clattering and tumbling the twenty or so feet to the bottom. He picked something up from the base of a prickly bush.

She scooped up his white straw hat. "What is it, Reb?"

He leaned over, craning his neck to study the inner cliff face. Finally he stepped back to the fence. He showed her a tattered piece of cloth. "Did you lose this?"

The cloth was a cotton black-and-white gingham print. Thin and tightly woven, it probably came from a shirt. She remembered the other night when Copper had been barking, and a frisson of fear tickled her innards. "It's not mine. I don't think it's Joey's either."

Absently Reb brushed thick hanks of hair off his forehead. He peered closely at the cloth. "It doesn't look all that old."

"Maybe somebody else is searching the property."

He lifted his gaze to her face. "Maybe they're looking for the duffel bag. Any ideas?"

Emily could only shake her head. God only knew what Tuff had gotten involved in. Or with whom.

Chapter Five

Emily set the platter of meat loaf in front of Reb. Without Joey around, the kitchen seemed extra quiet. Being alone with Reb caused an awkward silence that tangled her tongue and made her self-conscious about every move she made. Her T-shirt felt too tight; ragged strings on the bottom of her cutoff shorts tickled her thighs, but if she brushed them away, he'd look at her thighs. Even imagining him staring at her bare legs turned her insides to mush.

He smiled in gratitude. Warm light from the old-fashioned globe fixture overhead colored his eyes an electric blue. Dark rings surrounded the irises. She liked looking at him, liked the feeling of connection and understanding—liked the sexiness. He dropped his gaze, breaking the spell.

She loosed a long breath as she hurried to the other end of the table. She seated herself and flipped a napkin over her lap. Head down, she waited for Reb to finish loading his plate with meat loaf and boiled potatoes.

The scrap of cloth he'd found at the ravine lay on the table next to his plate. He picked up his fork, then touched the cloth with his little finger. "It doesn't look weather-beaten or sun-bleached. I'd say it hasn't been there long."

She put food on her plate. "It could belong to a hiker. A lot of folks like the backcountry off the trails. We're less than three miles from a national forest."

"Could be."

Emily focused on her food. Silence wore on her, increasing her nervousness. "Mind a question?" she asked. "Why are you here?"

He hoisted his fork. "I'm hungry."

She waggled a finger at him. "You know what I mean. Why are you on the Double Bar R, working for slave wages? I don't have anything to offer you. No promotions, not even job security."

"I'm a cowboy. I go where the work is."

She ate a few mouthfuls. He knew his way around horses and cattle, and was certainly strong enough for the work. Even so...she observed his nice manners. The way he put down his fork between bites and used his napkin made it easy to picture him wearing a suit and tie while dining in a fine restaurant. It struck her as odd how he knew so much about conducting a search, too. Never in a million years would it have occurred to her to mark out grids.

"What part of New Mexico did you live in?"

If her nosiness offended him, he gave no sign. "Grants. I worked for an outfitter as a hunting guide and wrangler. The boss decided to sell out, and I took it as a sign to move on."

"A hunting guide. I see." His explanation answered many of her questions. Though not the one about why a man of his quality worked for her. She supposed delving too deeply in the subject might embarrass him.

After supper she began clearing the dishes. Reb carried his plate to the sink and scraped it. "You don't have to do that," she said.

"I don't mind," he said. "I'll wash. You dry and put away."

"It might be a lousy old kitchen, but it's mine. I don't like anyone else working in here."

He whistled as he backed away from the sink, and then bent at the waist in a gracious bow. "My apologies, ma'am. Guess I'll go wander around the barn and see if there's anything I can do there. Thank you very much for the chow. It was fine as can be, as usual."

Shame nipped her. He was probably lonely, too, and he had been kind in helping her today. "Have a seat. I'll make a pot of coffee. I've got some cookies if you want something sweet."

"I never turn down a sweet," he said silkily.

"I can make something fancier if you want." For one of his smiles, she'd bake a pastry shop full of tortes.

"Cookies are fine." He sat back down and folded his arms over his chest. "So how long were you married?"

A few weeks ago his use of the past tense would have distressed her. Except she hadn't thought about Daniel once today. For a few disconcerting seconds she tried rousing feelings of loss and grief, but they eluded her. "Almost nine years," she said. Catching the quirk of his eyebrow, she added, "And yes, I was much too young. I had just turned sixteen." She squirted dishwashing detergent into the sink. After she started dishes soaking, she turned her attention to the coffeepot. "What about you? Married?"

He swung his head slowly in reply.

"Never?"

"Can't seem to settle down."

She wasn't certain she believed him. He was a nice man, and he appeared to like women. He didn't seem the type who used his attractiveness for meaningless conquests, either. Unlike her brothers, Reb wasn't vain at all.

"Do you have a girlfriend?" Her eyes widened. "I'm sorry, I don't mean to be nosy. Forget I asked that."

"I don't mind." He chuckled. "No girlfriends. No ties at all."

"What about your family?"

"None to speak of. I'm alone."

Even a weird, dysfunctional family like hers had to be ten times better than being all alone in the world. Her heart ached for him. "Joey probably told you our parents were killed in a car crash when he was only a baby. Grandpa raised us."

She prepared the coffee for brewing and hit the power switch. The smell of coffee reminded her of how Grandpa pounded on doors every morning at four o'clock sharp, even on Sundays. She remembered how his large, shaggy head bowed when he said grace and his uncanny way of saying an exactly one-minute prayer before every meal. He and Joey had been alike in possessing an accurate inner clock.

"Joey told me you and your grandfather didn't get along."

"I hated him when I was a kid. He ran the ranch like a boot camp. His philosophy was, if you weren't working, you were getting into trouble. And when there was trouble, he always took the boys' sides over mine. I was supposed to keep this house spotless and meals on the table and my mouth shut. Girls weren't allowed to have opinions. Or emotions.''

"So you ran away and got married."

She plunged her hands into the hot, soapy water. She laughed, softly, bitterly. "I did better than that. I married an out-of-state city boy who was much older than me." She peeked over her shoulder to catch Reb's reaction. He had none she could see. "Grandpa said if I married Daniel, he'd disown me. So I did and he did." Her chin quivered, and moisture burned her eyes. She focused on the dishes. "I didn't talk to Grandpa again for nine years, and by then he was dying."

"You made up with him, right?"

She closed her eyes, haunted by the memory of tears streaming down Garth Rifkin's weathered cheeks. "He did love me, but he never knew what to do with me. Cattle, horses and boys, that's all he knew. Me? I was from another planet as far as he was concerned." She dashed at her eyes with her forearm. "All I wanted was for him to love me."

"I'm sorry," he said.

She lifted her shoulders in a quick shrug. "After my husband had a heart attack, it hit me how much family means. It still took me a long time to work up the nerve to call Grandpa. I don't know if I can ever forgive myself for waiting so long."

"He was sick before you came home?"

"He'd had two strokes and surgery for a brain aneurysm. He was paralyzed on one side, and he suffered from seizures that caused periods of senility. He'd be lucid, then all of a sudden he couldn't remember who he was. It was horrible. He'd always been so strong. Seeing him in bed during daylight hours was too awful for words.'' Noticing a peculiar expression on Reb's face, she asked, ''What?''

''My mistake. I thought Joey said your grandfather became sick after you came home.''

She shook her head in wonder. ''Did he? I guess if he has to blame someone for Grandpa dying, it might as well be me. He blames me for everything else.''

''He doesn't hate you as much as you think.''

''You're kind to say so, but yes, he does. I was more like a mother to him than a sister, and then I deserted him. Before I left with Daniel, I promised Joey I'd send for him as soon as I got settled.''

''But you didn't.''

''I sent a plane ticket, but Grandpa sent it back and told me if I got anywhere near Joey, he'd have Daniel arrested. I wrote Joey a couple letters, but I never heard from him. I hurt Grandpa, hurt him bad, but I thought he didn't care. I was so stupid. I made such a mess of things. I don't blame Joey for hating me.''

''He thinks you stole the ranch.''

She envisioned Joey, fairly erupting with pent-up emotions, taking full advantage of Reb's friendly ear. It was to the man's credit he was willing to listen to her side, as well. She turned around and rested her backside against the sink. ''If I had stolen the ranch, I'd have dumped it a long time ago. I've had plenty of offers from developers who'd pay top dollar to turn the Double Bar R into ranchettes for rich folks.''

''So why don't you?''

''Because Grandpa made me promise to keep it for Joey. Grandpa knew Tuff was out of control. He got Grandpa's signature on some legal papers so he could sell off land. Tuff told Joey he did it to pay for Grandpa's medical bills, but it's a bald-faced lie.

When I got here, nothing was paid. This place was so deep in debt, Grandpa's lawyer advised me to declare bankruptcy. I've tried to explain it to Joey, but he won't listen. He's mad at me, he's mad at Grandpa. I guess he'll stay mad the rest of his life. The only person he isn't mad at is Tuff, and that's stupid because Tuff caused all this mess.'' She slapped the counter with the wet washrag. ''Sometimes I think Joey is too dumb for living.''

''You'll actually give the ranch to Joey. Free and clear.''

''As free and clear as I can make it. I wish I could do it today. I want to square things between me and Joey, and my leaving might do it. But Tuff will bleed the ranch dry. So if I can prove Tuff killed that man, all my problems are solved.'' Hearing how terrible she sounded made her wince. ''It's not like I *want* my brother to be a murderer, but he is. And if he goes away to prison, then Joey will be safe.''

Reb's mild expression and hooded, nonjudgmental eyes made her laugh.

''What's funny?'' he asked.

''You'd make a great therapist.'' When she saw the coffee was done, she reached for a mug. ''I bet you're thinking it sounds like a soap opera and we're all crazy.''

''I don't think that at all, ma'am.''

She poured coffee and put chocolate-chip cookies on a plate. She placed the mug and plate in front of him. In passing, her arm brushed his shoulder, and an electric thrill coursed through her. She figured it must be all the talking getting to her, the communicating. It had been a long while since anyone showed enough patience to listen to her. She brushed his shoulder again, this time on purpose. When he looked up, embarrassment over her boldness made her hurry back to the sink.

She didn't mean to lead him on. She didn't want a fling with the hired hand.

Kissing him again would be nice, though.

The telephone rang.

Tuff—she knew it had to be Tuff. She snatched the handset off the hook and held her breath, waiting for the inevitable mechanical voice of the collect-charges operator.

"Emily Farraday?" a man said cautiously.

Deflated, she sagged against the wall. "Yes, it is. May I ask who's calling?"

"A friend."

Nerves prickled along her spine. The gruff, whispered voice didn't sound friendly. "Who is this?"

"Stay out of the forest, Emily. I'm warning you. You're snooping around where you don't belong."

"Oh, God!" She nearly jumped out of her skin. "You're calling for Tuff! Well, you tell him I said—"

"You keep poking around those woods, you're gonna get hurt. Hurt bad. Maybe hurt dead. Don't say I didn't warn you." He hung up with a sharp click.

Emily's body jerked, but she kept the phone to her ear in case it was a bad connection and not a hang up. Silence rewarded her vigil, and she slowly placed the phone on the hook. Finding Reb at her elbow startled her again. "Put a bell around your neck or something," she snapped.

Reb cocked his head, his expression puzzled. "What's wrong?"

She hugged her elbows, and a shudder rippled through her from head to toe. Her gaze locked on the scrap of black-and-white-checked cloth lying on the table. "Tuff had one of his creepy buddies tell me that I'll get hurt if I don't stay out of the forest. Or killed."

Sapphire fire blazed in Reb's eyes and his jaw muscles tightened, flaring. His thick eyebrows lowered. "Did you recognize the voice?"

"No." Her throat ached with the effort of holding terror at bay. If Reb would only laugh or pass it off, then it couldn't be serious. His angry reaction made her feel worse. "Oh, jeez, I thought with him locked up, I'd be okay. Now I have to worry about his friends. Some of them are probably worse criminals than he is." She grasped Reb's forearm. It was unyielding corded steel under her fingers. "What am I going to do?"

He placed his hand over hers, and its weighty gentleness soothed her somewhat.

He said, "Call the sheriff."

"He'll just think I'm making this up." She sought answers in Reb's steely blue eyes, and found only anger.

REB WAITED until the lights inside the house winked out. The sodium arc bulb in the security light cast a silver glow over the house and turned the rocky yard in front of the bunkhouse into a moonscape of black-and-gray shadows. Reb sat on the bunkhouse porch, listening to the wind rustling through the trees and animals settling in the nearby barn.

The temperature had dropped sharply. Wispy clouds blew across the face of the quarter moon. Reb mused over how, if he lived a normal life, this would be a perfect night to court Emily. He'd stand under her window and sing a sappy song. Tease her into coming out to play, to dance in the dark. He squashed the thought as quickly as it had risen.

He had no time for romance—or for wishing. He had a serious problem. Having been over the property, he hadn't found a single piece of evidence Tuff had murdered Mullow. He hadn't found any trace of the money. Time was running out. The call threatening Emily meant Tuff was gathering troops.

He considered calling in his own troops, but only briefly. Without a casting sheet naming all the players, he had no idea who or how many were involved. Better to play this as low-key as possible.

He rose, keeping his ears alert and his eyes fixed on the house. He'd exchanged his boots for athletic shoes, and they helped silence his already quiet tread. He crossed the yard and mounted the back porch, taking care to avoid the squeaky boards he'd come to know. At the kitchen door he paused, listening. Hearing nothing to indicate Emily was up and moving around, he opened the screened door. In the assumed role of handyman, he'd oiled the hinges, and the door opened smoothly without a sound. He slipped a key into the inside-door lock and it turned easily. The inner door, too, opened silently. He let himself inside.

He crossed the floor and touched the wall-mounted telephone. A surge of chest-tightening anger caught him off guard. The irony of it didn't escape him. He was the last person in the world who should feel any concern about some hard case threatening Emily Farraday.

He lifted the handset and pressed it to his ear. He had to think a moment, to remember the local service number. By feel, he punched in star-six-nine. A mechanical-sounding voice told him the number of the last caller. The seventy-five-cent charge for caller identification would show up on Emily's next phone bill, but by then the job should be done.

FOR TWO DAYS Reb helped Emily search the forest. She kept looking around her, and she stuck close to him; the threatening call had shaken her. She even brought out her grandfather's shotgun, toting it as she searched. The shotgun made him nervous. He kept envisioning her finding the duffel bag and saying, *Thanks, Reb*. Boom.

Soon tree trunks and bushes sported red rag markers throughout the forest. Reb kept a sharp eye out for signs of other searchers, but though they left no stone unturned, no hole unexplored and no thicket unexamined, he didn't find so much as a boot print. He tried not to keep that sharp eye on Emily.

The distinct possibility existed Emily had already found and relocated the three million dollars. But every minute he spent with her, enjoying her company, liking her gentle sense of humor and admiring her perseverance, made it that much harder to picture her as a crook.

On the third day, while Emily served Reb's breakfast, she told him, "I've got to go to town today. I'll be back for supper, but you have to fix your own lunch. I can trust you to not mess up my kitchen, right?" Her dark eyes held dire warning; a gentle curve of her lips softened the admonishment.

Such a kissable mouth, he thought mournfully, as full and ripe as berries. If the sultry little glances and coquettish smiles she'd been tossing at him were any indication, it was a mouth wishing very much to be kissed. "Yes, ma'am. You won't find a crumb."

Her unruly curls were tamed into a single braid hanging down her back. A sleeveless blue chambray blouse tucked into white jeans showed off her full bosom and slender waist. Her arms were suntanned and finely muscled, her shoulders brushed with sprays of fine freckles. He noted the touches of mascara on her naturally lush eyelashes and glossy balm on her lips.

"You don't have to search the forest...." Her voice trailed off as she eyed him hopefully.

"I can keep searching."

"I'd be obliged." Her sunny smile stripped him of coherent thought. "You don't think it's useless, do you? I mean, we've covered acres and found nothing. I don't want you think you're wasting your time."

"I'm ready and willing, ma'am."

"You are an angel." She sat down and picked up a pen. Next to her plate lay a sheet of paper. "I'm going into Grand Junction. Do you need anything?"

"No, ma'am. Why all the way to Grand Junction?"

She gave him a cocky grin and held up an advertisement she'd torn from a newspaper. "I'm taking Joey's truck to put new tires on it. He's worked so hard, he deserves them." Her smile turned fetchingly sheepish. "They're having a sale, and it's too good a deal to pass up." She turned the paper so he could see it. She tapped a line she'd written. "This is the brand Joey needs, right?"

"Yes, ma'am." Confusion gave him a feeling like a fist around his diaphragm. He'd heard her complain about this old kitchen and its need for new appliances. A dishwasher would cut her cleanup time by half. It made no sense for a greedy, grasping woman to spring for new tires for her ungracious brother.

"I should be back before Joey gets home. If you want to use the washing machine to do some laundry, go ahead. Soap and such are in the cabinet over the machines. Clean out your pockets before you wash, please." She pushed a key toward the center of the table. "And keep the house locked up." She rolled her eyes. "I'm probably the only person in the valley who has to lock the doors."

He'd been waiting for an opportunity to search the house, and here she gave him carte blanche. Instead of satisfaction, his gut tightened with shame.

Shame lingered while Reb did his chores. Since his arrival on the Double Bar R, he hadn't found one shred of evidence Emily had anything to do with murder or theft—except for Tuff, Joey and Claude saying she was bad to the bone. She trusted him. She liked him.

This job was starting to get on his nerves.

By the time he finished working, Emily was gone. He entered the house, which was of wood construction and creaky with age. The floors beyond the kitchen were oak planks. Even Reb's practiced light tread made the floorboards creak. Hardening his jaw and his heart, refusing to look beyond the task at hand, he searched the kitchen, going through each cabinet methodically, ignoring no possible hiding place.

In the laundry room he threw a load of clothes in the washer. In case anyone came home early, it gave him an excuse for being inside the house.

He searched the small room. He found a stray sock behind the dryer, nothing more. He moved his search through the parlor, family room and the storeroom behind the stairs. Nothing. He didn't expect to find the money in the house. After all, Emily wouldn't want Joey finding it, either.

Still, he had to eliminate the obvious. He went downstairs to the basement. A single naked light bulb illuminated the narrow, low-ceilinged, dirt-wall cellar, which consisted of two rooms. The main room held the furnace, water heater and freezer; the smaller room served as a root cellar, containing bins of root vegetables and shelves of canned goods. He checked the freezer, examining each wrapped package. Braced for a possible meeting with a spider or snake, he felt around the walls and behind bins for hiding holes.

Behind a bin he found a plastic sandwich bag containing some marijuana. He guessed it belonged to Tuff. "Nice going, cretin," he muttered, tucking the bag in his pocket.

He climbed the stairs to the second floor. There were four bedrooms and a bathroom upstairs. Emily had closed the windows in the event of an afternoon thunderstorm. Even this early in the morning, the rooms were hot and stuffy. Reb picked out Joey's room immediately. It looked like a teenager's room. Ribbons awarded for 4-H animal-showing competitions and trophies won in bull-riding events were on proud display on shelves along one wall. Reb searched the room quickly and efficiently. He found nothing.

The next bedroom was larger. Tuff's room, Reb guessed, as he eyed a new television set and VCR. The closet was jammed with expensive clothing. Reb examined a hand-stitched Italian linen shirt. Two hundred bucks easy, retail. Tuff had a fondness for ostrich-skin cowboy boots and gold jewelry, too. Not bad for a cowboy without a job.

In the bottom of a dresser drawer he discovered some marijuana paraphernalia. There was no money in Tuff's room, though.

The third room was small and tidy. Work shirts and trousers hung in the closet. Denim jeans, socks and underwear filled a dresser. Boxes full of papers and other memorabilia were under the bed and on the closet shelf. Reb found a shoebox full of prescription pill bottles made out for Garth Rifkin.

One empty bottle had contained a blood thinner. The prescription had been filled eighteen months ago, which meant Emily, not Joey, told the truth about when their grandfather had suffered the first stroke.

He hesitated about calling Joey a dirty little liar, but apparently the kid didn't know the difference between truth and fiction. Or he didn't care. Or maybe he was so convinced of Emily's guilt that facts didn't matter.

He entered Emily's bedroom. He noted the dead-bolt lock on the door. Of shiny brass, it looked newly installed. Along with the bed, the room held two dressers, an armoire, a parson's table groaning under a junglelike collection of houseplants, a desk and a file cabinet. Her closet was jammed to critical mass with dresses, pastel-colored suits, lacy blouses and racks full of shoes.

The shoes took him aback. He'd only seen her wear sneakers and boots. He picked up a dainty red alligator pump with a gold tap on the toe and a slender spike heel. He caressed the glossy leather, rousing images of the elegant line of her calf and shapely sculpting of her ankle above the shining red high heel.

He quickly replaced the shoe.

Steeling himself, he checked pockets and felt around for hidden panels on the walls behind the clothes.

A dangling length of silk scarf brushed over his face, and as he moved to push it away, he couldn't help pressing it to his nose. Mellow sweetness redolent of vanilla and flowers filled his head with images of her wearing nothing but red shoes, sweet perfume and a smile, her arms open in welcome, her breasts bouncing softly. Heat flooded his groin, and every muscle tensed in thwarted pleasure. He sprang out of the closet as if it contained monsters. Chest heaving, fists on his hips, he shook his head to clear it.

In the file cabinet he found bank statements. She hadn't made a deposit in three months, but debits were numerous. He found an insurance file. Her late husband had owned a policy for one hundred thousand dollars. Reb couldn't find anything to indicate she'd inherited an estate worthy of note. Not much of a rich guy. He discovered she'd spoken the truth, too, about inheriting financial woes along with the ranch.

Reb wondered if Joey realized he could have lost the ranch to creditors if he'd inherited instead of Emily. Or if Joey realized his sister used her personal funds to keep this outfit afloat.

Troubled and beginning to feel like a low-down, belly-crawling sneak, he turned his attention to the desk. On top was a letter Emily had begun. In small, neat handwriting on lilac stationery she had written:

Dear Sharon,

I miss you so very much and if I can ever get ahead here, I'd love to take you up on your offer to visit. I miss the gang, but you most of all. I even miss Kansas City, humidity and all. Every morning around ten o'clock I still get the urge to pour a big cup of tea, extra sugar and milk, and spill my guts to you. Did I ever tell you that when Daniel was driving me nuts with his constant go, go, go and talking all the time, you were the only thing keeping me sane? I loved him so much, but he never listened! I wish you were here to talk to now. I could sure use a pal. I have made a friend, sort of. He's a cowboy my brother hired. He's very nice and polite, and cute, too. More than worthy of one of your "hunk alerts." His name is Reb, isn't that sexy? Am I a bad person for thinking about another man so soon after Daniel? When I'm with Reb, I don't think about Daniel at all. (Not with him in the biblical sense, silly girl! I know what you're thinking!) It's kind of embarrassing, but every time Reb is around, I start talking. I'm starting to think he's a psychiatrist incognito. I go on and on, worse than Daniel even. But it's good being able to say what's on my mind without starting a big fight, and he's so very sweet.

Conscience ripped through Reb like a lightning bolt. He replaced the letter where he'd found it and stepped back, hands on his hips, his jaw aching with tension.

Sweet. Nice.

He wasn't nice, he never had been nice and he had no intention or desire to ever be nice. *Nice* wasn't in his job description.

Chapter Six

"Who the hell do you think you are?" Joey demanded as he strode across the driveway. Gravel crunched under his boot heels. His eyes snapped with dark fury.

Seated inside Joey's old pickup truck, Emily pulled the key out of the ignition. Holding both hands on the steering wheel, she watched her brother's approach. Red-faced, fists clenched, knees stiff, Joey looked as if he meant to start swinging.

His blank, bulging eyes made him look so much like Tuff that fear paralyzed her. Common sense shouted at her to start up the pickup and escape. Her hands were clenched, white knuckled and aching, on the steering wheel. A key cut into her palm.

He jerked open the passenger door. Metal groaned and the truck rocked. "Get out of my truck!" His voice cracked. "You leave my stuff alone! I don't ever want you touching my truck! Nobody said you could drive it. Get out!" He grabbed her arm. His fingers dug between her biceps, and the pain snapped her into action.

"Joey! You're hurting me!" She slapped at his hand with the heavy ring of keys.

He tightened his grip cruelly and grabbed at the keys. Reb stepped behind Joey, caught the young man by the upper arms and hauled him away from the truck. Joey shouted, "Hey!" dropping his hold on Emily and kicking frantically. His boots clanged against the truck and flung gravel. Emily scrambled backward, dropping the keys onto the floorboard. Reb wrestled Joey to the side and kicked his feet out from under him. Joey hit the dirt with a thud and a cloud of dust. His good gray felt hat went skidding across the driveway.

Reb's eyes were steel; his expression was deadly calm as if knocking around an enraged cowboy was merely business as usual. He loomed over Joey.

"You stay out of this!" Joey shouted, and hoisted himself to a crouch. There he hesitated. "This isn't any of your business."

"I just made it my business."

"I'm not scared of you," Joey growled through his teeth. He made no move to rise.

Reb's fingertips twitched as if telling Joey to come on, get up and fight.

Emily supressed a sob, and her chest ached with the effort. She'd seen Joey angry many times, but never like this. Never had she considered she might need to fear him physically. She eased out of the truck, feeling carefully for footing. Looking between both men, she sidled away from the truck.

"I'm sorry, Joey," she said. "It was supposed to be a surprise."

"That truck is all I have. You've got no call to—"

"She put new tires on it, knucklehead," Reb said. "Look at them."

While Joey's expressive face ran the gamut of emotions from anger to surprise to suspicion before finally settling on wary sheepishness, Emily thought her heart would break. "They were on sale. I know you needed them...and you work so hard and I know you wouldn't take the money, so I thought I'd...surprise you."

Her brother cast a cautious glance at Reb before slowly rising. Always keeping an eye on the bigger man, he fetched his hat and swiped away the dust. "I can't afford brand-new tires...."

"They're a gift, free and clear. All I wanted was to see you smile." Emily gathered her purchases and the school information she'd picked up in Grand Junction and trudged to the house.

Only when she was safely inside did she allow herself to feel the inner and outer pain. She lifted her left arm and studied the darkening bruises. If not for Reb, Joey surely would have struck her. Then what? She couldn't live trapped between the threat of Tuff getting out of jail and Joey prowling around the house looking for an excuse to trounce her.

"Ma'am?" Reb stood on the other side of the screened door. He held his hat in both hands. "Are you all right? May I come in?" He entered before she could answer.

She dashed away hot tears building in her eyes. "Now isn't a good time." A lie—she wanted very much for him to come into the kitchen and let her fall into his strong arms. She wanted his husky voice soothing her, talking away her fear. "I'm all right, but I need to get supper started. I'm running late, so would you tend the cow for me? Put a cup of dried molasses in her feed."

"I'll talk to Joey."

Tempting, but then the problem wouldn't go away; it would only go into hiding until Reb went away. "Thank you for your concern, but it's between me and Joey." Tears rose faster than she could avert her face. Clapping both hands over her mouth did little to choke down the sobs.

Reb enfolded her in his arms. She let loose a wail and clutched his shirt while he stroked her hair.

"I can't live like this," she whispered between hitching sobs. "I'm scared all the time, and I don't know what to do and I don't know who to turn to. It's awful enough him shutting me out and giving me the cold shoulder and blaming me for everything that goes wrong. I love him so much, but I can't be afraid of him, too. I can't."

Reb swayed gently, rocking her, soothing her. She pressed her cheek against his shoulder, waiting for the sobs to subside. By virtue of size alone he offered comfort.

She reached for a roll of paper towels. Reb released her. She turned her back on him while she blew her nose and wiped her hot, sticky face.

He placed a heavy hand on her shoulder.

"I don't know how to tell him I'm sorry," she said, her throat sore from crying. "I was so young. I didn't mean to desert him and make him think I don't care. I was only a kid and I was hurting." She tossed the paper towels into the garbage can, then tore two more off the roll. "I love him, Reb, I do. But he's breaking my heart." She searched Reb's face—and found compassion. "I'll work this out with him. Some-how."

"Are you all right?"

She wondered if she'd ever be all right. Through the screened door she could see Joey's truck, but not Joey. Most likely he was hiding out in the barn. "I need to get to work on supper."

"I'll talk to him."

"I can't earn his respect secondhand." On impulse she thrust out her hand, reaching for Reb.

He grasped her hand, and they entwined their fingers. She searched his kind, handsome face, wishing he would hold her again. An expression akin to pain tightened his features, and a low noise rumbled deep in his chest. He pulled her to him and grasped the back of her neck, snatching her against his body. He kissed her. Hard.

The erotic possessiveness of his hands melted her joints. She clutched at his back. His mouth captured hers with bruising force. Greedy for the sensation of his slippery tongue and intoxicating taste, she met him with equal vigor, pressing the full length of her body against his. Fires ignited, filling her veins with liquid heat.

She suckled his lower lip, and his late-day beard rasped her chin. He smelled of hot sun and vibrant masculinity. He tasted wet and fresh like rainwater.

He released her hand, but tightened his hold on the back of her neck. She touched his hip, splaying her fingers in tentative exploration along the rough fabric seam of his jeans. He brought his hand to her face, and his touch turned tender against her cheek while the thrust of his tongue teased and tantalized, stoking her inner fires.

Breaking the kiss, she gasped. He caught the front of her throat in a wet, lusty kiss, and his teeth raked deliciously across sensitive skin. Her knees threatened to collapse.

Lifting his head, he gazed upon her through eyes gone dark and heated. All that showed of his irises were thin, electric blue rings surrounding smoldering pupils. He slid his hands down her neck to her shoulders. His fingers tightened. His thumbs caressed her collarbones.

Her heart thudded; all other sounds were muffled and far away. The heat of the kitchen was nothing compared to the fires inside. She panted softly through her mouth.

"I'm...I'm sorry," he said in a voice so soft it barely reached her.

"I'm not," she whispered back. An urge to add *Come to me tonight* was so overwhelming she had to close her eyes to keep from saying it aloud. Holding back the words gave her an unfulfilled ache.

He turned her loose and headed for the door.

"Reb."

He stopped with his hand flat on the screened door. His shoulders twitched.

"You aren't taking advantage of me or anything. I'm a big girl. I can take care of myself. I know what I want. At least, I think I do." She fingered her lower lip, and it was engorged, still tingling from his kiss.

"Yes, ma'am."

She wanted to tell him he touched her with his kindness and his strength. She didn't know if that was a basis for a relationship, but it felt like one and if he thought so, too, then nothing stood in their way.

While conflicting thoughts and emotions held her silent, Reb slipped out of the house. When the screened door slapped softly against the jamb, she sighed and absently wiped at her hot face.

Staying busy was her only cure for misery, so she dived into cooking supper. Her thoughts kept drifting to the bunkhouse and the narrow iron-framed bed where Reb slept. He slept naked, she guessed, or perhaps in his underwear. Either way, pictures in her head of his hard, gorgeous body gave her periodic chills.

While she was frying chopped beef for chili, Joey crept into the kitchen. His hat was pulled down low on his forehead, his hands were jammed into his jeans pockets and his shoulders were hunched. Her back muscles crawled, growing taut along her spine.

"Emmy?"

The childhood nickname opened a floodgate inside her chest, spilling painful emotion. She wanted to run to him and gather him in her arms. She stirred the frying meat; the spoon clanged against the cast-iron pot.

"I'm sorry for grabbing at you. I'm—I'm ashamed of myself. I had no call."

That's all right, hovered on her tongue. But it wasn't all right, and if she said so, it never would be all right.

"You can't ever do that again, Joey. Not ever, not for any reason." She set the spoon aside and faced him. "I know you don't think I love you, but I do. I want the best for you. But I won't accept threats—or abuse of any kind."

SUPPER PROVED surprisingly tame, outwardly at least. Except for a few troubled glances and excruciatingly polite pleases and thank-yous, Joey ignored Emily. He talked to Reb about Denver and the cattle sale.

Emily managed to not embarrass herself with Reb, but awareness of him left her feeling sticky and un-balanced inside. It was as if their kiss had left behind an aura or shadow, a lingering psychic scent trail. Having him so close stripped the air from her lungs, making every breath a chore. Each time he looked her way, she craved another touch.

Having Claude Longo arrive at the back door was almost a relief. The old cowboy entered the kitchen with a bandy-legged swagger and a gleam in his eyes. Emily resisted the urge to stand even taller so she could look down on him; it would only make him act more obnoxious.

"Hello, Claude," she said. "You're just in time for coffee and pie."

"Cream and sugar in the mud, and ice cream on that pie, girl." Claude clapped Joey's shoulder in passing and nodded a friendly greeting at Reb. He took Emily's chair at the head of the table.

He's old, she reminded herself, *set in his ways.*

Claude slapped onto the table a thick sheaf of pa-pers bound with a rubber band. "Receipts, expenses, invoices, checks. All here. I'm tired as a hound dog after a bear hunt, but I'll go over this with you, girl. Step-by-step, so you know I'm honest." His taut grin dared her to say a single word refuting his honesty.

She bit back a sharp retort and forced a smile. "I'm sure everything is in order."

He patted his shirt pocket. "I cut my own check." His eyes narrowed in challenge. "You want to look at it?"

"No need." Catching a questioning look in Reb's eyes, she was embarrassed. No doubt he was wonder-ing what kind of wimp she was. She hurried through serving pie and coffee, then grabbed the paperwork and made her escape upstairs.

She tossed the papers onto her desk, then unzipped her jeans and worked them off her hips and legs. She reached for a pair of shorts on the foot of the bed, and froze. The bed didn't look quite right. Cocking her head this way and that, she studied the way the bedspread was tucked under the pillows.

Goose bumps rose on her arms and across her shoulders. Turning a slow circle, she felt it. Someone had been in her bedroom. Someone had *touched* her belongings.

No doubt when Joey got home and found his truck missing, he'd come in here seeking revenge. She hurried to the closet and tore open the door. A quick scan of the hanging clothes told her they'd been moved. She'd always been organized and efficient; disorder made her a little crazy. Even though her clothing was hanging okay, it wasn't exactly right. She grabbed her jewelry box off the shelf and opened it. To her relief, nothing was missing.

She pulled on the shorts. When she sat down before the desk, she knew it had been touched, too. Nothing missing, nothing horribly out of place and if she weren't so neurotic about everything being just so, she'd never notice. Seeing she'd left the unfinished letter to Sharon out in full view made her cringe. So now Joey knew she had a crush on Reb.

Marvelous.

She set to work on the papers from the sale. It relieved her to see Claude had already countersigned the checks over to her. They'd received a good price for the cattle. Barring catastrophe, the proceeds would bring all the current bills up-to-date. Armed with a calculator and an eye for detail, she checked Claude's figures. He'd miscalculated the net profit by eighteen hundred dollars and shorted his own bonus by ninety-five. He'd forgotten Reb's sale bonus completely.

Head figuring! If it didn't mean hours of extra work and a few long-distance phone calls to double-check figures, it would be funny.

It took her all evening and most of the next morning to get the paperwork straightened out. When Joey and Reb appeared for lunch, she handed Joey an extra check along with the envelope holding deposits for the bank.

He held the check in both hands and scowled at it. "What are you giving me a check for?"

"It's not for you. Ninety-five dollars of it goes to Claude. He shorted himself, and I don't feel like getting into a shouting match with him over his math. I don't care what you tell him, make up a story, but give him his money." She flashed an apologetic smile at Reb. "The rest is Reb's bonus. Claude forgot, I guess."

Color rose from Joey's neck, up and over his cheeks. Even his ears burned with a fiery blush.

"*Joseph,* you forgot, too?" Emily rolled her eyes.

Reb peered suspiciously at her. "Bonus?"

"It's a Double Bar R tradition," she said. "When cattle are sold, hands get a bonus. It's not much, but it's a way of saying thanks for the extra work. I'll give you your regular pay in cash, too, if you want. That way you don't have to hassle with the bank."

"I guess I did forget, Reb," Joey mumbled, tucking the check into the envelope. "It's been a while since we've had hired hands."

"Claude forgot, too, and he's got no excuse. We have to face the truth. He's seventy-six years old."

"You can't fire him," Joey whispered. Stricken, eyes wide, he looked about six years old. "This is his home. He's as much part of the ranch as Hannah Peak."

"I am not going to fire him or get into a fight to make him quit or anything. For as long as he wants it, this is his home." Her jaw tensed uncomfortably. Claude was another legacy from her grandfather. "But I can't let him take care of the bookkeeping anymore. He makes math errors. He forgets to file papers. He wants to fight with the IRS and the land-management people even when he's in the wrong."

"Claude's the manager. He's supposed to do the paperwork."

"Not anymore."

Joey pushed back his chair. "I can't tell Claude you're taking over his job! No way! He's the manager—"

"*You're* taking over," she interrupted in a mild, matter-of-fact voice. She picked up her sandwich. Joey's shocked expression almost made her laugh. "While I was in Grand Junction, I picked up some class information," she continued. "You can take courses in bookkeeping and accounting. It's not that hard, and I can help teach you."

"Me?" He looked to Reb as if the cowboy had something to do with Emily's decision.

Reb stared at his plate and ate steadily. Emily thought she detected a twitch of a grin on his supple lips.

"Yes, you. Face reality, Joey, you're not Grandpa's cowhand anymore, you're a rancher. Claude isn't going to be around forever. Neither am I. If you're going to stay afloat with this outfit, you'd better learn the business end."

"I reckon," he mumbled, and concentrated on his food.

Joey hurried through his lunch, grabbed his hat and scooted out the door. His truck engine roared to life, and he raised a cloud of dust as he sped out of the driveway.

His silent acceptance of her decree made her uneasy. She never won arguments without a major battle preceded by a lengthy campaign.

"Oh, boy," Emily said, and rested her chin on her fist. "I think I just stepped in it big-time."

"What do you mean?" Reb asked. He folded his napkin and laid it beside his plate.

"He took that too well. He's up to something."

Reb laughed. The sound of it startled Emily. His laughter was rarer than his speech. Charmed, she peered at him questioningly.

"The kid has some mind changing to do. Maybe a few words to eat. You're reaching him."

"Do you really think so?" she asked hopefully.

"You might make a man out of him yet." Reb rose and nodded graciously. "Good food as usual, ma'am."

"Are you making fun of me?" Still with her chin on her fist, she gazed up at him, admiring the way a shaft of sunlight made blue sparks in his hair. "You're calling me 'ma'am' again. You make me sound like a grand old dame."

"Being polite."

"I see."

"My mama always told me, I can't be completely worthless as long as I use good manners."

"Did your mama teach you to kiss a girl then run off like she bites?" As soon as she spoke, she was sorry and wished she could take back the words.

"I'm sorry you think..."

"I don't know what to think," she said. Warmth crept over her face. "I never actually dated or had a boyfriend. I married Daniel quickly, without a long courtship. Am I doing something wrong?"

Reb lowered his face and caught the back of his neck in his hand. His knuckles flexed. "I don't know how long I'll be around...Emily. No sense starting something I can't finish."

"I see."

"You aren't doing anything wrong."

She swallowed hard, mustering courage. "Neither are you. Truth is, I'm not looking for anything or demanding anything from you. A big part of me still feels married." When she said the words aloud, she heard the untruth. She'd loved her husband with all her heart, and she still loved him, but he was gone. She glanced at her left hand, now bare of her wedding ring. She'd removed it to wash dishes several days ago and forgotten to put it back on. She hadn't missed it.

"I respect that." He dropped his hand to his hip and hooked his thumb in a belt loop.

"I like being with you. Talking to you." She prayed Reb didn't misunderstand. She didn't want a quickie affair or loveless sex no matter how passionate.

But she very much wanted Reb Tremaine.

He took a step closer to the door. "I've got to set out salt licks this afternoon. Don't go into the forest alone."

She knew he worried about the anonymous caller who didn't want her searching for whatever Tuff had hidden. "I'm not that brave. I'll wait until you get back. Maybe we can go out after supper before it gets dark."

He settled his hat squarely on his head and left the house.

His escape—and *escape* fit his departure perfectly—hurt her feelings. Maybe she wasn't pretty enough for him. Maybe he only kissed her because he thought she was loose.

Trying to push him out of her mind, Emily spent the afternoon harvesting beans, squash and cucumbers from her garden. Then she went to the barn in search of canning supplies. While she rummaged in a storage room looking for jars without cracks or chips, she heard Joey's pickup truck rumbling up the driveway. A box of old jars caught her attention. The glass had turned blue and green over the years. She imagined they'd fetch a decent price in an antique store.

"Did you get it?"

Reb's voice startled Emily. She hadn't realized he'd returned. She picked her way through the clutter to the open storage-room door and peered out. Reb and Joey stood in the wide middle aisle near the barn door. Joey cast furtive glances toward the house.

"I got it," Joey said. He looked angry and sounded sullen. "I don't like this. I don't like it at all." He put something into Reb's waiting hand.

Emily squinted, trying to see what her brother gave Reb, but the man slipped whatever it was into his pocket.

"You're doing good, kid. Trust me."

Joey shook his head and turned away. "It doesn't feel good. I don't know how I let you talk me into it."

"You came to me."

Meeting in the gloomy barn to pass goods couldn't be a good thing. Emily stepped out of the storage room and called, "Just a minute, you two!"

Chapter Seven

Joey stood frozen, his eyes wide and his mouth hanging open. Reb merely watched Emily stomping down the barn aisle. Emily focused on her brother. He looked guilty as sin. She was so afraid he'd turn out like Tuff that her heart threatened to explode.

"What did you just give him?" she demanded.

"I, uh, none of your damn business."

She stopped before them. She glared at Reb, and the unwavering way he returned her gaze increased her fury. The man didn't possess an ounce of shame. He didn't care about her or her brother.

"The only thing I gave Reb is his bonus money," Joey said. "Just like you told me to."

She looked for lies, but he stared at his boots and his hat brim covered his face. "Money, right. Sneaking around the barn. I saw you looking at the house like you didn't want me seeing you."

Reb pulled a wad of bills from his jeans pocket. "Bonus money, ma'am."

Uncertain but having no choice except to believe them, she said, "I can't take chances. Joey, you realize that, don't you?"

"I earn my money honestly," he returned. He peeked at her, revealing traces of the earnest child he'd once been.

She eased a step backward. "I apologize, then." Intuition screamed she was acting the fool. She was sure there was more to this than met the eye. She returned to the storage room to collect the jars.

Search Joey's room, common sense urged her. *Make sure he really is keeping his nose clean.* She fretted over the problem while she loaded a box with jars.

"Emily?"

She brushed hair off her face, and looked over her shoulder. Reb stood in the doorway. "I don't like lies, Reb Tremaine. So if you're involving Joey in anything illegal, then pack your gear and get off my property. I warn you, if I find out you are doing anything illegal I will call the law."

"I'm not," he said as mildly as if they were discussing the weather. "Neither is Joey."

She jumped to her feet. Hands clenched, she approached him. "You don't need to sneak around to make sure I don't see him give you bonus money."

"True."

"I'm not stupid. You two are up to no good. I saw him give you something, and it wasn't money." She sighed in frustration and jammed her hands in her pockets. The unfairness of it all heightened her anger. She'd grown to care deeply about Reb, even depend upon him. She hoped for some kind of romantic entanglement, too—but he was lying to her. Worse, he'd involved her brother in the lie.

"You're right." He reached into his pocket and pulled out a small cardboard box. He held it on his open hand.

The flat box was printed with the silhouette of a couple embracing against a lush sunset scene. It took a few seconds before she realized what the box contained. "Condoms? He gave you condoms?"

"I asked Joey to pick them up for me in town." He slipped the box back into his pocket. "He doesn't exactly approve of what I intend to do with them."

As his meaning sank in, warmth on her face turned into a blaze. "Oh." Her voice dropped to a whisper. "You told my *brother* you want to sleep with me?"

He quirked an eyebrow. "No, ma'am. He jumped to that conclusion all by himself. I apologize. I don't mean to embarrass either one of you."

A giggle tickled her throat, and she quickly turned away. Knowing he carried sexual protection in his pocket was akin to having a stupid song locked inside her head—it played around and around and around in her thoughts, refusing to go away. "I think you are being a bit presumptuous," she said tartly.

"Only if I do intend to make love to you."

She gasped and whipped her head about. "You aren't?"

Grinning, he backed out of the doorway. "Have chores to do, ma'am. See you at supper."

She ran to the doorway. "Maybe I don't care a bit who you *intend* to sleep with!" she called. "It's none of my business, and don't think for a moment I want to make it my business."

He kept walking, but his shoulders hitched. One quick hitch, enough to let her know he laughed.

FROM HIS VANTAGE POINT inside the bunkhouse, Reb watched Emily lug a box of glass jars onto the porch and into the house. The sway of her hips, snugly encased in ragged cutoffs, fixated him. When the screened door closed behind her, Reb returned the box of condoms to Joey. He could kick himself for being so sloppy. Not a good sign him being careless around Emily.

"She fell for it, huh?" Joey said.

"Trust me," Reb said, "she won't ever mention it again. From now on, when you have something to give me, do it here."

Joey stared at the box for a moment. He slowly raised his head. His dark eyes glittered. "Sure you won't be needing these? I've got plenty more in my truck."

The kid's hostility washed over Reb like a wave of hot air. A guilty twinge squeezed his gut. When he'd shown the condoms to Emily the look on her face, wide-eyed and appreciative and dewy mouthed, had tempted him to slam the door and pin her against the wall. He wanted to kiss her senseless and hold her beautiful body and have those long, elegant legs wrapped around his hips. Lying to her was ripping him up inside.

"I see the way you look at her," Joey said after a moment. "The way she looks at you."

Anger crept over the back of Reb's head, tightening his scalp and forehead. He was too good at his job to let a woman affect him this way. Especially a woman who was a target.

Reb said, "I thought you don't care what I do to Emily as long as I get her out of the way. I quote, 'Get her lying, thieving butt off this ranch.'"

Joey slumped with his back to the wall. He hooked his thumbs in his belt. "Maybe I was wrong."

"About what? The lying part or the thieving part?" Reb pulled the wad of cash out of his pocket. "Tell me again how dishonest she is. Or how about we take a ride in your truck on those brand-new tires, and you can tell me how greedy she is?"

"Shut up, Reb."

"I'll shut up when you grow up."

Joey kept his head down. His jaw tightened stubbornly. Stubbornness, Reb decided, was a family trait. Joey and Emily were both as persistent as mosquitoes on a summer night, and taking out his irritation on the kid accomplished nothing. Reb turned back to the window and watched the house.

Guilty or not, Emily was still a target, and Reb never cared about or got involved with targets. The cleanup man survived by avoiding messy relationships and emotional entanglements.

A man like him never made the mistake of falling in love.

AT SPOTTING Mickey Thigpen's patrol car, Emily groaned. She'd just spent hours in the forest with Reb, fantasizing about his hot hands and hotter mouth having free rein over her body, and now she wanted to be alone. But Reb was still beside her. She didn't dare so much as glance his way for fear of jumping on him and ravishing him in the dirt. None of which put her in the mood for bantering with Mickey.

Mickey had parked beside the house. Lights blazed inside the kitchen. Since Joey had gone into town after supper, she imagined Mickey had let himself inside the kitchen and helped himself to a drink.

She and Reb crossed the creek. Sloppy splashing announced Copper bringing up the rear. The dog raced past her, spraying her with icy water, then he loped along the path and disappeared into the barn.

"What do you think the sheriff wants?" Reb asked.

A hot date and bragging rights, she thought sourly. "Who knows?"

She trudged down the path. After a few steps she realized Reb didn't follow. Instead, he sat upon a boulder. Shade from a cottonwood dappled him in hues of purple and gray. Looking as if he hadn't a care in the world, he plucked a long stem of grass and chewed the end of it.

"Nice evening," he said. "Think I'll sit here and watch the stars come out." A slow grin teased her and set her heart to racing. "When you finish with the sheriff, come on out and join me."

A hunch said he didn't want within a hundred feet of the law. It could be he didn't want to interfere between her and Mickey or he wasn't sociable. Or he truly did enjoy the evening, which had cooled to balmy sweetness while stars popped into the cerulean sky like Christmas lights. Still, she suspected he avoided the sheriff because he didn't want the sheriff asking questions. Was Reb hiding something from her?

"Sure." Troubled, she headed to the house, hurrying so she could get the visit over and done with.

Mickey waited inside the kitchen. He had one leg propped on his knee, and his big, black, shiny boot gleamed under the light. He'd helped himself to a glass of lemonade and the remainder of an apple pie. Crumbs littered the tabletop around the scraped-clean pie plate. His hat hung on a peg near the door, and his salt-and-pepper hair curled luxuriously around his ears and neck.

"Make yourself at home," she said dryly, moving to the sink to wash her hands. She was glad she wore a baggy T-shirt and blue jeans; they protected her from his probing gaze. "What brings you here, Mickey?"

He glanced at the pie plate. "Best apple pie in the state." His smile acquired a solemn tinge. "I need your help."

"There's a switch. Do you have a problem with Tuff?"

A manila folder lay on the table. Mickey opened it, revealing a stack of Wanted posters. "The real problem with being in law is it makes me itchy." He fanned the posters with a sweep of his hand. "So I'm sitting there, nothing going on, shooting the breeze with Tuff. Say what you want about him, he's pure entertainment. Except him having more visitors than the pope, he makes a good prisoner. He's a character."

Emily sat so she could see the posters. They looked of the same type displayed in the post office.

"So I'm cleaning out my desk, getting rid of outdated material. I shove a stack of these at Tuff and ask him if he knows the whereabouts of any of these outlaws. Joking, right? We're talking about rewards and bounty hunters. Nothing to it."

Interested and curious, she turned a poster around to read it. It showed a Hispanic man with a Fu Manchu mustache who was wanted for armed robbery.

"Tuff reacted, Emily. Not much, didn't say anything, but it made me itchy. I got to thinking about you and the phone calls you made to us the night before we arrested Tuff. Call it a hunch, but maybe that so-called murder victim of yours is in this stack of photos. Take a look. See if you recognize anybody."

"What did Tuff say?" she asked as she gathered the stack of posters.

"Nothing. Not a word. That makes me extra itchy. Tuff can talk the ears off a deaf man, so when he shuts up, I listen. Take a look for me."

She went through the stack of posters carefully. The photographs were terrible, worse than ill-lighted Polaroids on drivers' licenses. Some of the people pictured were wanted by the state police, some by federal officers. Crimes ranged from traffic offenses to homicide. On her first pass no one looked familiar. On the second pass she picked up a sheet and peered closely at the man pictured in frontal and profile mug shots.

"This kind of looks like the man I saw." She turned it for Mickey to see.

"Hmm, James Richard Mullow, also known as 'Jimmy Wheel.'" He frowned. "Are you sure? This one's wanted by the FBI. Armed-robbery and weapons charges. Doesn't sound like Tuff's choice of pastimes. Didn't you say your boy had a tattoo?"

"On his arm, some kind of big cat."

"No mention of it. This sheet is over a year old. Maybe I can get an update. Anyone else in there look familiar?"

"No, I'm sorry. Truth is, I didn't get that good a look at his face." She clamped down the urge to tell him what he should be doing right now, such as scouring the forest with her. Doing so would only lead to arguments. She settled back on her chair instead and waited.

"Idea," he said, scowling at James Mullow's mug shots. "If you're willing, write me out a statement. Write down everything you saw and heard that night."

"What good will it do?"

"Give me something to nudge Tuff with. Who knows what I can drag out of him."

"You believe me, then." She smiled. "You finally believe I saw something that night."

Mickey wagged a finger in admonishment. "I don't believe anything. Not yet. You can't even give me a positive ID on this fellow. And you still don't have any proof Tuff was here that night. Only thing I have right now is an itch. Give me a few days to scratch it, and see what happens."

"Fair enough." She intended to keep searching with Reb, though, with or without the sheriff's blessing.

She fetched a pen and a pad of paper, then sat at the table, ready to write. "If Tuff murdered this man, will I have to testify in court?"

"I won't pull a Pollyanna on you, honey. It won't be easy. You'll have to look your brother in the face and swear you saw him with Mullow. But that's only if a murder did happen and I get enough evidence to prove it."

"What if Mullow is alive?"

"Then we have to prove he and Tuff committed a crime." His smile turned patient and condescending. "Something worse than disturbing your beauty sleep, that is."

How about a duffel bag that contained heaven knew what? she wondered. She kept her thoughts to herself. If Mickey refused to get excited about a possible murder, he'd be positively catatonic concerning the duffel bag.

She concentrated on writing out her statement. She'd replayed in her head that horrible night so many times it took her only forty-five minutes to fill five pages. Proud of herself, certain once he saw it in black and white he'd have no choice except to open an investigation, she handed the pages to Mickey. He requested she sign, number and date each page. Only as she signed the last page did it occur to her what Joey was going to think. He idolized his older brother. If this snowballed into an investigation, and her testimony sent Tuff to prison...

"What's the matter, honey?"

"Nothing." She scribbled her signature on the paper and shoved her statement across the table. She supposed Joey hating her forever was a small price to pay for his safety.

"I know you're thinking I'm a dumb redneck who doesn't know squat about solving crimes," he said as he carefully folded the papers into thirds and tucked them into his breast pocket.

"I don't," she protested.

"There are limits to what I can do. Resources, manpower. Family squabbles are always tricky. Things have a way of getting twisted around. My job is to wear a cool head and keep matters untwisted. Even out here in the sticks, folks have rights. Despite my feelings for you, I have to respect Tuff's rights. I play by the rules. Do you understand?"

"I suppose."

He patted the pages and they crackled. "If I thought for a minute you were in any kind of danger, I'd do something."

She debated telling him about the threatening telephone call. In light of his current lecture and her not mentioning the incident when it happened, it would only make her sound foolish.

"I understand, Mickey."

He stood, smiling down at her. "So are we square again? Friends?"

"Sure."

"Prove you still like me. How about dinner tomorrow night?"

She seriously considered saying yes. Mickey was a nice-looking, hardworking, decent man. She'd known him practically all her life. She knew his history and his family and where he went to church.

Irritation at Reb running hot and cold tickled the devil in her. She'd love to see his face if she dressed up in her fanciest clothes and announced she had a date. That would show him he couldn't get away with kissing her, then pretending nothing had happened.

Except she couldn't make herself stoop to dating one man in order to spite another.

"Thanks for asking, but I can't." She headed for the door, hoping he took the hint.

He put a hand below the back of her neck. She stiffened.

"Saturday night, honey," he said. "I'll show you the best time of your life. Promise." He flexed his fingers, kneading the gone-tight muscle between her shoulder blades.

She stepped aside, reaching for the door. He caught her wrist, turning her about to face him. His gray eyes appeared thoughtful, and his lips parted, becoming soft. Just as he lowered his mouth to hers, she jerked her head aside. His lips grazed her chin.

"Don't," she said.

"You can't stay hidden away forever." He touched her cheek with a large knuckle, stroking her skin. "You need a man. It's not natural for a beautiful woman to stay tucked away. So you wear something pretty." He touched her earlobe with his fingertips. "I'll pick you up at seven sharp."

She pulled away and, when he started to follow her, she thrust out a hand, keeping him at bay. "No. I'm sorry, Mickey, but I can't. I'm not ready to date." She hurried to the sink, putting the table and chairs between them. "We're friends, Mickey. I want to keep it that way."

His narrowed eyes and the way he kept fiddling with his hat brim made her nervous. "All I'm asking for is a chance, honey. Ever since you've come back to the valley, seems like all I can think about is you. You're a beautiful woman."

"I'm flattered, but the timing is wrong." She tried not to look at her statement poking out of his pocket, feeling afraid that he might ignore it if she hurt his feelings.

"Are you seeing someone?" Anger tinged his speech. "Found yourself another rich man with one foot in your bed and the other in the grave?"

Her vision blurred and her back ached from tension, but she kept her voice calm. "Daniel Farraday was a good man, hardworking and kind. He wasn't rich, either. Both of us worked eighty, ninety hours a week in our restaurant. I know what folks say about me around here, but they're lies. And you of all people know they're lies."

He lowered his face and shuffled toward the door.

"You want to know the truth about me, Mickey Thigpen? I'm not looking for a rich husband. I don't need one and I don't want one. If I start seeing a man, it'll be because I care about him. So don't you *dare* come in here acting like I should be grateful because you want to date me."

"I'm sorry, hon—Emily." His neck blazed crimson. "I can't seem to get off on the right foot with you."

Despite his posture, she heard the false note in the apology. He wasn't sorry for hurting her feelings; he was sorry she'd called him on it. She wasn't sorry a bit when he crept out of the house and drove away.

Drained, she sat at the table and rested her head on her folded arms. A soft knock on the door made her lift her head. Reb stood on the porch. She gestured for him to come inside.

"Is everything okay?" he asked. He hung his hat on the peg where Mickey had hung his.

She invited him to sit and then told him what Mickey had told her. "I wish I'd been more certain about the picture. I still don't know if Mickey will do anything for me." She grimaced, imagining the sheriff tearing her statement into teeny-tiny shreds and washing his hands of her completely.

Reb scratched his chin. He tapped his fingers on the tabletop. His eyelids remained at half-mast, revealing nothing of what he felt.

She sensed all was not well. "What's the matter?"

"Did you tell him about the man who threatened you on the telephone?"

"No. Maybe I should have."

Reb waited.

"It wasn't the right time," she said lamely.

"How do you know the sheriff is on the up-and-up?"

She laughed. The offended narrowing of Reb's eyes made her laugh harder. "Mickey Thigpen is always on the up-and-up! Good heavens, he's been sheriff for something like fifteen years. He's a fourth-generation rancher here in the valley. What could he possibly gain from lying to me?"

Reb lifted a shoulder. "Maybe he wants to find the duffel bag for himself."

"He never mentioned it. He's not convinced Tuff was here that night, much less with another man. What are you getting at?" She leaned closer to him and stared until he met her gaze. "Is there some reason you don't trust the sheriff?"

"I don't know the man."

"And you don't want to know him, either. Or is it you don't want him knowing you? Are you in trouble with the law?"

"No."

"This is the second time you hid out when he showed up."

"I'm not hiding. I get tired of the hassles, that's all." His tone turned mocking. "What's your name, boy, where you from, got any insurance on that Jeep?" Reb sighed. "It gets old."

Caught in the spell of his bright blue eyes, she murmured, "Oh."

"But the way he ignored your complaint seems strange. If I were sheriff, I'd take you seriously. You're talking about a possible murder, and he's doing nothing."

"Tuff has constitutional rights, including the right to not be hassled." The wry curve of his lips told her the point struck home. "I don't have any choice except to see things from Mickey's point of view. It's my word against Tuff's. The sad fact is, around here my word doesn't mean much.''

"If there's evidence of a crime on this property we'll find it.''

His steadfast support made her feel better. "Maybe there is no body," Emily said. "I know I saw blood, I'd stake the ranch on it. But Tuff could have fallen. The other man could have been waiting in the car while Tuff washed up.''

"The duffel bag.''

"If the other man is alive, then as soon as he found out Tuff was locked up, he'd have come back and grabbed it. He was probably the one who called me.''

"Are you willing to take the chance and drop it?''

As much as she'd love an excuse to drop the matter and not have to worry about murders—actually finding a body would probably give her nightmares for life—or bags full of contraband, she knew what she'd seen.

"I didn't think so," Reb said, and rose to his feet.

She didn't want him to go away. He didn't look eager to bolt out the door, either. Ornery impulse gripped her. Giving her head a flippant toss, she said, "I think the real reason Mickey came out here was to ask me out on a date.''

Reb made a noncommittal noise.

"Maybe I should go. Can't hurt, and I hear he's a great dancer." She gave Reb her most innocent look.

His eyes narrowed and his brow lowered, not much but enough to tell her she struck a nerve. She examined a small scratch on the back of her hand. "Not that I get that many offers. Guess I shouldn't be too choosy.''

The rumbling of Joey's truck engine saved her from herself. She smiled, earning a questioning look from Reb. *This love-starved widow lady won't be throwing herself at you tonight, cowboy,* she told him with her eyes.

Churning gravel and skidding tires made her wince. She began shaping in her mind lectures about driving responsibly with safety foremost. The truck door slammed.

Reb said, "See you tomorrow, ma'am."

Joey's boots thudded on the porch, and he nearly ripped the screened door off its hinges.

"Joey!" Emily snapped. "Just what in blazes do you—?"

The look on his face knocked the impending lectures out of her head. He'd lost color from beneath his suntan, turning his face yellow except for mottled blotches of feverish redness. His eyes were red-rimmed and swollen as if he'd been crying.

"Joey? Honey, what is it?"

He tore off his hat and flung it at the peg rack. It hit the wall with a thud and fell. That he didn't so much as glance to check for damage to his treasured hat heightened Emily's alarm.

Emily caught his arm. "Joey," she whispered. "What happened?"

"Tuff." He dragged in a long, snuffling breath. "The fool broke out of jail."

Emily shot Reb a startled, disbelieving look.

"He escaped. He jumped Tim Patterson, took his gun and escaped." Joey wobbled, groping for a chair. "They're calling him armed and dangerous, Emmy. They'll shoot him on sight."

Chapter Eight

Emily moved woodenly through the routine of milking the cow. She hunched inside a heavy coat, and the backs of her hands were reddening with the cold. Steam roiled from the surface of the frothy milk, carrying its rich scent to mingle with the grassy smell of the cow's hide. Blossom twitched her tail and stamped her right hind hoof, but Emily paid little heed to the cow's irritability. Worrying about Tuff and the implications of his escape occupied her.

Last night around seven o'clock, Joey had gone to the jail. The doors had been locked, and no one answered his knocks or calls. He had figured the deputy on duty had gone to supper. He'd returned in an hour, but still no one answered; by that time some of the townsfolk had gathered, wondering why no one was in the sheriff's office, no lights were on and no one answered the telephone. Unable to raise the sheriff, they'd finally found the other deputy. When he opened the office, he'd found Deputy Tim Patterson lying on the floor. Tuff had disappeared, along with the deputy's service revolver.

The all-points bulletin called Tuff armed and dangerous. Emily easily imagined doors locked throughout the valley and nervous drivers eyeballing the roadsides. No one could possibly be more nervous than she.

Where she rested her forehead against the juncture of Blossom's flank, Emily felt a twitch. The cow's hoof struck the nearly full bucket of milk, and Emily lost her balance on the one-legged milk stool. She fell backward into the straw.

Reb's soft chuckle sounded. "A roll in the hay, ma'am? You do it different in Colorado."

Emily lifted her baleful gaze to Reb. He rested his forearms on the stall wall and grinned at her, his eyes gleaming with amusement. Roll in the hay, indeed, she thought, but failed to muster indignation. Instead, her thoughts drifted to imagining Reb on his back, next to her on the straw, and he was bare chested, wanton, reaching for her, holding her.

Blossom grumbled and returned to her feed bucket, and Emily levered upright to a sitting position. Her breath emerged in wispy puffs, and she shivered. It had clouded up and turned cold overnight.

"Don't you have chores to do, Reb?"

"Finished. Where's Joey? I haven't seen him this morning."

Her heart fluttered uneasily. "You haven't?" Tuff's escape and the subsequent manhunt had Joey in a royal state. Reb stepped around the stall wall and extended a hand. She took it and he pulled her upright.

"His horse is gone," Reb said.

She realized Copper wasn't hanging around, either. Usually the dog vied with the feral barn cats for a chance to drink fresh milk. Copper must have followed Joey.

"I better check on him. Do you know how to milk a cow? She might have enough left for coffee."

Reb nodded. "I can take care of her. You don't think Joey is off doing something stupid, do you?"

"He probably headed over to Claude's place." She turned her worried gaze to the barn doorway. Frost glittered on blades of grass. Thanks a lot, Reb, she thought, for now she imagined her younger brother searching for her older—armed and dangerous—brother. Even worse, Joey resembled Tuff. Both had dark hair, worn collar length. It would be conceivable for some overzealous rancher sighting Joey through a rifle scope to congratulate himself for doing a good deed by bagging Tuff.

"He doesn't want Tuff killed. Oh, God, Reb, I don't want him killed, either. But I'm afraid Tuff'll come back here, too."

"Not in a million years," he said firmly. He lowered a hard gaze on the shotgun Emily had propped against the stall wall. "He can't be that stupid."

Apparently Mickey Thigpen hoped Tuff would come back to the ranch. He'd returned to the house late last night. He'd installed a caller-ID device and a tape recorder on the telephone in case Tuff called. He had refused to answer her questions; the only thing he said was to keep the doors locked tight and to call immediately if she saw any sign of Tuff. She prayed Tuff wouldn't come home. She doubted if she had the nerve to shoot her own brother.

She sighed, wishing the fear would leave her. She'd barely slept last night. In every squeak, rustle and creak, she'd heard Tuff sneaking up the stairs, gun in hand, to shoot her. "They'll never catch Tuff," she finally said to Reb. "Not if he stays in the mountains.

I better find Joey. Somebody might mistake him for Tuff.''

As she passed, Reb caught her arm. She stopped in her tracks. "Can you," he said slowly, now grim faced, "think of any reason Tuff would come home?"

Her anxiety worsened, knotting up her insides, making it hard to breathe. "He doesn't need to. He can survive in the mountains. He knows every trail, every watering hole. Besides, he must realize I'd turn him in as soon as I spotted him." She shrugged away from Reb. "I hope Joey went to Claude's. I want to check and make sure."

"I'll saddle the horses. We'll stick together."

By the time she finished her chores, Reb had Strawberry and Jack saddled and ready to go. Lithe as a dancer, Reb mounted in one fluid up-and-over motion. Emily handed him the shotgun. He checked the bore and the load, and shook his head.

"When's the last time you cleaned this?"

"It's clean. I don't think it's been fired in years."

He made a disgruntled sound as he gathered the reins in his left hand. Emily gave the roan mare a hard look. *Please don't embarrass me,* she entreated silently, and climbed onto the saddle. Except for a huffy snort, Strawberry stood quietly until Emily was firmly seated.

Reb turned Jack east and urged him into a canter toward a pine-covered ridge. Emily gave Strawberry her head to follow. Ahead of her, Reb rode with the relaxed, slightly forward posture of a man who could anticipate his mount's every move.

When they reached the trees, Emily heard a bark. The distinctive wavering quality of the dog's voice told her it was Copper. She reined the mare to a stop.

"Copper? Here, boy!" She whistled, listened, then whistled again.

A flash of red-gold on a nearby rock formation preceded the dog bursting into the open. Pointed ears laid flat, his mouth wide open in a doggy grin, he pranced circles around Strawberry.

She smiled at Reb. "Claude's dog doesn't like visitors, so Copper never comes this way on his own. He must have followed Joey."

"Let's make sure," Reb said. He touched his heels to Jack's side, and the gelding obediently stepped out.

"Wait! Reb, wait." She held the reins tightly, preventing the mare from following Jack. Strawberry shook her head and stamped a hoof. When Reb stopped and turned to face her, Emily said, "Joey must be visiting Claude. I should leave him alone." She wished Joey trusted her enough to come to her when he needed comforting.

"I want to make sure."

"If I go barging in on him and Claude, he'll think I'm babying him. I don't want to make him mad. He might go looking for Tuff just to spite me."

Reb nodded east. "To the edge of the trees, then. We can see Claude's cabin from there. If we see Joey's horse, we won't go any farther."

His worry showed in his face. He cared about Joey. Warm gratitude replaced some of the fear in her chest. Closemouthed or not, Reb Tremaine was a good man with a big heart.

"Only to the edge of the trees." She clucked her tongue and put her heels to Strawberry's sides.

Up the ridge Reb kept Jack to a slow pace. The big gelding picked his careful way up the rocky path. Water from the morning fog dripped off the trees and turned the pine straw black, as if it had been burned. Emily kept her gaze fixed on the ground, mindful of the treacherous footing. Copper trotted alongside, his ears pricked forward and his nose working busily, drawing in scent.

Once over the ridge, the trail narrowed and dropped steeply. Emily hung on tightly to the saddle horn and braced her feet against the stirrups. Up ahead Jack seemed to glide down the path, his rider easy in the saddle.

When they were on level ground, Jack broke into a lazy lope. Emily gritted her teeth in anticipation of Strawberry's jarring trot; the mare didn't disappoint her. Her hooves thudded against the hard pack, each jolt whomping up Emily's spine.

Reb glanced over his shoulder and did a double take. He hauled back the reins, slowing Jack to a walk. When Strawberry slowed, too, Emily groaned in relief. Catching the look on Reb's face, she hung her head.

"I'm not a very good rider." She patted Strawberry's neck to show her no hard feelings. "When I was a little girl, I was terrified of horses. I don't know why. It embarrassed Grandpa no end having a granddaughter who wouldn't compete in rodeos or help with the cattle." She smiled sheepishly. "So now you know my deepest, darkest secret. I'm a rancher who can't ride. Don't laugh at me, okay?"

"I'm not laughing," he said solemnly. "It takes courage to do something you hate."

"I'm not courageous, trust me. Just stubborn." Realizing Copper had disappeared, she looked around. "Speaking of stubborn, did you see where my dog went?"

"Sorry."

She guessed the dog had figured out she was headed for Claude's and he'd retreated. Claude's border collie tolerated no trespassers—especially not Copper.

They reached the edge of the forest. The land opened onto rolling hills marked by dark green knots of scrub oak and granite boulders that looked like monstrous eggs half-buried in the dirt. Claude's cabin, the original ranch house for the Double Bar R, perched on a low hill. Thin blue smoke curled out of the stone chimney. Joey's horse cropped grass in the small yard beside the cabin.

Relief drained Emily's energy. She slumped on the saddle and closed her eyes.

"What about Claude? Will Tuff go to him for help?" Reb asked.

"No way. Claude doesn't like Tuff any better than he likes me." She chuckled. "Joey's fine. He's probably eating those sorry biscuits Claude is so proud of baking. And drinking his coffee. Have you tasted Claude's coffee yet?"

An almost imperceptible wince rippled through his broad shoulders. She guessed he had tasted Claude's syrupy, bitter brew. She reached for Reb, and placed her fingers against the sleeve of his denim jacket. "Thank you for coming with me. Thank you for caring about my brother. And about me."

"No problem."

He sounded uncomfortable, so she let the matter rest and turned Strawberry toward home. She rode a few yards before realizing Reb didn't follow. He stared at something to the south. Under the shade of his hat brim, his face appeared carved from stone.

"What is it? What do you see?"

"A vehicle parked on the main road. I can see the back end of it through the trees."

"It's probably a police car. That's the only road leading into the ranch." She rode to his side. By standing in the stirrups, she could see a glint of chrome and white-painted metal shining through the trees. "It's a car from the sheriff's office," she announced. "That's the only way a vehicle can get onto the property. Too many washouts and ridges block other ways. It's a roadblock."

"I don't like this."

His comment puzzled her. It brought back her suspicion Reb was in some sort of trouble with the law. Straightening her spine, she said, "Look, if you're in some sort of trouble, you have to tell me. I have a right to know if I'm harboring a fugitive. Please tell me the truth, Reb."

He flashed a grin. "No fugitive, ma'am."

She wanted to believe him. "What's the matter?"

"I've taken part in posses before."

"You have? Because you were a hunting guide?"

He nodded. "Jailbirds are like homing pigeons. They head back to the roost. If it were me, I'd be sweeping every inch of this ranch and posting a lot more than one patrol car on the road. What did the sheriff tell you last night? Did he say if anyone helped Tuff break out?"

"The only thing he said was to keep the doors locked. Tuff wouldn't dare come back here." A sickening thought occurred to her. Joey had visited Tuff in jail, and Mickey had been unfriendly when he'd returned to the house last night. He'd refused to answer her questions. He hadn't even flirted with her. Did he think Joey had helped Tuff make his escape?

"Tuff will come back if he thinks it's worth the risk," Reb said.

She gave his comment careful consideration. *Joey is worth the risk.* Worried anew, she studied Claude's cabin, seeking signs of life behind the window glass.

"The duffel bag," Reb said.

"Not a chance. Tuff is way too smart to risk getting shot over a duffel bag. No matter what's inside it."

"So why did he escape?"

"Because..." Darn good question. Tuff hadn't been suffering in Mickey's jail. He'd had hot meals, a comfortable cot, unlimited television and visitors. Besides, his sentence was almost up. "Do you think Joey told him I'm searching the forest?"

"Somebody did," Reb answered gravely.

"So he escaped in order to stop me."

"Can you think of a better reason?"

Nothing came to mind. Strawberry shuffled her hooves and strained against the bit. Emily patted the mare's neck absently, ruffling her brushy mane.

Reb looked around at the ground. "Tough land. Bedrock a few inches under the soil. Tuff needed a shovel and pickax to bury the duffel bag. And it's dangerous to negotiate the forest in the middle of the night."

Emily forced herself to continue. "Even if we found Mullow's body on the ranch, it would still be my word against Tuff's as to how it got here."

She turned her sights west, seeing in her mind's eye the forest on the far side of the creek. "If the bag is full of drugs, how much would it be worth?" She remembered Mullow as he hoisted the duffel bag. A man with bulky shoulders and massive arms, but he'd struggled under the weight.

"Could be worth thousands," Reb said evenly. "Millions."

She tightened the reins and turned Strawberry toward the road. "I have to make Mickey listen to me now. He can arrange for drug-sniffing dogs. They can stake out the—"

"Stop."

The soft-spoken command halted her in her tracks. Strawberry gave a little hop and swiveled her ears.

"Don't trust the sheriff," Reb said.

She laughed. "Oh, come on!" A hunch said Reb was jealous of Mickey. The idea pleased her as much as she thought it was ridiculous. "I can't say I approve of all Mickey's methods, but he's completely trustworthy."

"Do you trust him not to confiscate your ranch?"

She scowled in confusion. A strand of hair had worked loose from her braid, and she pushed it off her neck. Reb returned her scowl with an inscrutable neutrality she found annoying. "What are you talking about?"

He crossed his forearms on the saddle horn and leaned against them. His blue eyes gleamed with solemn light. "If illegal drugs are found on a property, drug agents can confiscate the property automatically. *Even* if no arrests are made. Drug-enforcement agencies are having a field day raking in fancy cars and boats. And homes."

"Whatever's in that duffel bag isn't mine."

"Prove it. Government agents are determined to do their jobs. They take the property, *then* figure out who the players are."

"It's not right," she said, her indignation rising. "They can't do that."

"Right or wrong, they can and they do."

She shook her head fiercely. "No. Mickey wouldn't do that to me. He knows me and he knows I'd never mess around with anything illegal." Even as she spoke, she wondered if she knew the sheriff as well as she thought. After the little scene last night, his attitude about her couldn't be all that generous.

"It might be out of his hands. The federal agencies have a lot of power in these matters."

"How do you know all this?"

He lifted a shoulder in a lazy shrug. "I've seen agents in action. When I guided hunters in national forests, I always had to be on the lookout for marijuana crops and drop points. Stumbling into one is a good way to get killed."

"So what am I supposed to do? If I can't trust Mickey, who can I trust?"

"Trust me."

She averted her face, but still heard the echoes of *Me...me...me...trust me.* She did trust him. He was her friend. "I never wanted any of this, Reb. I just wanted to come home, get my bearings and pull my life back together. Everything is going wrong. If I lose the ranch, I'll lose Joey, too. He won't blame Tuff, he'll blame me."

Reb urged Jack to move head to tail with Strawberry. He picked up Emily's hand and gave her fingers a gentle squeeze. "Let's just try to find the duffel bag ourselves, then we'll figure out what to do." Reb sighed. "If Tuff's caught on your ranch with the duffel bag and if it's full of drugs, the Feds could still confiscate your property. The ranch is in your name.

You're supposed to be responsible for whatever happens around here. They could prosecute you as an accessory. I don't think they can make charges stick, but you'll end up selling the ranch to pay the legal fees."

He smiled ruefully. "I'm sorry, I don't mean to scare you. When we find the bag, we could take it off the ranch, dump it on the road and then call in an anonymous tip to the authorities." He waggled his eyebrows. "They love covert stuff."

"We don't know for sure it is drugs," she said, gazing at Reb. *Definitely an angel,* she determined. He'd appeared when she needed him most, when she was at the limits of her mental and emotional resources. Gratitude welled within her like a warm tide, filling her to overflowing. "I'll do anything to protect Joey and the ranch. I trust you, Reb." She squeezed his hand.

He glanced at their entwined fingers, frowned and turned her loose. "Let's go. We have a lot of ground to cover."

She lifted her gaze to the glowering sky. Clouds shrouded the mountains. The breeze cutting through the trees had a bite to it, carrying the scent of rain. She set her heels to Strawberry's sides. The mare stepped out, her hooves ringing on small rocks.

Back at the house, she left a note for Joey telling him where she and Reb were going. Since the horses were already saddled and warm, she and Reb rode across the creek to the forest. At the tree line she studied the strips of red rag that marked the areas they'd already searched. She may as well set out a big sign for Tuff: Here I Am, Bro, Looking For Your Goodies. Come Shoot Me!

On foot, making good use of probes, they resumed the methodical search. The going was hard, mostly uphill, and rock formations meant they climbed as much as they walked. Copper made periodic appearances to see if Emily was doing anything interesting. Then he would trot away to follow a deer trail or chase a tufted-eared squirrel.

Around noon the clouds covered the sky and blotted out the surrounding mountain peaks. Moisture gathered on leaves and darkened the ground. Chilly air made Emily shiver inside her nylon coat. She dropped onto a boulder overhanging a small spring. Full of minerals, the spring pool had a crystalline quality, and the air smelled tangy. White clumps of crystals glittered around the edge of the pool. The water was tepid, warmed by its source deep below the ground.

Reb leaned against a tree trunk and idly twirled his broomstick probe, making circular patterns in the dirt. The shotgun resting near his feet gave her a measure of confidence. That warm tide of gratitude washed through her again. She wondered what life might be like if Reb stayed on and made the ranch his home. "Do you think we'll find the duffel bag before Tuff does?"

"His advantage is he knows where to look. Our advantage is the cops are looking for him." He pushed away from the tree, picked up the shotgun and, with a graceful hop, joined her on the boulder. He sat beside her and stretched out his legs.

"This is hopeless. The more ground we cover, the more we have left. What if the police track him here?"

Reb tossed a pebble at the pool, watching as the rings spread. "There's something I need to tell you."

His tone of voice made her scalp prickle. *Here it comes,* she thought with a rise of panic. A sudden premonition told her after sunrise tomorrow, she'd never see him again.

"I—"

"Wait!" She twisted and placed her fingertips against his lips. "Wait a minute," she whispered. She studied the hard, straight line of his cheeks and the lines etched into his forehead and the way the reflection from the pool put greenish lights in his eyes.

"I know what you're going to say." She reluctantly pulled her hand away from his face.

"No..."

"Before you say anything, I need you to know something first." Unable to bear the brilliance of his gaze, she turned her eyes to the pool. "I lost my husband and Grandpa, two men I loved very, very much. Now I feel Joey slipping away from me. I don't know how to reach him. It's hard trying not to think I'm being punished. It's really hard to remember life goes on and will probably get better." She placed her hand atop his. "I don't know you very well, Reb, but I feel close to you anyway. When you're around, I don't feel so...alone."

"Emily, wait."

She shook her head. "I need you to know you've made things better for me. And I'm grateful. And I'm..." *Falling in love?* "I know you're only passing through. A year from now you probably won't even remember my name. But I'll never forget you." She made herself face him. "You've helped me remember I can be strong. Even though you're only going to be here a little while, I'm glad you're here. You mean a lot to me."

That said, she felt drained, but lighter somehow.

"Ah, Emily."

"I know you're leaving me. I don't know why, but you don't have to explain if you don't want to. Maybe it's better if you don't."

His eyebrows had lowered; the corners of his mouth turned down. She sensed she'd hurt his feelings, but couldn't imagine why. She shifted uncomfortably on the rock.

"That is what you're going to say, isn't it? You need to leave?"

Unable to bear his silence pressing around her like a blanketing fog, she laid her hand against his cheek and kissed him.

Chapter Nine

Emily loved kissing Reb. He touched only her mouth; his hands remained still. She adored the wet, strong, passionate thrust of his tongue and the supple press of his lips. His hot, masculine scent intoxicated her. She rubbed her fingertips over his cheek, savoring the rasp of midday beard and the movement of muscle under his cheek.

One night, she told him with her kiss. She wanted more, so much more, a chance to start anew and a chance at forever. But one night would sustain her. One night in his arms, one night of his love, one night of memories to cherish forever.

She started to pull away, and he wrapped his arm around her shoulders and held her tightly. They kissed and kissed, and she drowned in sweet sensation. He lowered her to the rock so she rested against his arm. A soft clunk accompanied him setting down the shotgun and he held her, his fingers clutching her above the waistband of her jeans.

Her body shed weariness. Worries and fears dropped away one by one until the only thing that mattered was Reb. His lips claiming hers, his tongue engaged with hers in a tender duel of thrust and parry, the solid strength of his arm around her shoulders, the smell of him, the taste of rain-freshness and man-sweat.

When he finally came up for air, she opened her eyes. Her eyelids felt weighted. Air swirled within her, each breath capricious and quick. Desire darkened his eyes. Never had she seen such beautiful eyes. She could stare forever into his eyes, imagining the thoughts behind them.

She loved him.

Not the way she'd loved Daniel. Theirs had been a comfortable kind of love. A settled love. The type of love built over time in shared tasks and a life without secrets.

Reb's love was only for today. It jumbled her up inside and made her thoughts flitter to match her fluttering heart. It scared her and filled her with joy. Even knowing tomorrow would break her heart, she felt happy.

"This isn't a good idea," he said, his tone mournful.

"Probably not." She reached upward for another kiss, but he drew his head aside. She rested against his arm. "You are leaving, aren't you? Moving on."

"It has to happen, Emily."

"I know." *Give me time,* she silently urged him. A day or a week or a month, long enough to show him being settled didn't mean being bored. Enough time to prove happiness wasn't always waiting in the next town.

He dotted her cheek with a bird-swift kiss, then pulled them both upright and turned her loose. He drew in his legs, his boot heels scraping on the rock. "There are things about me you don't know."

No mistaking the sadness of his words. Her heart went out to him. "I don't want to know, Reb. It doesn't matter."

His eyes darted, flashing sapphire fire. "Don't imagine I'm some kind of hero." His back tensed. "You might feel like you can depend on me, but a couple kisses don't make me a good guy."

His rise of temper startled her. She tugged at her coat sleeves and smoothed her hair. Her suspicions about him returned, and loss filled her. She pushed off the boulder. "You must be hungry," she said. "Let's go back to the house. Get some lunch and something hot to drink."

He turned his head slowly. Turbulent emotion darkened his face. "I don't want to hurt you, Emily. God knows, I don't want that."

Behind the words, she heard he was leaving and she'd never see him again for as long as she lived. Maybe he was right to stop before they began. No sense prolonging the agony.

"Emily," Reb said, "I'm not running out on you."

"Then what are you doing? What aren't you telling me?"

He touched her back. She hadn't heard him rise from the rock. She squeezed her eyelids shut. A gust of cold air heavy with dampness ruffled against her face, making her shiver while filling her nose with the scent of wet pine.

"As long as Tuff is loose, I won't leave you alone. I'll help you find whatever he hid."

She waited, each breath taut and self-conscious, for the *but* surely to come. When Reb remained silent, she opened her eyes. "With a posse crawling all over the place, is there a chance you'll get in trouble? Please tell me the truth, Reb. I won't hold it against you. I promise."

"I promise you," he whispered, his breath warm against her ear. "The law isn't my problem."

She turned slowly. The shotgun held loosely in his right hand reminded her of why they were in the forest and the potential danger they faced every minute until Tuff was taken into custody. Still, all she felt was the pain of impending loss.

"I don't want to get you in trouble." Pain swelled within her and lodged in her throat. "I don't want you to leave." *Ever. Never.*

"Ah, Emily." The words emerged as a sigh. Under the shadow of his broad hat brim, his eyebrows crinkled. His mouth skewed in a rueful grin. "I'm not the man for you. You deserve better than me."

"What makes you so sure?" Her fingers twitched, struggling against the impulses her body craved. She itched to run her hands over his chest, inside his shirt. To comb his hair with her fingers and feel the coarse heaviness of the raven strands. She wanted his touch, his hands and mouth and legs, reaching for her, holding her, claiming her. "Maybe I'm as bad as Joey says...."

His anger flashed again. "Your brother's a few bubbles off center."

She had to agree. Besides, deserving or undeserving, what was the difference in matters of the heart? She dropped her gaze to the pine-straw-covered ground, where stubborn little weeds, bright with tiny star-shaped flowers, grew.

"Even if I'd known Daniel would die so young," she said carefully, "I would have loved him anyway.

Losing him hurt, it still hurts. But at least I had what I had with him.''

''This isn't the same thing.'' Reb's voice held a poignant note. ''I'm not Daniel. I'm not the man you want. I'm not steady or settled. Or whatever it is you're imagining.''

But he was lying to her and to himself. The fact that he stood his ground, so close she could count every eyelash and smell the heat on his skin, emphasized his lie. The rough note in his voice and the twist of his eyebrow told her he wanted her as much as she wanted him.

Reckless defiance rose, thrusting its wings, filling her with heady power. ''Kiss me again, then tell me you're not the man I want.''

He shook his head. ''You're a dangerous woman, ma'am.''

''I must be,'' she said, lifting her chin. ''I sure put a yellow streak down your back.''

The corners of his mouth twitched, and his eyebrow relaxed. A soft chuckle rumbled in his chest. He caught her chin, holding her fast. Liquid heat filled her veins. The recklessness grew in power, consuming her. Her clothing felt too tight, too restrictive. Her body was too small to contain every emotion roiling within her. He squeezed her lower face gently, his callused hand roughly erotic against her skin. She drowned in his eyes.

Suddenly he tensed.

Before she had time to think or protest, he'd swept her to his side and brought up the shotgun. Snake swift, he chambered a shell with a deadly clack. She stumbled against a tree and caught the rough bark with both hands. In numb fascination she watched him jam the butt against his shoulder.

"Emily?" Joey's call echoed off the trees. "Reb?"

Reb lowered the shotgun. He cocked back his hat, giving her a smoldering sideways look that sent a tingling along her spine. Down below, iron-shod hooves rang against rock, then footsteps.

"Over here," she called, watching Reb. She held not the slightest doubt if it had been Tuff instead of Joey climbing the hill, her older brother would be a dead man.

A few minutes later Joey climbed over the rocks. He stopped next to the spring, his breath emerging in long white plumes. The expression on his face freshened Emily's fear. He looked twenty years older and as hard as the mountains. He settled his grim gaze on a red scrap of cloth marking a bush.

"Do you need Reb?" Emily asked. "We were just coming down to the house for lunch." She wanted to ask him if he was all right, but obviously he was far from all right.

"I'm leaving," he said. "I'm going to look for Tuff."

"Joey, no—"

"I have to. I don't care what he's done. They're going to shoot him. I can't let them do that. I won't."

"He's dangerous," Emily said gently. "You can't interfere with the sheriff's search. You'll get hurt."

"I've got no choice. I'll be back when I find him." He turned abruptly and headed down the hill.

"Joey!" Slipping on pine cones and rocks, she hurried after him.

By the time she caught up to him, he'd mounted his horse. The saddle was laden with a bedroll and bulg-

ing canvas bags. His deer rifle was sheathed in the
boot. His poncho and sheepskin coat were tied behind his bedroll.

She caught the horse's bridle. "No."

"Let me go."

"You don't know what you're doing. The mountains are full of state police and search parties. Someone could mistake you for Tuff and shoot you. Or
even worse, you'll find Tuff. He won't care that you're
his brother. He could use you for a hostage. If he
doesn't kill you first."

"I'll make him turn himself in."

Reb materialized silently at her side and he, too,
took hold of the horse's bridle. The big animal flicked
his ears and rolled his eyes. "Listen to your sister,
Joey," Reb said calmly.

"I have to find him." Joey's mouth turned soft and
vulnerable. Moisture trembled on his lower lids.
"Don't you see, they'll kill him."

Emily tightened her grip on the bridle. "He's coming back here."

"He's not stupid." Joey's face twisted in pain. "He
knows you'll turn him in."

She licked her lips. It was futile to argue, but she
had to try. "Listen to me. Tuff buried a duffel bag up
here somewhere. I think it's full of drugs. He'll be
back to get it."

"You're crazy." Joey looked at Reb as if he expected Reb to call Emily crazy, too.

"Did you tell Tuff I'm searching the forest?" Emily asked. The guilty dart of Joey's eyes told her he
had. "That's why he escaped, Joey. It's the only reason he'd take such a chance. You've got to stay put,

Joey. Or you could be in danger. Reb, tell him. He'll
listen to you. Please.''

REB SENSED Joey was about to bolt. The kid had returned to the barn and dismounted, but he made no
move to unsaddle his horse. Rain had started while
they were riding back, and the sky had darkened,
shrouding the land in misty gray. Joey shifted his gaze
between the ominous clouds and Reb. With his
bloodshot eyes and haggard cheeks, he looked as if he
hadn't slept in a week. Reb refused to feel sorry for
him. Joey didn't need pity; he needed a reality check.

Reb caught Joey's shoulder. "No more lies, kid.
Not to me, not to yourself."

"Leave me alone." A flash of lightning preceded a
thunderclap, making Joey jump. The horses nickered
nervously. "You don't know what it's like around
here. People are right out of the last century. They
believe in mountain justice. They'll kill him. I can
make him turn himself in, I know I can."

Reb felt dismayed. He wondered if he'd been this
hardheaded at age nineteen. "Listen to me. The reason Tuff wants Emily dead has nothing to do with
your grandfather. And you know it. You've been lying to me from the start."

"She killed my Grandpa. She stole the ranch."
Neither Joey's voice nor his expression held conviction.

"Your grandfather was sick long before Emily came
home. He had surgery almost a year before she
showed up."

"He was getting better."

"You're lying again. She didn't steal the ranch, she
saved it. Do you know how much money she had when

she came here? About a hundred grand. Do you know how much she has left? Less than a fourth of it. She pulled you out of debt and paid your grandfather's medical bills.''

''She's lying—''

''Emily didn't tell me. It's all there in black and white if you'd only look. Tuff is the liar. He doesn't care about you, and he doesn't care about this ranch. All he cares about is the duffel bag he hid. I doubt if Tuff lost any sleep over the man he may have killed, but he isn't about to let your sister find that bag. Think about it. Why did he break out of jail?''

Joey said nothing, so Reb continued, ''Wake up! He knows exactly what to say to you. Oh, yeah, she's a killer. Oh, yeah, only good old Tuff can keep her from throwing you off the ranch. He's using you, Joey, playing you like a puppet.''

Joey struck Reb's forearm a stinging blow. Reb tightened his jaw and his grip.

''Let me go!'' Joey swung with a wild roundhouse, aiming for Reb's chin.

Reb merely ducked, and Joey stumbled against a stall wall. He sat hard in the dirt, his legs sprawled. The three horses skittered down the aisle, heads high and trailing reins.

''You want to beat me up?'' Joey asked, even though Reb hadn't made a move on him. He slammed a fist against the ground. ''Come on, if it'll make you feel better.''

Reb clamped his hands on his hips. He'd broken his number-one rule: never care. Joey had a lot of growing to do, plenty of mistakes to make before he became a man, but the pain in his dark eyes spoke of a deep-seated decency worth salvaging. "What will make me feel better is for you to listen."

"You're sleeping with her," Joey said, his voice now an octave higher and cracking. "That's why you believe her. You're the one getting fooled, not me."

Joey couldn't see past his own pain. It'd be easier changing the course of the Mississippi River than changing his mind. Still, Reb felt compelled to try. "Remember when we first talked? Tuff's blowing smoke, you said. He doesn't really mean it. But down deep in your heart, you knew he meant it. So you came to me instead of a goof like Pat Nyles. You're scared for her."

Joey opened his mouth. A ragged exhalation shook his entire torso.

"Emily had nothing to do with your grandfather's death. The first stroke damaged his brain."

"He was getting better," Joey said.

"I've seen the medical records and the autopsy report. Nobody could do anything for him."

A tear trickled from the corner of Joey's eye. "He wasn't supposed to die. He's all I had."

Reb lowered himself into a crouch and dangled a hand over his knee. "I know. And you're angry. You don't want to believe he was doing right by you when he gave the ranch to Emily. The fact is, you didn't have the money or the experience. If you inherited, you'd have lost everything."

"He shouldn't have left me," Joey whispered. "I need him and he left me."

"Nothing I say is going to make you feel better. Only time will do that."

"Why didn't Grandpa tell me? Why did he let me think he cut me out of his will?"

"I didn't know him so I can't speak for him. All I can tell you is what I see with my own eyes. She loves you. She'll do anything to make sure you're safe. Your grandfather must have known it, too."

Joey pressed his face against his shoulder.

"She's telling the truth about Tuff." Reb paused, uncertain about how much he dared tell Joey. Instinct won out; the less Joey knew, the better off he'd be. "Tuff will be back to get the duffel bag. Help us find it."

"What's in it?" Joey asked, his words muffled by the awkward angle of his face.

"Whatever it is, he'll be back. I need you here. Trust me."

"I did trust you. You said you'd make everything all right. You said you'd help me."

Reb waited a beat. "But? Why don't you trust me now?"

"Her," he growled between his teeth. "You're sleeping with her."

"No."

"You're in love with her."

Reb opened his mouth to deny that, too. Except the words refused to form. A twinge of conscience caught him off guard, and he had to look away.

"Jesus," Joey breathed. "She's done caught you by the tail. Have you told her the truth? Does she know who you are?"

"I'm not in love with her." Saying so made Reb's chest ache. Odd thing. He was a practiced liar; he survived by lying, by being whatever targets desired him to be. Easy lies, skillful lies, lies with enough truth to keep him from tripping himself up.

Lies never hurt him.

Until now.

An idea formed that Emily need never know the truth. She never had to know how he meant to betray her. He'd find the money and disappear, leaving her unharmed in her ignorance. The idea built steam; he began to believe it. He could make it work. He stood upright, looking down at Joey. "She's a victim in this. The less she knows, the better."

Joey breathed hard, his gaze gone remote, focused somewhere beyond the barn door. Reb smelled trouble brewing, and it scared him. "Let's unsaddle the horses," Reb said. He reached for Jack's saddle cinch, and Joey began unsaddling the roan mare.

The rain increased, battering the barn's metal roof like gravel poured from a bucket. The air turned clammy, redolent of wet straw and grass. Perfect weather for a fugitive. The heavy rain and lightning grounded helicopters and made tracking dogs useless. Reb pictured Tuff trudging through the rain, drawing closer to the duffel bag.

Family, Reb thought with a mixture of disgust and disquiet. Since he had no family of his own, the dynamics eluded him. He understood loyalty, but he understood self-preservation better. How could Joey be so blind to his older brother's behavior? Even more confusing was Emily's devotion to a dead man's promise and to a sullen younger brother. He tried to rouse disdain, but felt instead a sense of shame for the empty place inside him. He yearned for someone to fill it.

Reb shook his head to clear the unsettling thoughts as he led Jack into a stall, but the thoughts remained, along with knowing Emily held the power to change him. She could forge a bond with him strong enough to erase the past and make him whole. If he allowed it.

Joey trotted his still-saddled horse to the barn door. He shot Reb a glare and swung onto the saddle.

"Joey!" Reb lurched out of the stall.

"He's my brother," the boy said, jerking his hat down low. He spurred his mount and galloped into the driving rain.

As Reb ran to the doorway, Joey spurred his horse through the meadow toward the creek. A shift of wind sent rain against Reb's face. With a sinking feeling, he knew by the time he saddled his horse, the kid would be long gone, swallowed by the forest where he had the advantage of knowing every trail.

The screened door slammed, and Emily rushed across the porch. Grasping a post, she watched her brother's receding form. Reb ran into the rain. By the time he reached the porch, he was soaked. The look on Emily's face made him feel lower than a worm in a mine shaft.

"I'm sorry," he said.

Her chin trembled. "Other than shooting him in the leg, there's nothing you could do. He's stubborn as a Brahma bull and determined to protect Tuff."

"I'll go after him."

"You'll never find him. He knows these mountains almost as well as Tuff does. Oh, Reb, why won't he listen to me? What am I going to do?" She pushed away from the post and opened the door. "You best come inside. You're wet."

He followed her into the kitchen. "I thought he was listening to me."

At the sink she rested against the counter. "He's just like Grandpa. He never listens to anybody. No patience. Always has to be doing something even if it's wrong." She lifted her eyes to the telephone. "I can't even call Claude. He doesn't have a phone."

"Will Claude know where to find him?"

"I don't know."

"Chances are slim to none that Joey will find Tuff," Reb said. "We've got a better chance of finding him." The assurances tasted dry and weak as dust. He was frightened for the kid, too. The flat, soulless look he'd once seen in Tuff's eyes told him the older brother wouldn't have the slightest sympathy or mercy where Joey was concerned.

They ate a tense, silent lunch. Emily kept staring hopefully at the door as if she expected Joey to appear at any moment. Reb kept his eyes off Emily. Each glimpse of her made him think about family and settling down and the emptiness gnawing his insides. His damp shirt clung icily to his skin, but the cold he felt outside was an inferno compared to the dread building inside him.

"The rain is letting up." She rose from the table, carrying her plate. "I want to go back out."

Reb plucked at his damp shirt. "Give me five minutes to change my shirt and grab my poncho."

By the time they went outside again, the rain had stopped. Wind whistled shrilly over the barn, lowering the temperature. Once inside, they retrieved the broomsticks, and Reb checked the shotgun for moisture inside the barrel.

"Did you drop some money?" she asked.

He turned around. She held out a limp, tattered twenty-dollar bill.

"I found it on the ground." She dangled it by the corner. She turned the bill back and forth, frowning.

Her frown focused on the floor behind Reb and deepened.

He followed her line of sight and spotted another bill. A tightening in his gut told him where the money had came from. He picked up a soggy twenty-dollar bill with teeth marks in it. "I think Copper got hold of something."

"My dog robbed a bank?" Emily loosed an incredulous laugh. But she called the dog.

Copper emerged from a stall at the far end of the barn. His red-gold, mud-splattered fur was plastered to his tough body. He grinned widely, his tongue lolling with every rapid pant.

"What have you got there, boy?" she asked. At the edge of the stall, she stopped in her tracks and gasped. "Where in the world did you find that?"

Chapter Ten

On his knees in the straw, Reb sorted through a pile of twenty-dollar bills. Emily stood behind him, looking over his shoulder. Copper had chewed the money into a sodden, mangled green mess. Many of the bills were in pieces, but there were a lot of pieces, perhaps hundreds of dollars' worth. She looked down at her dog, wishing he could talk. Copper watched Reb, his amber eyes bright with interest and his tail wagging slowly. He appeared pleased with himself and eager to get back to chewing up the money as soon as the man was finished playing with it.

"Do you think he hijacked a backpacker?" she asked, nervously, then she gave up trying to crack jokes. "How much is there?"

"Hard to tell. It looks like he ate some of it." Reb showed her a bill that had been chewed in half. "Looks like thirty bills all together."

She crouched and picked up a bill. Despite being wet, it looked new. "Why in the world would Copper chew up money?"

Reb shrugged and placed the messy stack of bills inside a feed bucket, out of Copper's reach.

"A duffel bag full of money." She laughed uneasily. If Tuff had robbed a bank, surely she'd have heard or read about it in the news. "Tuff buried money. That's why he escaped, to get it before I do." Uncertain what to do, she looked toward the barn door. "I better call the sheriff. He has to realize this is evidence."

"If you show up with this much money, word will get out about a hidden stash," Reb said. "You'll end up with a thousand treasure hunters crawling over your property."

Knowing they were in way over their heads, she backed up a step. "It'll be better than Tuff getting away with murder. Mickey can bring in tracking dogs. If I give him the money and tell him I suspect drugs might be involved, no one will think I'm involved. I have to trust Mickey on this one."

"What about Joey?"

"What about him?"

"Tuff didn't break out of a locked cell by himself."

"Watch your mouth, Reb Tremaine."

He held up his hands, showing his palms. "I know Joey wouldn't help Tuff, and you know it. But the sheriff has to blame somebody. Joey was in town when Tuff escaped. Now Joey's taken off to find him. The law might claim he's gone to join him."

Lightning flashed, brightening the barn doorway. Inside their stalls the horses shuffled restlessly. Reb's poncho rustled as he moved. "Put a leash on Copper," he said. "Let's see if he can lead us to the duffel bag."

They headed out again. Copper protested his lack of freedom by grabbing at the leash and playing tug-of-war. The storm had blown east, and the sky over the mountains was black, flashing with lightning. Howling wind twisted the trees, making it look as if the storm might shift and come back this way. At the creek Emily stopped and stared. The water overflowed its banks, surging against the rocks, carrying broken branches and clumps of leaves. Even Copper balked at crossing.

"Head upstream," she said to Reb. "We might find a place to cross."

As they trudged through the sopping grass, the storm shifted as Emily had feared. Beneath her poncho and heavy sweatshirt, she could feel the temperature dropping. Wind ripped at her breath and pummeled her eyes. She tried not to think about the hay crop that still needed harvesting or about Joey.

Lightning struck Hannah Peak, making the air vibrate and blinding Emily for a second. The rain exploded from the sky as if a mighty hand had turned on a fire hose. She wore one of her grandfather's cowboy hats, but its broad brim gave only the illusion of protecting her face from the driving rain.

She slipped in the mud and grabbed Reb's arm. "This is nuts!" she yelled above the wind. "Copper is miserable." Ears pressed flat to his skull, the dog hunched his back. "Even if we get across the creek, he won't be interested in looking for anything."

Reb stared longingly at the trees on the far side of the creek, then turned back to the house. By the time they reached the house, Emily's socks were soaked inside her boots, her hands were red and stinging cold and her teeth chattered. Joey, she thought miserably, out there alone, without a chance of finding dry wood for a fire. On the porch, she dried off Copper, then made sure his water bucket was full and put extra kibble in his food dish.

"I'm going over to the bunkhouse," Reb said from the doorway as she peeled off her dripping poncho and hat.

"Stay here. I'll get you a towel and a robe. You can use the shower upstairs." The invitation held a suggestive ring she told herself she didn't mean. She merely didn't want to be alone. She was scared and wanted Reb by her side. "There's nothing we can do out there. No sense you putting on dry clothes just to run back here through the rain. I can wash and dry your clothes while you wait." She clamped her lower lip between her teeth to stop the rush of justifications.

"Throw in some hot coffee and it's a deal."

She hurried to fetch him a towel before he changed his mind. After starting a pot of coffee, she went upstairs to shower. The heat of the pounding water made her worry all the more about Joey. He was tough, and living on a ranch meant he'd been out in worse weather than this, but still she imagined him wet and cold and sick. Her only consolation was she doubted if he could find his own hand, much less Tuff, in this storm.

In her room she pulled a robe from her closet. Daniel had given her the robe on her birthday. Made of heavy emerald green satin, it tied under her breasts, and the skirt flowed over her feet. It was warmer than a sweat suit, she reasoned. Modest. She wasn't trying to look pretty for Reb. She plaited her hair into a loose braid.

Downstairs Reb sat at the table. He had wrapped the towel around his waist. The sight of his heavily muscled arms and powerful chest turned her joints heavy. Head down, she mumbled, "I left a robe in the bathroom for you. First door on the right at the top of the stairs."

"Thank you, ma'am," he said in that cool, amused way of his.

As he left the kitchen, she peeked, eagerly noting the smoothly working muscles in his back. Not a trace of fat softened the hard lines of his waist, and his legs were as she imagined, chiseled and covered with black hair.

Smoothing a hand over the soft robe, she knew before he left her, she was going to make love to him. She would beg him to stay, pride and sensibility be damned.

She put their wet clothing into the washing machine.

A sudden knock at the back door made a scream rise in her chest. Back arched, she clutched the washing machine. The knocking continued, turning insistent.

She peeked around the edge of the laundry-room doorway. Through the glass in the upper half of the kitchen door she could see a hulking man-shape. She glanced at the shotgun propped against the wall.

The water stopped running upstairs. Pipes clanked.

Steeling herself, she went to the door. Mickey Thigpen stood on the porch. Unable to leave Mickey cooling his heels, she invited him inside, but she wished she knew if her suspicions about Reb avoiding the sheriff were valid. As much as she didn't want to admit it, she wanted to cover for Reb—even if he was in some kind of trouble.

"I didn't hear you come up," she said. "Is everything all right? Did you find Tuff?" She spoke loudly, hoping Reb heard and stayed upstairs.

Mickey brushed off his hat, holding it low in an effort to keep the water from dripping on the floor. "Not yet. My guess is he's headed for Mexico."

As she helped Mickey out of his poncho, she glanced guiltily at Reb's boots turned upside-down on the rack by the door. "Has he been spotted?" she asked.

He grimaced. "Phones are ringing off the hook. Folks have seen him in barns and in cars. One fellow swears up and down he saw Tuff flying a plane. It's a doggone mess." He made a clicking noise with his tongue and teeth. The puffy circles under his eyes made her wonder if he'd had any sleep since the escape.

Her gaze drifted to the window, where it looked dark as dusk outside. Rain sheeted against the glass. She imagined Tuff heedless as a demon, drawing ever closer to his duffel bag. Lightning flashed, turning the world bright for a moment; seconds later thunder rattled the house.

"Emily?"

The urge to tell him about the duffel bag was so strong she could almost hear the words hanging in the air. She cleared her throat. "How is Tim?"

Mickey shook his head. "Good thing he's got such a thick skull. Got his head cracked a good one, but I still had to give him an official order to take a few days of sick leave. He's fretting at the bit, and I can't say I blame him." He cocked his head, frowning at her. "Strangest thing. He was sitting at his desk, filling out a report, and suddenly Tuff came at him. But his desk faces the door, so no one could have gotten past him."

She didn't like the way he looked at her when he spoke. "Tim smokes, doesn't he? Maybe somebody slipped into the building while he was outside taking a break."

"I already figured that—is that coffee I smell?"

The pot had finished brewing, and she poured him a cup.

He sat at the table. "Funny seeing you in night-clothes during the day. Are you sick? There's a flu going around."

Heat rose on her cheeks. What if Reb appeared, also wearing a robe? Mickey had been annoyed at her before. She could well imagine what he'd think if he found her dressed like this with another man. She busied herself at the sink. "I got caught in the rain, and I needed something warm to wear. Drink your coffee while I change."

"Don't bother on my account. I think you look just fine."

"All the more reason to change," she said tartly, and hurried upstairs.

Steam billowed lazily through the open bathroom door. She whispered, "Reb?"

He poked his head out of her bedroom. She shooed him inside again, then closed and locked the door.

"It's the sheriff," she whispered, eyeing him in dismay. Her grandfather's flannel robe fit Reb as if it belonged to him. With his wet hair and flushed skin, he looked as if he'd spent the morning romping with her.

"I know," he whispered back. "I saw his car."

"I can't let him see you like this."

"Fine by me."

She refused to even consider what he meant by that. "Face the door and don't peek. I have to change my clothes."

He faced the door squarely and locked his hands behind his back. She dressed quickly in gray sweats, watching him all the while, making sure he didn't peek. To her disappointment, he didn't.

Downstairs Mickey had almost finished his coffee. Forcing down her impatience, she joined him at the table.

"Aren't you having coffee, honey?" He held out his cup for a refill.

"I only drink tea." As she freshened his cup, she realized her mistake and waited for him to ask why she'd made coffee if she was alone. "So how is the search going?" she asked. "Is the posse having any luck?"

"It's out of my hands. As soon as I reported the breakout, the state police took over. I'm just a penny-ante gofer these days." He spoke lightly as if it were amusing, but anger showed in the taut lines around his eyes.

Emily couldn't blame him for taking the escape personally.

"Helicopters are grounded, and they've pulled the dogs. The posse is threatening mutiny because everyone's worried about their hay crops." Mickey shrugged. "Plus the media has lost interest. As soon as the reporters found out Tuff's crime was only being drunk and disorderly, they packed up their cameras and went home." Mickey gazed solemnly at the coffeepot. "Where's Joey?"

"Why?"

"Somebody helped Tuff. I intend to find out who."

"Don't be ridiculous," she said hotly, scared all over again. "Joey didn't help Tuff escape."

"Where is he?"

She stared at her hands. Mickey wanted a scapegoat. He was angry, his pride affronted, and he probably felt taken advantage of, too. Locking up both Rifkin boys would go a long way toward assuaging his anger. Her urge to tell him about the duffel bag withered. No way could she explain why she'd withheld the information in the first place. "He's out," she said. "Checking cattle."

"You're expecting him."

She shook her head. "No."

His smile turned tight, and his eyes glittered. He stroked a hand over his damp, shiny hair. "Who are you expecting?"

"In this weather? Nobody." She tried to control the guilty pitch of her voice. She knew he knew she lied.

He stared so hard she felt needle-pricked. The old clock hanging over the sink ticked slowly, loudly, echoing the thumps of her guilty heart. The horrible idea that Mickey knew everything grew in power. She pressed the back of a hand to her forehead.

"Is there someone in the house?" he whispered.

Tuff. Mickey thought Tuff was holding her hostage. "You don't need to whisper, Mickey, there's no one in the house."

"Maybe I should take a look-see for myself."

"Maybe you should just take any ideas about getting upstairs into my bedroom right out of your brain!" The ease with which she mustered indignation surprised her. But it had the desired effect. Mickey's face flushed and he scowled, his eyes darting.

"When are you going to get it into your thick head that I think of you as a friend, nothing more?"

"Now, darn it, honey, that's not what I was thinking."

"That's what you're *always* thinking." She clamped her arms tightly across her chest and gave a wounded little sniff. "And I'd like you a whole lot better if you'd just stop thinking that way about me and start treating me with a little respect. If for no other reason than because you respected Grandpa."

"I can't help it if you're beautiful. You've got that effect on a man. It makes me a little . . . randy."

"Is that supposed to be a compliment?"

He visibly considered her question. "Do you consider it a compliment?" he asked cautiously. He pulled his head against his shoulders. "Reckon not." He tapped his fingers on the tabletop, restlessly toyed with his coffee cup and fiddled with his tie.

Emily almost felt sorry for him. On occasion he acted like a jerk, but he had a good heart and meant her no harm.

"Actually," she said, "I am hoping Joey will come home soon. I'm worried about him. He's on horseback, and this lightning makes me nervous."

He shifted his gaze to the shotgun propped in the corner. He nodded as if it confirmed something, and his shoulders relaxed. "Where did he go exactly?"

"I don't know . . . exactly. Probably the north pasture. If you absolutely have to find him, I can loan you a horse. You can't get there by car. Or you can check over at Claude's place. Except Joey might be outside with Claude." She shut up before she tangled herself in the lies.

"I suppose it'll keep." He lifted his gaze. All traces of good humor were gone.

Yes, Mickey definitely knew she was lying.

"Have you seen Pat Nyles lately?" he asked.

The name alone made her grimace. Pat Nyles had been the only boy in her seventh-grade class who needed to shave and had a license to drive. He'd been a hulking, sullen boy who carried cigarettes inside his shirt pocket in open defiance of school rules, and masked his stupidity behind a vicious temper and ready fists. "I didn't know he still lived around here."

"Oh, yeah. He's one of Tuff's running partners."

"Do you think he helped Tuff break out of jail?"

"Could be. He came by almost every day. I'm changing my policy, that's for certain. This escape is turning me into a laughingstock. That idiot over at the newspaper is having a field day with cracks about my 'open-door policy.'"

"Why ask me about Pat?"

He glanced at the shotgun again. "It's probably nothing. Pat's only running his mouth and acting like a big shot. But rumor has it that Tuff hired Pat to come after you."

Uncomprehending, she shook her head. "What do you mean?"

"Tuff was madder than hell about you calling the law on him."

"So he asked Pat to...hurt me?" Fear closed in on her, settling square in her chest in an ice-cold knot.

"It's probably not true, but Pat's disappeared and no one knows where he went. The timing is peculiar, know what I mean."

"Wait a minute. *Peculiar?* Tuff hired Pat Nyles to kill me, and you're worried because he's disappeared?'' Her entire body went numb. Her own brother had hired a man to kill her!

Mickey waved a hand lazily. ''This is exactly why I didn't want to tell you. Now you look like you've seen a ghost, and you're getting all excited about something that's nothing more than a rumor.''

''So why *are* you telling me?''

''For one thing I never said Tuff hired Pat to kill you. Rough you up, maybe, or scare you. Has Pat tried to scare you? Threats? Phone calls? Any hint at all he intended to help Tuff get out of jail?''

''I haven't seen Pat since high school.''

''Even so, with Tuff on the loose, maybe it's best if you took off for a while. I don't have a man to put out here to guard you. I'd stay myself, but I'm too busy.''

''I can't leave. It's impossible.''

''Go visit your friends in Kansas City for a week or two. We'll have Tuff in custody by then.'' A sharp squeal cut off whatever else he meant to say. He worked a pager off his belt. ''Mind if I use your phone?''

''Help yourself.'' She rested her face on her hands. Putting Tuff in jail hadn't lessened the harm he could do to her in the least. While in jail, he may have hired a man to hurt her—maybe even kill her. She wasn't surprised. But she was very frightened.

Mickey dropped a heavy hand on her shoulder. ''I have to go, honey. Duty calls. If you want, I'll come by tonight.''

''I'll be all right. Joey will be back soon.''

His eyes narrowed. ''Right. As soon as he walks in that door, you tell him to get his butt into my office.'' Mickey retrieved his hat and settled it carefully on his head. He worked his arms into his rain poncho.

She saw him out the door and turned the dead bolt. It locked home with a soothing clunk. She remained at the door, watching him drive away. The rain had eased off again, but the wind had picked up so it shuddered and howled against the house. Down at the creek the cottonwood leaves had been blown inside out, so the silver sides showed.

"Emily?"

She broke out in goose bumps from head to toe. Shivering, she hugged herself. "Were you listening?"

"I caught part of the conversation," Reb said.

"Mickey thinks Joey is in cahoots with Tuff. *And* there's a rumor that Tuff hired a man to hurt me, maybe kill me." Saying the words aloud made her feel sick and scared all over again.

"You should follow the sheriff's advice." He helped himself to a cup of coffee. "Leave until this blows over."

"I can't. Despite what Joey says, he needs me." She pushed away from the door, and Reb rubbed her shoulder. She looked up at his face and loved him all the more for his worried eyes and the unhappy pull of his mouth.

"Think about yourself for once," he said.

She laughed bitterly. "I thought about myself when I married Daniel. Look at the mess I caused. I can't desert Joey. If I do and Tuff comes here, then Joey will help him."

"Putting yourself in danger will make things better?"

"You don't understand."

"You're right. I don't."

She wasn't certain if she understood fully, either. "He's my brother. I let him down once, and I've regretted it ever since. It won't happen again."

"Your grandfather had no right to make you promise to watch out for Joey."

"He had every right. We're family." She pulled away from him. "I need to finish the laundry."

He followed her to the laundry room. Leaning his shoulder against the doorjamb, he crossed his arms. His eyes were indigo, shadowed by narrowed lids, and his disapproval shone through loud and clear.

She transferred her and Reb's clothes from the washer to the dryer, then she measured out soap and started another load in the washing machine. "Haven't you ever loved anybody? What's the use of living if you've got no one to care about but yourself?"

"Look how Joey treats you," Reb said. "If you think acting the martyr is noble, think again. He doesn't deserve what you're doing for him."

"You really don't understand." She faced him, and the sight of him filled her with regret. He was good and strong with gentle hands and gentle ways. She knew deep down where it counted he was capable of great love and loyalty. She suspected he knew it, too, and it spooked him.

"I know exactly what Joey is going through. When my husband had a heart attack, it was sudden, no warning. One minute he was in the restaurant, laughing and talking the way he always did. Then...he wasn't. He was dead. Gone." She snapped her fingers. "Like that. After the shock wore off, I was angry. Every night I'd cry into my pillow. When I sold the restaurant, I swear a part of me was saying, *See, that's what you get for leaving me.* It took me a long time to get over being angry."

"That excuses the way Joey treats you?"

"Not exactly. But it doesn't make me love him any less."

He snorted. "I don't know whether to admire you or think you're an idiot."

"I'm not saying I'm smart, Reb. I'm just telling you how it is." She shrugged. "Speaking of stupid, maybe we should discuss why you're hanging around."

His mouth curved into a slow, sheepish grin. "*Touché.*"

"I won't think any less of you if you do the smart thing and skedaddle. I'm guessing you weren't looking for trouble when you hired on."

"There's that little matter of the yellow streak down my back. I resent the implication."

It took a moment to understand what he meant. "Oh, I get it. Proving you're a big, strong, brave man is so much more sensible than my family loyalties." Thankful for the touch of lightness, she managed a smile. "Truth is, doing the smart thing doesn't make you chicken."

"I don't want to leave."

The poignant note behind the statement touched her. Maybe he never had any intention of caring about her and Joey, but he cared anyway. Maybe, just maybe, he loved her a little bit, too. She held out her arms to him. He averted his gaze.

"I'm scared. Hold me, Reb."

His features tightened, turned dark and pained. He pushed away from the doorjamb and gathered her into his arms. When she reached upward for a kiss, he captured her mouth with a mixture of ferocity, yearning and soulful sweetness. Embers of desire caught fire, stripping her of any thought except of him. He caught her waist in both hands and hoisted her atop the washing machine. Moist heat seeped through her sweatpants, and the vibration of the motor heightened her excitement. She kissed and kissed him, absorbing the wet freshness of his mouth and the soapy scent of his skin. She wrapped her legs around his hips, and he thrust his pelvis at her, leaving no questions about his arousal. She raked her fingers through his damp hair and worked her other hand inside his robe. Her breasts ached, grown turgid, and she felt silently desperate for Reb to work his hands underneath her shirt.

But he abruptly broke the kiss. She stared into his eyes and was lost in their black, gleaming depths. He stroked her waist and ribs, and his thumbs grazed the sides of her breasts.

"We shouldn't do this," he said, his voice raw. "The timing is bad. Your defenses are down."

"I don't need any defenses against you."

He cocked his head, his expression touchingly puzzled.

"Do you think this is spur-of-the-moment?" She nuzzled her nose against his. "You're not that dumb, Reb Tremaine."

He slipped both hands under the hem of her sweatshirt. Her back arched in a spasm of pleasure as his hot palms resumed lazily, sensuously caressing her sides.

She wanted to tell him they should do this because she loved him...to say that a little while with him was far, far better than never being with him at all. But words were inadequate. She clasped his face in both hands and drew him toward her for another kiss.

"Ah, Emily," he whispered, and kissed her again.

Chapter Eleven

Reb made love to her slowly, thoroughly, passionately. What he refused to say with words, he spoke with his hands tenderly against her skin, with his lips hot against her mouth. Lost in his loving, she cried out her pleasure and whispered his name and begged him to stay with her forever. He answered her pleas with gracefully expert hands, holding back nothing, drowning her in the intensity of his passion and the depths of emotion in his eyes.

Afterward they lay entwined on her narrow bed, tangled in the sheets and blankets. She sprawled half-atop him, with one leg thrown over his thighs. Cold air against her cooling skin tingled pleasantly. She breathed in his sweet, musky scent. Reb lay on his back with an arm hooked behind his neck. His expression was remote, his gaze troubled.

His distance saddened her. A few minutes ago they'd been as one. He'd denied her nothing of himself. Now it was as if a wall had dropped between them. She saw regret in the thin set of his mouth. Or perhaps guilt.

She searched for light words, reassuring words. She had no regrets. The only guilt she felt concerned being warm and happy while her brother was out in the storm.

His chest rose and fell in a heavy sigh.

Did he love her? she wondered. A little bit? She wanted to ask if he'd ever been in love, and if so, had the woman wounded him and turned his heart stony.

"The rain stopped," she said. Though still cloud covered, the sky had lightened. Moisture made lace patterns on the window glass. "I hope the sun comes out. Every bit of hay we can harvest is that much less I have to buy." She frowned. "Do you know if Claude called the haying crew yet?"

He merely grunted softly.

"You were right before when you said I don't like ranch living," Emily mused. "There's too much stuff to worry about. Running a restaurant is ten times easier."

He turned his head to look at her.

Subdued, she asked, "Do you want me to be quiet?"

He petted her hair, fingering the long curls. His silence wore on her nerves. Uneasy laughter rippled through her as she remembered the box of condoms he'd purchased. Protection neither of them had mentioned in the heat of the moment. She debated mentioning it now, but if he wasn't thinking about it, she sure didn't want to bring it up. No sense giving him more cause for regrets.

She struggled upright, clutching a corner of the bed sheet over her breasts. The floor was cold under her bare feet. "Guess I ought to finish the laundry."

"Finishing the laundry is how this got started."

She looked over her shoulder. He smiled at her, relieving her greatly. Warmth filled her. With it came a yearning for a child from this union. Even if Reb left her, she wanted a piece of Reb to keep forever. She placed a hand low over her belly, and hoped.

Crazy hope, ridiculous hope, unrealistic and selfish hope—but she hoped anyway.

Tearing away from him, she slipped on the emerald green robe, went downstairs and started water boiling for a cup of tea. Then she stood at the window. Backed by pale silver clouds, the mountains looked sharp, as if they'd been carved by a razor. The landscape was fresh washed and bright, the colors having an extra sparkle. Tiny chickadees and juncos gathered at the edges of puddles. Hens scampered around the chicken house.

"Any coffee left?" Reb asked.

She reached for the cupboard where she kept cups. She couldn't make herself look at him. As a child she'd been deeply superstitious, seeing signs and omens in every night-bird cry and oddly grown flower. The childish beliefs filled her now. If she turned too fast or looked too hard at him, he'd disappear. Ergo, if she didn't look at him, he had to stay.

She filled a cup and set it on a counter, keeping her back to him.

"I want to drive over to Claude's. He may have an idea where Joey went."

"We need to talk," he said.

She thrust out a hand, showing him her rigid palm. "No, we don't."

"I'm not going to hurt you, Emily."

He had that dead wrong. He was going to break her heart. For now it didn't matter. What mattered was the scent of him clinging to her skin and the sweet memory of him kissing her.

"Let's just be quiet for a while," she said. She wanted the luxury of believing that what they shared would last.

The teakettle began to whistle. While she fixed a cup of tea, chair legs scraped the floor. His image was burned in her brain; his scent and the feel of him and the sound of his loving were fixed firmly in her heart.

"Our jeans aren't quite dry yet. You might as well run over to the bunkhouse and get dressed in fresh clothes. We'll drive my car over to Claude's place. That is, if you'll go with me."

"Emily..."

She shook her head and cradled the teacup in both hands. "We're not going to talk about us, Reb. Not right now." Emotion climbed her throat. She wanted to fling herself onto his lap and cover him with kisses. She really wanted to talk about tomorrow and the day after and babies and couldn't he at least *consider* settling down?

Behind her she heard the chair legs scrape again. The back door opened. She tensed, wondering if he was angry, frustrated or what—and unable to make herself turn around to see. The door shut softly.

"You're acting like an idiot, Emily Farraday," she murmured. Nothing new. Daniel had always teased her about being naive. A country girl who once upon a time believed in fairy tales and fortune-tellers and Sasquatch. The best person at fooling her had always been herself, though. She wanted to believe in a better tomorrow and the goodness in most people, and if they weren't good, then they were bad guys who always got what they deserved. Sometimes reality was too hard to contemplate.

She carried the tea upstairs. Sipping tea, warming her face in the steam, she looked at her bed. She was half-tempted to never wash those sheets again. She could store them away, and when the nights were too lonely, she'd bring them out, wrap herself in memories and take comfort from Reb's scent.

Except, she knew, in the end she'd be practical. She'd wash the sheets and do her mourning in private. She sighed. Where men were concerned, she had no luck at all.

She dressed warmly in jeans, a flannel shirt and sweater. Reb waited for her in the kitchen. Now fully dressed, she could look at him. He wore clean jeans, a striped shirt and a denim jacket. He'd combed his hair, but unruly hanks escaped to fall over his brow and ears.

"Are you all right?" he asked.

"Couldn't be better."

"I'm sorry," he said.

"For what?"

"For putting the sadness back in your eyes."

She tried to smile, but her face refused to cooperate.

He held out a hand. For a long moment she stared at it. He had big hands, scarred by hard work, burned brown by the sun. Tendons and veins stood out in sharp relief. Gentle hands, clever hands, unselfish hands... loving hands. She placed her hand against his, palm to palm. Her body reacted with a heavy thump in her midsection and shivery weakness in her knees. He closed his fingers over hers and drew her gently toward him.

He kissed her. A tender kiss, and sweet. In the gentle play of his lips against hers, she felt his goodbye.

WHEN REB TRIED TO PULL open the garage door, the damp wood resisted him. He gave the door a good jerk to open it all the way. Emily's Oldsmobile shared the building with a 1949 Ford pickup. She unlocked the driver's door to the Olds. This far into the country with the car safely inside the garage, she shouldn't have to keep it locked. Except she had no one to trust.

Least of all, him.

Every lie Reb had told her gnawed at his soul. And mingled with the pain was the lingering pleasure of making love to her. Sex, he tried to correct in his head. Made *love,* came the insistent reply. He wouldn't walk away from her unscarred—if he could walk away at all.

She invited him into the car. Despite being three years old, it was as clean and fresh smelling as a new car. He buckled his safety belt.

To reach Claude's house they had to drive out to the main road, follow it around the ridge, then negotiate a rutted, twisting path barely wide enough for the car. Emily inched around the worst potholes and washouts, but still bottomed out several times. She winced with every jarring jolt.

Reb kept an eye out for official vehicles, but saw no sign of any. Manpower shortage, he guessed.

"Another item for the to-do list," she muttered, looking anxiously at the rearview mirror. She searched the road behind them as if expecting to see transmission parts strewn in their back trail. "By spring not even the cattle trucks will be able to get up here."

"Rent a grader and I'll do it." Surprised by his impulsive offer, he scowled.

"You know how to do road work?"

"Jack-of-all-trades," he murmured. Now he feared looking at her. No telling what might fall out of his mouth next.

She parked in front of Claude's house, clutching the steering wheel with both hands. Lights were on inside the house. Claude's border collie lay on the porch, his muzzle on his paws. His unnervingly intelligent eyes were alert and watchful.

"I always feel like an idiot around Claude," she said, and pulled the key from the ignition. "He's the meanest man in the world."

"Why do you keep him on?"

She shrugged. "Where would he go? He's too old to find another job and too cantankerous to live with relatives. If he has any." A bright laugh bubbled from her mouth, and she shot Reb a mischievous glance. "If he were forty years younger, I'd march that old goat off this ranch at gunpoint."

Her expression turned thoughtful. "But a long time ago he saved Grandpa's life. There was a blizzard. He and Grandpa were checking the cattle and got caught in an avalanche. It killed their horses, and Grandpa hurt his leg. They were snowed in and couldn't use the roads, so to get help, Claude would have had to ride or walk twenty-five miles. Instead, he carried Grandpa off the mountain." She shook her head, her eyes filled with wonder. "Grandpa was your size, maybe a little bigger. But Claude carried him off the mountain. Grandpa never forgot. I can't, either. So I'm stuck with him."

"You're an amazing woman, Emily Farraday."

"I don't feel amazing," she said as she got out of the car.

The border collie rose to his feet.

"It's me, Paco," Emily said, her voice soft and soothing. She and Reb climbed the porch stairs with measured steps. The dog watched their every move. She rapped her knuckles against the weathered door.

When Claude appeared, he made no effort to conceal his dislike of Emily. Openly reluctant, he invited her inside. He smiled at Reb and offered coffee.

As Emily moved gingerly to the center of the room, Claude launched into a diatribe about ruined hay fields, managing to make it sound as if Emily had conjured the rainstorm and freezing weather to make life hard for an old man. With a tight little smile on her face, she folded her arms and said nothing. Her eyes glazed.

When the older man finally ran out of steam, she said, "I appreciate your concern. But I have a more pressing problem right now. Joey took off."

"I know. Sheriff's looking for him. What's this about him being up at the north pasture?"

"Joey's looking for Tuff."

Claude lifted his fleshy upper lip in a snarl. "Why?"

"Because he's scared. He's afraid the posse will shoot Tuff."

"Good riddance, I say. Tuff is devil's spawn. He ought to be shot. If he shows that mug of his around here, I'll shoot him myself." Claude handed Reb a cup of coffee so black it looked like paint. Then he snorted, his wiry shoulders shaking with disgust. "I thought you had a firm rein on Joey, girl."

"Do you have any idea where he would go? He's on horseback and he headed west. You know better than I do where Joey thinks he might find Tuff."

"Ain't that a fine kettle, huh?" Claude cracked his oversize knuckles. "My joints are telling me this dang storm is more than a blow-by, and you let Joey go running off.'' He sniffed derisively in the direction of a radio. ''Weathermen say it'll clear. Ha! Be snow before the week is out. Count on it. Why, I recall back in '56—''

''Listen to me!'' Emily interrupted. ''He's out there alone and he's scared and he's worried to death about Tuff. If you don't want to look for him, then tell me where to look.''

Claude shrugged irritably and dropped into a chair. He picked up a leather awl and examined it.

''Blame me all you want,'' Emily continued, ''but I know you care about Joey. So help me. He was here this morning. Did he tell you where he's going? Did he even hint about what he's up to?''

''Nobody'll find Tuff unless he wants finding. Kid's got the sneak of a cougar. And I sure wouldn't want to be the cowpoke who crosses his path.''

''Exactly my point, Claude. I don't want Joey finding him. Tuff stole a gun. He'll use it.''

He looked her up and down, his pale eyes sharp behind sagging folds of weathered skin. ''You can't find him, and that's a fact.'' He heaved a martyred sigh. ''Reckon I can go take a look-see for the boy.''

''Reb and I will go with you.'' She turned for the door. ''I'll meet you—''

''I'm not in the mood to play nursemaid. You just scoot on back to your kitchen and let me handle Joey. Harrumph, most likely he'll come dragging back before the day's out anyway. He knows how hard it'll be to find Tuff.''

Emily looked at Reb, her eyes begging for his help. He agreed with the older man. Emily and her roan mare couldn't keep up with Claude. Stubborn determination wasn't enough to make her search effectively. As much as Claude's hurtful words and unfair attacks irritated him, Reb kept his mouth shut.

"Fine," she said wearily.

"Wait a minute, girl. I got something to say to you." Claude set down the awl and clamped both hands on his knees. "Think about this while you're baking a pie."

She closed her eyes. Her lips moved as if she were counting down her temper.

"Sell me the Double Bar R."

Reb lifted his eyebrows, and Emily turned slowly to face Claude.

"You can hightail it back to the city," he continued. "Me and Joey will get along fine without you."

"I can't sell the ranch."

"You won't be selling it out from under the boy. I'm more family than you are. I'll leave it to Joey in my will."

Emily sighed. "I have no intention of taking the ranch away from Joey, Claude. Now, please go find him." She put her hand on the doorknob.

"Pay you fair market value. Cash. That's what you want."

"Even if I did, you don't have that kind of money. I've been offered nine-fifty. And that's just the starting bid."

Claude cocked his head, his incomprehension plain.

"Nine hundred and fifty thousand dollars, Claude," she said patiently. "Another real-estate broker told me the land could be worth as much as a million-three to the right buyer."

His mouth fell open.

Reb didn't share Claude's surprise. He'd seen the high-priced vacation homes sprouting throughout the valley. There must be a dozen developers licking their chops at the idea of buying the Double Bar R. If Emily had a dishonest bone in her beautiful body, she'd have been long gone. It did surprise him Claude didn't realize it.

Claude recovered with a shake. "That's big-city prices, but I just want the land. You find out what it's worth, and I'll pay up. Cash, fair and square."

"You don't need to buy the ranch, Claude. Not even for a nickel on the dollar. It belongs to Joey. If I can keep him alive long enough to grow up, I'm giving it to him, no strings attached. So, please, go find him and bring him home."

Reb thought he detected a trace of softening on Claude's seamed face. The old man popped to his feet. "Reckon that's what you told Garth, but I'm not falling for it."

"Let's go, Reb." She opened the door.

"Shoot," Claude continued. "I don't drink, don't honky-tonk or gamble. Only weakness I got is for fancy painted horses, and ain't bought one of them since 1973. Been saving my money for my old age, but hell, I'm old and still got nothing to spend it on. Only thing I have left is Joey. You and Tuff are nothing but heartache. Any luck at all, Tuff'll get himself shot for a varmint."

"I'll think about it, Claude," she said in a small, troubled voice. She hurried out the door.

Reb studied the cowboy. Claude was nearly eighty years old and set in his ways. Still strong in body and spirit, but weak inside his closed-tight mind.

"Watch out for that woman, Reb," Claude warned. "She'll drain you like a spider drains a fly."

Once outside, Reb inhaled the fresh rain-washed air. Then he followed Emily to the car and slid onto the passenger seat. She leaned against the steering wheel with her head on her folded arms. He rubbed her shoulder.

"I never did anything to Claude," she said. "I don't know why he hates me." She pushed upright, gave herself a shake and started the engine.

Reb settled back on the seat as she carefully maneuvered the car in a circle. "You could take him up on his offer. Sell out to him."

She surprised him with a laugh. "Get real. He doesn't have the money. It wouldn't surprise me a bit to find his mattress stuffed full of cash, but I know what he makes in wages. Even if he's saved every dollar he ever earned, he couldn't buy the ranch." She kept both hands on the wheel and her gaze focused on the road. "He has no concept of today's prices. He still thinks a dollar should buy a steak dinner and a round of beer. So trust me, even if I'd sell, he couldn't buy."

"So, let him make an offer and take it."

"That would leave Claude and Joey with nothing. Neither of them have a clue about the business side of running this operation. Joey's smart, he can learn, but losing the ranch isn't the lesson I want to teach him."

"You're underestimating Joey."

"I can't take the chance."

He rested a hand on her arm. "This is guilt talking, not reason. You're trying to make up for running away with Daniel."

She snatched her arm from his grasp and shot him an angry, wounded glare. "You're the last person I expect to understand! You don't know anything about responsibility. Or—or loyalty."

Her barb cut straight through him.

The rear end of the car dropped into a pothole. Reb bounced hard on the seat, and his teeth clacked. Emily jerked on the wheel. The tires thump-thumped into another hole.

"My car!" she cried. "I wrecked my car." She jammed hard on the brake.

"Emily, calm down."

A word he never expected to hear from her slipped out of her mouth. Tears glazed her eyes, and her chin quivered. Reb braced for a storm as she inched the car forward. An ominous rattle shook the rear end, and a tear slipped down her cheek.

"It's probably only the muffler. Do you want me to drive?"

She ignored him. Her hands were white knuckled on the steering wheel. He knew her tears had nothing to do with the car and everything to do with Joey's disappearance. Not to mention Claude's unwarranted abuse. He searched for something, anything to say. All that came to mind were justifications about how he was both responsible and loyal and if she'd give him half a chance, he'd prove it.

As soon as she parked the car inside the garage, she raced around to the rear end and dropped to her knees on the gravel.

Reb looked down at her as she peered anxiously underneath the car. He didn't trust himself to say anything wise. He ached to offer comfort, but he knew where that would lead. A hug, then a kiss, then into her bed with nothing resolved and his culpability increased. He crouched. With a hand on the bumper, he examined the muffler, which hung so low that it touched the ground.

"You lost a bolt. Nothing serious. I can fix it in ten minutes."

She sat back on her heels. "I'm sorry for snapping at you," she said. "I didn't mean what I said."

She had meant it. And she'd spoken the truth; it couldn't hurt so much unless it was the truth. Being responsible professionally and loyal to whoever paid him meant nothing. Any dog could show loyalty to a man with a feed bowl. "Get me a flashlight so I can look at the fittings."

"I really am sorry. Please forgive me. I don't want you mad at me, too."

"I'm not mad." *Except at myself.* He understood perfectly now what Garth Rifkin had seen in her and why he'd entrusted her with the ranch. She possessed decency, honesty and a capacity for caring. Her grandfather had known as soon as the words *I promise* slipped from her lips that she'd keep her word no matter what it cost her. Garth had used her.

As Reb used her now. He hated himself for it.

As Emily headed toward the house, he set his hat on the trunk and lay on the ground so he could get a better look at the muffler. Propped on an elbow, he watched her climb the porch steps. The time had come for him to tell her the truth. She wasn't involved with Tuff or the money or the murder. Keeping her ignorant served no purpose. In some ways it only made his job more difficult.

She was going to hate him. She'd look directly at him, her big brown eyes hiding none of her hurt or anger, and she'd loathe him.

Emily wouldn't scream and pummel him with her fists. No, she'd be understanding. She'd listen quietly as he explained how she'd been designated a target for murder because her older brother wanted her dead and her younger brother thought she was a murderer. Reb was going to have to tell her that Tuff was even worse than she thought, too. Not only was the man a thief, but Reb knew he'd been involved in more than one murder. All along, Reb had used charm and lies to gain Emily's trust so she would lead him to the money. Maybe Emily would pretend to forgive him—and say she realized he had a job to do, that it was dirty work but somebody had to do it.

And yet the adoration in her doe-soft eyes would extinguish.

She'd turn frigid to his touch.

If her mouth didn't say it, the rest of her body would: you're a low-down, dirty-stinking, rotten liar, and I'll never, ever forgive you.

Emily burst through the doorway. The screened door slammed with a bang against the house. Her feet thudded on the wooden porch. Catching a post in one hand, she vaulted across the steps and hit the wet ground hard. She slipped, regained her balance and churned grass, racing toward the garage.

Reb scrambled to his feet.

Arms outstretched, she ran to him. "Somebody's in the house!"

Chapter Twelve

Whoever had been in the house was probably long gone, but despite Reb's assurances Emily tiptoed into the kitchen, even after Reb had searched the house from top to bottom. Wide-eyed, she looked around the room, then her fearful gaze followed a faint trail of muddy boot prints across the floor.

"It could have been Joey," Reb said. He crouched and swiped a finger across one of the prints. "Dry." He glanced at the clock. "We weren't at Claude's that long. Maybe Joey was hanging around, waiting for you to leave so he could fetch dry clothes."

Emily gave a start when she realized how late it was. Between Tuff and Mickey, Joey and Claude, it seemed as if a lifetime had dragged through the day. Yet here it was almost fully dark. "I doubt it's Joey. He knows better than to track mud on my floors." Shivering gripped her. "It had to be Tuff. The door was locked, so whoever was here used a key."

"If it was Tuff, why didn't he take the shotgun?" Reb nodded at the weapon resting against the wall. "Check around. See if anything's missing. I'll take care of the animals."

"Pardon me for cowardice, but I'm not staying in this house alone. Come with me." She steeled herself and crept through the kitchen. The muddy prints petered out in front of the staircase, but still clearly pointed to the intruder going upstairs.

Displaying none of her reluctance, Reb went past her. He checked Joey's room a second time. Nothing was disturbed, and there were no damp clothes in the hamper.

Emily cautiously opened the door to Tuff's room.

"Anything missing? Out of place?" Reb asked. In the center of the room he turned a slow circle, his eyes darting, searching.

"I wouldn't know. I never come in here, not even to clean." She rubbed her chilly arms. "He doesn't want me in here."

She knew it had to be Tuff. He must have been watching the house, waiting for her to leave, and used his key to enter. Why? She checked his clothes hamper. Empty. Nothing inside the closet indicated he'd changed clothing.

Why?

She never kept cash in the house, and Tuff knew it. The only weapons they had were Joey's deer rifle and the shotgun. The kitchen was undisturbed, so he hadn't come back for food. His car was locked up in the county impound lot.

"Joey's truck." She ran across the hall to Joey's room, straight to his desk, where he kept a spare set of keys for his truck.

"His spare keys are gone," she called out. Suddenly sensing someone behind her, she jumped—only to find Reb standing right there. She clasped a hand over her pounding heart and cast him a glare.

"I'll start whistling," he said, his smile contrite.

She pawed through the clutter of pens, paper clips, old school notes and rodeo schedules, but couldn't find the keys. She checked all the drawers and his bedside table. "Gone." She looked out the window and, even in the dusky darkness, could see the old pickup parked in its usual place under the long branches of a cottonwood tree.

"Joey could have hidden the keys to keep you from taking them," Reb said.

A reasonable assumption. She chewed her lower lip. "If not the keys, then what?"

"Come on."

She didn't bother putting on her coat, and the cold bit her as soon as she followed Reb outside. Carrying the shotgun, Reb didn't appear in the least disturbed by the rapidly dropping temperature. He stood tall, outwardly relaxed, as he looked around.

A sense of exposed vulnerability kept Emily pressed against the wall. In every shadow she imagined Tuff, lean and deadly, caressing the barrel of a gun, waiting for a chance to put a bullet in her head.

"I'll call the sheriff," she whispered. "He can stake out the truck. Let's get out of here, Reb. I'm scared."

"He'll be expecting a trap."

Reb hopped silently off the porch and strode to the pickup. She heard him open the truck's hood. Curiosity overcame caution, and she hurried to his side. He handed her the shotgun, fiddled around with the engine, then gently lowered the hood. He leaned on it to secure the latch. He held something.

"What is that?"

"Distributor cap. Cheap trick, but effective. Tuff isn't going anywhere. Any spare keys to your car?"

"None Tuff knows about. Reb, we need to get out of here. You have to believe how dangerous he is. If we get in his way, he'll kill us."

"Not a chance. Trust me."

A cold, wet blob thrust against her hand. She screamed and would have dropped the shotgun if Reb hadn't caught it. Copper woofed and laid his ears flat, turning in tail-wagging circles as if in apology for frightening her.

"Tuff doesn't need to kill me—you two will give me a heart attack." She crouched and grasped the dog's big head by his furry ruff. He tried to lick her face. He acted as unconcerned and friendly as usual. If Tuff were around, Copper would be cowering in the barn. "Okay, Reb." She rose. "Tuff isn't here."

"Will Copper bark at your brother?"

"No, he'd be digging a hole to hide in. What do you suggest?"

"Go back in the house. Lock up. I'll take care of the animals and check around."

Once inside the kitchen, she stood at the sink, watching through the window as lights went on inside the barn. Weariness draped her shoulders. The adrenaline rush had faded, leaving her heavy and dull minded.

Still, something was wrong. She was sure Reb didn't want the sheriff here, but that didn't make any sense. At this very moment Tuff could be digging up the duffel bag. He'd come back here to steal the truck, and when he couldn't start it, then what?

Reb didn't want the sheriff's help.

Reb, she decided, was out of his ever-loving mind. She reached for the telephone, but hesitated.

If she called the sheriff and a hundred cops showed up, Tuff would know. He'd hear them coming from miles away. He'd never be caught—and she'd always be in danger. She sighed, still not sure what to do. She fixed a simple supper of leftovers, and had it hot and ready on the table when Reb returned. He held Copper by the collar.

"Copper," she said. "Get in here."

"C'mon," Reb urged as Copper came inside.

"Did you see any sign of Tuff?"

"Nope." Reb propped the shotgun next to the door. "He'll show up."

"We'll be ready for him."

"And if he doesn't show?"

"Then I'm going after him."

THE WIND ROSE AGAIN, rising and falling, one moment a gentle rustling, another moment a thundering gust rattling the house and whistling down the chimney. Restless and fearful, Emily kept wandering the house, compulsively checking the door locks and window catches. Outside, within the ragged circle of light cast by the security lamp, nothing moved except leaves tripping across the driveway.

Each time she entered the kitchen, Copper would leap to his feet and stand with his nose touching the door, waiting for her to let him out. She'd tell him, "No, Copper, down." He'd lower his head and creep back to the corner, giving her his best woe-is-me look.

Reb's coolness began wearing on her nerves. He sat in the living room, his long legs stretched out and crossed at the ankles, his arms folded loosely over his chest, while he watched television. She brought out the mending basket and made a halfhearted effort at patching the knee of a pair of Joey's jeans. After pricking her finger with the needle twice, she gave up. It started to rain again. Drops pattered at the windows, and echoes inside the chimney sounded like a drum.

"Do you think Joey's okay?" she asked.

Reb cocked an eyebrow. "He's probably at Claude's. Even teenagers get tired of being wet."

Around midnight Emily began to doubt if she'd get any sleep. Jittery with nerves, she joined Reb on the sofa.

Reb played with her hair. He watched an old Gregory Peck movie on television, his expression unreadable, so she couldn't tell if he even realized what his fingers were doing. Knowing exactly what she was doing, she shifted on the couch and ended up with her head resting against his shoulder. He made no objection, but continued finger-combing her long curls. She picked lint off his thigh.

"Emily."

She froze, her hand hovering an inch above the worn-soft denim sheathing his thigh.

"You're driving me crazy."

He drove her crazy, too. She turned her face and met his sparkling blue eyes. Hot blood pulsed hard through her veins, warming her from the inside out, making her quiver in anticipation. All the desire she'd felt earlier coiled inside her, fresh and hungry and new.

Reb kissed her tenderly and placed his hand against her face, his long fingers hot. She returned his kiss with eagerness, twisting on the couch to find a less awkward position. Television, wind and worries forgotten, they necked, making the old sofa groan. She climbed onto his lap and straddled his thighs. He worked his hands under her shirt, always kissing, teasing, testing, tasting, a melody of slick teeth, wet tongues and the smoky scent of arousal. He unhooked her bra. Her body ached for his touch. She silently chanted her love for him, willing him to hear with every move of her hands and lips.

Lips bruised, her cheeks and chin burning from rasping his late-day beard, she let her head fall back. Each breath was a struggle, though her body sang, thrumming with life. He worked her shirt up her sides, and she lifted her arms, helping him. He stripped off her bra and tossed it behind him. Bathed in the silver light from the television, his face glowed.

"You're beautiful," he whispered, his voice tinged with awe.

She felt beautiful.

He grasped her shoulders in both hands, holding her fast, her breasts thrust proudly forward. Her blue jeans felt excruciatingly tight, chafing skin that had grown overly sensitive with his touch.

"Are you going to look at me or make love to me?" she asked.

"Both." He eased her backward, holding her steady until she had her feet on the floor.

She straightened, loving the heat in his eyes and his hungry smile. Slowly she unzipped her jeans while he watched every move. She wriggled to push denim and her panties off her hips and down her legs, then she stepped out of her clothes and between his legs.

He swept her onto his lap, playfully rough, erotically tender. She tore at his clothing, impatient in her eagerness to feel his skin against hers, to taste him and revel in the contrast between his hard muscles and her soft curves. The sofa was too small, and several times they nearly tumbled to the floor, but the intimacy of the confined space heightened her arousal. He whispered her name huskily between kisses.

Only afterward, content within herself to feel the ebbing echoes of her climax and his, did she feel the cold. Reb lay atop her, with one hand on the floor holding his weight off her, his head resting against her neck.

"We're insane," she said.

When he lifted his head, the troubled, distant look was missing. He wore a crooked, sleepy grin. "Have to say I agree, ma'am."

She wanted to tell him she loved him—so much that the words ached in her throat. But the sweet spell of his mellow eyes was too precious to break.

With grace incongruous to his size, he rose. He stood for a moment, his tall, gorgeous body outlined in silver by the black-and-white movie playing on television. Emily melted all over again. She sat up and wrapped her arms around her knees as he pulled an afghan off the back of a rocking chair and tenderly tucked it around her nakedness.

"Don't want to get caught with my pants down," he said reluctantly. He picked his jeans off the floor and turned the legs right side out.

Watching the sinuous line of his back made her hot. If not for Tuff lurking around the ranch, she'd drag Reb upstairs to her bed.

After he dressed, he resumed his seat on the couch. Now sleepy, she snuggled against his side. Her eyelids drooped as she tried to figure out what movie played.

"My parents abandoned me," he said, his voice devoid of emotion.

For a moment she thought she was dreaming. Was Reb really going to share intimate details about his life with her? But it was no dream.

Reb continued, "You're right, I don't understand families. I understand responsibility and loyalty, though."

Feelings of sympathy rose within her, but Emily squashed the urge to fill the silence with chatter. Reb was offering her a piece of his carefully guarded self, and it was a gift she'd spoil with thoughtless words or misplaced pity.

"Might say I learned by bad example. My father split when I was little. I don't remember him at all. Mom never recovered. She drank. She finally dumped me with her sister and took off. My aunt had her own problems, her own kids, so she couldn't take care of me. I grew up in foster homes and on a boys' ranch."

Emily allowed a tear of sympathy to slide down her face. She grasped his hand.

"I liked the ranch. They kept us busy with school and hard work, but the counselors cared. They were good people."

"Do you ever see your mother?"

"Not in years. I remind her too much of my father."

Her loss, Emily thought. Any good woman would be proud to have a son like Reb. Though he spoke in a mild, almost sleepy way, she knew he hurt.

EMILY AWAKENED with a start. Disoriented, she stared into the darkness, unable to recognize any shadowy shapes, but knowing the windows were in the wrong place and her bed felt all wrong. Gradually she remembered she was in the living room, on the sofa. She must have fallen asleep. The afghan had tangled around her feet, and her toes poked through the crocheted stitches. Wind hammered the house, whistling under the eaves.

She stretched out her feet, seeking Reb. Unable to find him, she sat up, huddling inside the afghan, listening.

"Reb?"

Only the wind answered.

Imaginings tumbled through her groggy brain. Tuff had returned and drawn Reb into a showdown. Reb had decided this was too much closeness for comfort and had taken off, never to be seen again. Joey had returned, and he and Reb were seated at the kitchen table.

She found her jeans and sweatshirt, but not her socks or panties. Unwilling to risk turning on a light, she dressed as quietly as she could. She felt around for the shotgun, which had been lying on the floor next to the sofa. It was gone, too. She tiptoed to the kitchen doorway and cocked her head, listening. An anxious whimper told her Copper was still in the house. He scratched at the door. She noticed a light on inside the bunkhouse.

More curious than frightened, she moved to the kitchen window and stared at the bunkhouse. She longed to know Reb better. He'd given her a taste, a morsel about his background, but she didn't even know how old he was or his birthday or if "Reb" was a nickname or his given name. She didn't know whether or not to take his desertion personally.

She started to turn away when the silhouette of a man appeared in the bunkhouse window. Then two men. Startled, she grabbed the sink and stood on tiptoe, nearly touching her nose to the window glass. The shapes disappeared. She blinked, wondering if the glass had distorted what she'd seen. The light winked off, plunging the bunkhouse into darkness.

Troubled, uncertain what she'd seen—or hadn't seen—she poured a glass of water. When she looked outside again, Reb was striding quickly across the driveway to the house, with his head down, holding his hat, and his shoulders hunched against the wind.

A key turned distinctly in the lock. She startled.

Reb slipped inside, accompanied by a swirl of gelid air.

"Where did you get a house key?"

He sidestepped away from the outside light that shone through the glass and melded into the shadows. She took two long steps and hit the light switch. He squinted at her from beneath his hat brim.

Pained by the light, she averted her face. For a few seconds neither of them spoke or moved. When her eyes adjusted, she glanced at the clock. It was after six in the morning. Cloud cover hid the dawn.

She asked again, "Where did you get a key to my house?"

"Joey gave it to me." Calmly, without guilt or shame, he returned her gaze.

Fear crept into her belly. "Why?"

"In case of emergency when he went to Denver. I forgot to give it back." He held out the key to her. "Here, I'm sorry. I thought you knew I had it."

A nasty little inner voice told her he was lying—but why? She'd already given him the run of the house. "Finding you gone scared me. Why didn't you wake me?" She wondered if she'd really seen another man with Reb.

"You needed your sleep." He set the shotgun next to the door, then pulled off his hat and pressed it to his chest. He wore a heavy parka instead of his denim jacket. The fingers of his leather work gloves were dark with moisture. He gave her an endearing smile that stripped away her suspicions and weakened her knees. "I was doing the chores. What I'm hired to do."

The glass must have distorted what she'd seen. If Joey had been in the bunkhouse, Reb wouldn't drag out her worry. Uncertainty subdued her. If she asked, it meant she didn't trust Reb. Joey distrusted her, Claude thought she was the devil incarnate, her friends were hundreds of miles away, all the sheriff did was pat her on the head and Tuff wanted her dead. The only person who believed in her was Reb, and she needed desperately to trust him. "Did you get any sleep last night?" she asked.

"Enough." He rolled his head and kneaded the back of his neck. "Not too comfortable, though."

"Did you see any sign of Tuff?"

"Not a one." He shivered, and his smile turned mischievous. "It's cold out there. If the wind wasn't so mean, there would be frost." He cocked his head as if listening. "Hand me the bucket. Blossom's sounding anxious. I'll tend her for you."

Undone by his smile, Emily dropped a lid on her suspicions. He left the house again, this time with an eager Copper hot on his heels.

By the time the sun had climbed high enough to lighten the sky despite the clouds, the wind had subsided to a brisk breeze. Fog crawled down the mountainsides. Emily dressed warmly before making breakfast.

Claude arrived while Emily and Reb ate. After tying his horse to the back-porch railing, Claude walked into the kitchen as if he owned it and sat at the table. His attitude rasped like sandpaper over her frayed nerves as she poured coffee and set out the cream and sugar.

"So the boy never came home," Claude said. "I've got to check the fence and the cattle anyway, so I'll keep my eyes peeled for him."

Despite his gruff voice, Emily heard a note of worry. No matter what his feelings for her were, Claude loved Joey and would go to the ends of the earth for him. Her dislike of the old cowboy eased a little.

"I've an ache in my joints that says there'll be snow before the day's out. Bad sign, yessiree, bad sign all the way around. Snow this early in the fall means blizzards are on their way." Claude sighed. "You sleep on my offer for the ranch, Emily?"

She had more important matters to worry about. "We'll discuss it later."

"You betcha we will." He nodded sharply. "Get saddled up, Reb. Day's a-wasting."

She exchanged a worried look with Reb. "I need him here."

Claude snorted. "Get your hat, Reb. I want to make sure we didn't lose any calves."

"No, Claude, I need him. I think Tuff came by yesterday. He might be looking for a chance to steal Joey's truck."

"Tuff's mean, not stupid. He won't come here."

"I don't care about the cattle," Emily continued. "I want you to look for Joey. If you'll hold on a minute, I'll call the neighbors and see if he stayed with any of them last night."

"Ain't that a pickle! You don't care about the cattle. Living in that big city with a rich feller makes you think beef grows in supermarkets? What do you think puts food on this table and those fancy duds on your back?"

His sneer was the last straw. She slapped both hands on the table. "I do! I put food on this table! Not to mention money in your pocket and hay in the barns."

Claude's eyes widened in an expression of clownish surprise. If Emily weren't so angry, she'd laugh.

"Now you listen to me, Claude Longo, and you listen good. I own this ranch and I work my tail off keeping it out of bankruptcy. It's costing me almost every penny I own, not to mention my self-respect, and I'm not taking any more crap off of you. You work for me. You will not come into my home and insult me! Get off that chair. Get out of my house. Go look for Joey."

"Yes, ma'am," Claude muttered in shock.

Huffing with fury, she stomped after him. The screened door shut in her face. "And when you find my brother, tell him to get back home, pronto!"

Tugging his hat down low, Claude hopped like a cricket onto the saddle of his horse. "Yes, ma'am."

"And watch out for Tuff. If you see him, get to the nearest telephone and call the police."

She stood glaring out the door, watching Claude's wiry figure atop the fast-moving horse until he disappeared from sight. As soon as he was gone, her anger drained away. Reb cleared his throat.

Wincing, she faced him. His smile stunned her.

"You think this is funny?"

"No, ma'am," he said, swinging his head and fighting the smile.

She rubbed her fist against her aching chest. "They push me and push me. Picking and prodding until I could just scream. What am I supposed to do? I try to be fair. I'm nice as can be. I hate losing my temper like that."

"Ought to do it more often."

She plopped into a chair. "Oh, please."

"You spend too much time trying to make up for the past. Claude and Joey know you feel guilty, and they take advantage of it. They walk all over you."

"So I should yell more often?"

Reb shrugged lazily and sipped his coffee. "Might not hurt. Especially with Claude. He respects a good row."

"I'm trying to be nice to him."

"Uh-huh. And the more you bend over backward, the harder he stomps on your toes." He rose and stretched, catlike, arching his spine and flexing his shoulders.

Remembrances of last night infused her body, twisting her up inside. For a moment she forgot what they were talking about. Visions of him naked, long and muscular and lean, graceful as a dancer, hard as stone, gave her shivers.

"You think I'm a wimp."

He shook his head. "If you want their respect, stand up for yourself." He arched his eyebrows. "You earned mine. Let's go." He picked up the shotgun and checked the load.

That snapped her back to the present. "Where?"

"To find the duffel bag."

"You're kidding, right?"

"We still don't know for sure if Tuff came here last night. I don't feel like waiting around for him. Unless you want to stay here alone."

She hurried to dress in a warm jacket and made sure her gloves were in the pocket.

"I'll put the leash on Copper. Pack a lunch and something to drink so we don't have to break off searching. If we're lucky, the storm knocked something loose."

His words proved prophetic. A few hours later Copper playfully pounced on the tattered remains of a duffel bag. Emily had almost given up hope of the dog finding anything. They'd let him sniff and paw at the money he'd found, and he'd seemed excited about the possibility of finding more, but then he'd merely meandered through the forest. Having Copper actually find something left Emily speechless.

Reb examined the remains of the olive green canvas bag. The bottom had been ripped off. The sides had been ravaged by teeth and claws. It had been lying in a rut formed by a rivulet, now dark and hardened into mud. Emily followed the path of the water up, lifting her gaze to Hannah Peak.

Chapter Thirteen

Exhausted, Emily flopped into a chair. She and Reb had climbed, crawled and dug across the base of Hannah Peak until sunset. They had poked inside caves and fissures, pushed into thickets and dislodged loose rocks. Now she plucked a dried oak leaf off her shirt. Her muscles ached, and she was frozen to the bone. She couldn't recall ever feeling so cold and miserable.

On the table in front of her lay a note. On a scrap of newspaper, in large, messy script, Claude had informed her he hadn't found Joey, but that he would continue looking. Apparently she'd rattled the old cowboy—at least enough so that he'd worded the note politely.

Reb slumped on a chair and rested his cheek on a fist. He stared at her; she stared at him.

"Nothing," he said.

"I know. I was there." She sighed. "Let's face it, Tuff's long gone. And I say, good riddance."

"Uh-huh." Reb turned his gaze in the direction of the barn, where Emily had insisted he leave the empty duffel bag. "Animals got into that bag."

Emily had already figured that much out. The mountains harbored a large population of bears, coyotes and foxes, along with smaller scavengers such as weasels, skunks, crows and magpies. Mountain lions occasionally scavenged, too. Hungry animals readying for winter would go to great lengths to dig up any possible source of food. "Well, whatever was in the bag is gone now."

Emily lowered a baleful glare on the telephone. It was too late to call the sheriff. Small consolation knowing there were no drugs left to endanger the ranch. Tuff had wreaked his havoc and was getting away with it, free and clear.

She pushed to her feet. Her back twinged, sending biting pains down the back of her left thigh. Rock climbing called for muscles she didn't use every day. "Five minutes in the shower, then I'll fix something to eat."

"I'd like to take you to dinner." His eyes widened as if he surprised himself with his own offer.

"Tonight?"

He shrugged. "Sometime."

He seemed sad, as if *sometime* would never come, and it saddened her. "I'd like that, Reb." Hope built. If he saw her in a setting outside the ranch, removed from her family problems, perhaps his thinking about their relationship would turn onto more permanent avenues. She smiled. "I clean up pretty good."

"I know." Reb tapped the tabletop with his fingers. "I haven't always been a cowboy. You might not approve of some things I've done."

His caginess set off her inner alarms. "Are you...a criminal?"

He shook his head.

He was going to make her guess. In no mood to play, she said, "Cruelty is the only thing I can't forgive, and I know you aren't cruel. But you're not looking for my approval. Be straight with me, Reb. The idea of settling down scares you, and that's the real problem here. So if you think you're letting me down easy, forget it."

He lifted his eyes to her.

Shut up, she told herself, you're delving into areas where you don't belong and looking for answers you don't want.

Still, she wanted to assure him that she wasn't anything like his parents; she'd never abandon him. "I understand...I think. You've traveled a lot of places, know a lot of people. You're like one of those sailors with a girl in every port. Itchy feet and a restless heart."

"Not exactly."

She waited for elaboration, but none was forthcoming. "Fine, deny me the juicy details. It's beside the point anyway. What I'm trying to say is I don't want to put a harness on you." A lie. If Reb wanted a commitment, she'd hitch herself to him in a second. She suspected if Reb tasted true commitment and could learn to trust, he'd like it, too. "You're a good man, Reb Tremaine. A mysterious man, true, but I suppose it's part of your charm. I'd like to change your ways, but I'm thinking it's impossible. So let's drop it."

"You're too good for me."

Common sense said to take his statement at face value. Her heart flung away sense with willful abandon. She lifted her chin. "I know what's good for me.

I also know I hate being treated with kid gloves. If you're staying, then stay, if not, then go."

His eyes acquired an icy glitter. She'd struck a nerve, but he'd started this stupid conversation, and it was only fair he share the pain.

"Some things aren't meant to be, Emily."

Arguments rose like noisy children, waving hands and shouting for attention. He was strong and decent and mannerly. He was smart and hardworking, with integrity. He treated her and Joey with respect. Which didn't begin to cover his handsome face and exquisite lovemaking. Or how, when he looked at her, she felt beautiful and powerful and alive.

"Whatever," she said, turning away. Her pride ached worse than any sore muscles.

"Don't say that."

"What?"

Reb sighed. "Emily, I'd give anything not to hurt you."

"Yeah, right." She walked out of the kitchen.

He followed her up the stairs. "Don't blow me off."

"You started it, Reb." She stepped into the bathroom and turned, holding the door. His pained expression made her chest ache. She wondered if they even spoke of the same things or heard each other, or if both of them were trying to be so careful they might as well be speaking gibberish. "I don't understand you at all. I'm used to people speaking their minds. I'm tired and irritable and not in the right frame of mind for your pussyfooting around."

"I'm trying to explain."

"Don't bother. Either you'll stay or you won't. Neither decision needs an explanation." Without another word she closed the door.

ONCE WASHED AND DRESSED in clean, dry clothes, she went downstairs. Reb was gone. Her heart caught in her throat until she looked through the window and saw lights on inside the bunkhouse. She supposed if she somehow wheedled him into staying, she'd always remain on edge, wondering when he'd leave for good. Other horizons, other places were calling to him, tempting him with new sights and fresh adventures. His past was probably filled with women like her, loved and left, wondering if someday, somehow he'd wander back into their lives.

She made a solemn promise to leave him alone.

Still, without plan or conscious thought, they ended up in her bed. She held nothing back of her mouth or body or passion, except the *I love you* she longed to say. Those words she intuited would send him fleeing into the night.

When she awakened to find his blue eyes mellow and soft, and his smile sweet, she rejoiced.

Good feeling fled when she saw it had snowed in the night. Snow blanketed the ranch and the surrounding mountains, turning the dark morning landscape into a Christmas card. Tree branches still wearing summer leaves drooped under heavy loads of snow. Hannah Peak looked like a charcoal drawing, stark black-and-white.

On the radio an announcer read off a list of school closures. After he finished, he warned motorists about snowplows and tire-chain requirements.

''Wow,'' Reb said, staring out the window over the sink.

She prayed Joey had found warm shelter in the night. She couldn't help thinking about what this was doing to the hay crop. Having to buy hay could very well deplete her remaining bank accounts and force her to take out a loan. With a sigh she dressed and headed outside to do her morning chores.

When she finished, Emily slammed around the kitchen, taking small satisfaction in making the old cupboard doors bang. Reb cradled a cup of hot coffee in both hands and focused his attention on the steam curling from the surface.

When she set breakfast in front of Reb, he asked, "Want to talk about it?"

She swiped hair off her shoulders. "Nothing to say."

He smiled gently. "You're not very good at hiding your moods."

She slid into her chair and stared at her plate. "Everything is the matter," she said. "I can't win. If it isn't my brothers, it's the weather." *And you,* she added silently.

He gave the radio a nod. The newscaster was predicting warming temperatures. By the weekend they could expect a return to Indian summer. Owners of ski resorts were rejoicing, boasting about record early openings. "The snow won't last long."

She turned her gaze to the window. Dawn colored the sky in a pastel medley of pinks and oranges. Where outdoor color mingled with the interior light, it brushed the old cabinets in gold. "Neither will the hay. I don't know if I can do this anymore. It's just too hard."

"So sell out to Claude."

"Don't start—"

"You don't have to have cash up front. Hold a mortgage. Work out a deal to get back what you've put into it. Make him put Joey on the deed."

"What about Tuff?"

"To put it bluntly, he's going to end up dead or in prison. No other options. Either he found his goodies and left or he didn't, but he's not your problem anymore. As for Joey and Claude, make it a part of the deal to hire an accountant. At least until Joey learns the bookkeeping."

The more she considered Reb's suggestion, the more it made sense. No law said she had to sell the ranch for what the developers would pay. She could recoup her money and start fresh. Joey would certainly think it a grand idea.

Except... "I can't see making Joey buy what rightfully belongs to him in the first place."

"He's willing enough to make you foot the bills."

"That's different."

He cocked his head, and half his mouth pulled into a sad smile. "I get it. You're buying off your sins."

She bristled. "You don't know what you're talking about."

"In a way your grandfather blackmailed you. But you don't owe him. You don't owe anyone."

Reb made it all sound so simple. Sell the ranch, walk away, everybody was happy, the end. "What if Claude dies before Joey is capable of handling the ranch?"

"What if he doesn't?"

Emily had to admit that Reb had a point. Before she could respond, Copper barked, high and yodeling. Emily went to the door. The dog stood in the partially open barn doorway, staring down the driveway. He leapt at the snow, sank up to his hocks and jumped back. Barking, he disappeared inside the barn only to return again. Emily stepped onto the porch.

A riderless horse trotted up the driveway, throwing up clumps of snow as he headed for the barn. Copper bounded across the snow, exhaling fat clouds of steam. Despite Copper's antics, the horse paid him no heed whatsoever.

Emily shook her head in mute, futile denial.

"That's Joey's horse," Reb said beside her. He thrust her coat at her in passing and hopped off the porch into the snow.

The horse reached the barn, but the door wasn't open wide enough for him to enter. He turned his head and whickered plaintively at Reb. Emily struggled into her coat, and she and Reb ran through the snow. Reb pushed open the barn door, and the horse trotted inside.

"Where's Joey?" she whispered.

The horse waited in front of his stall. His tail was coated with clumps of snow, and sweat darkened his neck and chest. Steam rose from his hindquarters. Reb worked quickly in getting the animal stripped of tack.

"We've got to find him," she said.

Hard at work rubbing down the now-trembling horse, Reb said, "Get yourself dressed for riding. I'll ready the horses. We've got to move before the sun melts the snow and erases his tracks."

She ran back to the house. Moving on autopilot, she dressed in a heavy parka and rubber boots. By the time she was ready, Reb was, too. His eyes were grim under the brim of his hat, and his mouth set in a thin line. Emily mounted Strawberry, and Reb swung onto Jack. As if sensing his rider's urgency, Jack moved out sharply.

As the sun rose over the mountains, each sparkling ray burned against the snow. Mist rose off the rolling meadows, hovering like steam off a boiling pot. All around them water dripped and clumps of wet snow fell from tree branches.

Joey's horse's tracks followed the driveway, then angled toward the creek before heading due south. Giving Strawberry her head to follow Jack, Emily sat tall in the saddle, anxiously scanning the horizon for any sign of her brother. The tracks formed a dark line aiming directly for a stand of trees. Reb urged Jack into a lope, and the powerful animal lunged through the snowdrifts, breaking a trail for Strawberry to follow. Copper bounded behind Emily.

At the tree line the trail thinned, and the path turned icy. No longer impeded by snowdrifts, Copper raced ahead of the horses. The dog seemed aware this was no mere romp, but a mission. Ears flat, head low, he followed the swiftly melting spoor.

The trail disappeared on a rocky outcrop where the trees and wind had prevented snow from accumulating. Emily forced down her panic as she watched Reb and Copper circle. Sniffing at the ground, the dog coursed back and forth.

Staring hard at the earth, Reb whistled sharply, then called the dog. Copper loped to the man, stopped in his tracks and stared, his ears pricked. Suddenly Copper loosed a howling bark, lunged at an oak tangle and wriggled into the brush.

Reb leapt off the saddle. Following the dog, he used his shoulders and hands to sweep aside the thick branches.

They found Joey wedged in a dirt hollow between the roots of a pine tree, his body hidden by brown oak leaves. When Emily reached him, Copper was licking furiously at the boy's pale, blue-lipped face. Reb shoved the dog away and crouched, feeling at Joey's throat for a pulse.

He is not dead, Emily told herself. *He isn't.*

"He's in bad shape," Reb said. "Bring the horses around. Move!"

She ran back the way she'd come, barely feeling branches whipping her icy cheeks. She caught Jack and Strawberry and led them on a wide path around the oaks.

When she reached Reb and Joey, Reb hoisted Joey's lanky body over his shoulder. A drop of blood fell from Joey's head, splattering like a crimson flower on a patch of snow.

Down a hill lay a ramshackle cabin once used by cattle drovers. A track led from this stand of trees to the cabin. Joey must have taken shelter in the cabin before attempting to ride home.

"The main road is about a quarter mile that way, Reb. It'll be easier getting him there than back to the house."

"I'll take care of Joey. Ride Jack back to the house. He's faster. Call the paramedics and get an ambulance to meet us on the road." Reb cradled Joey against his chest.

Emily held Strawberry's bridle while Reb draped the boy over the saddle, then Emily mounted Jack. The quarter horse gelding was warmed to his task and trembled eagerly as she gathered the reins.

"I'll take care of him, I promise," Reb said.

She turned Jack for home, gave him his head and slammed her heels into his sides. Clinging to the saddle horn for dear life, she leaned low over his neck, trusting Jack's surefootedness as he galloped between the trees.

Snow flew in huge sprays and clumps from his hooves. She could hear only the steady huff-huff-huff of Jack's breath and the crunching of snow. Sunshine hit the snowy fields and burst into millions of prisms, blinding Emily.

"Go faster," she whispered over and over, never daring to loosen her grip on the saddle to wipe the streams of tears from her pained eyes. "Go faster."

Reaching the driveway, she spotted a figure standing next to the house. Snow-blind, all she saw was a blur moving to intercept her and the horse. Her hands had gone numb, but she fumbled with the reins. She tried to shift her stance in the stirrups, but they were adjusted for Reb's longer legs. Jerking her body backward, she flailed for footing and hauled up on the reins. Jack obediently tucked his hindquarters, sliding like a skier in the slushy snow.

Emily jounced hard on the saddle. She lost the right stirrup completely.

The figure waved his arms and shouted, "Hiyup, there!"

Jack planted his forehooves, threw up his head and stopped. Emily lost her balance, grabbed wildly for the saddle horn, missed and fell.

She hit the ground hard. Slush melted through her jeans. Dazed but unhurt, she lay on her back in an icy puddle. Blinking hard, she gazed up at the man looking down at her.

"Damnation, girl, what are you doing riding a real horse? You tore up here like a tornado. Don't you know you can ruin an animal that way?"

"Claude," she whispered breathlessly, and struggled to rise. He grasped her parka front and hauled her upright. She clutched his arm until she felt confident about remaining on her feet. His tirade continued, buffeting her ears, but she pushed him away and staggered toward the house. Cold and the hard ride had numbed her legs.

Grousing and grumbling, the old cowboy dogged her heels. At the base of the porch, she turned on him. "We found Joey!" She gasped in a breath. "He's hurt, Claude. Just take care of Jack."

Claude's mouth fell open. "My boy can't be hurt," he whispered.

"He's unconscious and bleeding. Reb's with him, carrying him to the road." Terror caught up to her. "I have to call the paramedics. Take care of Jack." Thinking, *He can't die. I won't let him die,* she stumbled up the porch steps and into the house.

Chapter Fourteen

The Blue Creek Volunteer Fire Department paramedics met Reb, Emily and Joey halfway to Humbolt. The paramedics took one look at Joey's blue face and sprang into action. All business, they strapped him onto a stretcher and threaded an IV line into his arm. They announced their intention to take him to the Humbolt hospital. The hospital was little more than a clinic, so Emily knew they doubted he'd survive the longer trip into Grand Junction.

Reb drove the car, following the ambulance along the icy road. Emily hunched into her parka, watching the flashing lights in front of them.

"He'll be all right," Reb said.

She fervently hoped so. But once they reached the hospital, there was nothing to do except wait. Emily paced the corridor, keeping her gaze fixed on the ornate wooden door separating her from Joey. Reb offered her coffee from a vending machine. She sipped it, tasting only the waxy cup and her own dread.

The doctor finally came out of the treatment room. Dr. Cort Nelson had been her grandfather's primary physician. At the sight of his bright red hair and florid face, she mustered a smile.

His bushy ginger eyebrows tangled in a scowl. "I think he's been shot, Emily."

She shook her head in mute denial.

"The X rays show a crease in his skull and a severe concussion. It looks as if a bullet entered his scalp just below his ear, then bounced off his skull and exited at the top of his head. Not much bleeding because of the cold, but he's got some hairline fractures. We're getting him stabilized. I've got the receptionist calling the sheriff." He lowered his voice. "Is this Tuff's doing?"

She blinked back tears. "I don't know. Will Joey be all right?"

"Probably. You Rifkins are a hardheaded bunch. I've patched him up for worse after a bull ride."

Dr. Nelson wasn't given to false optimism. Emily's smile widened. "When can I see him?"

"His body temperature is still below normal. I've got to keep an eye on the brain swelling. Worst case, we'll have to transport him to Denver."

"Brain surgery?"

"Worst case, Emily," he said kindly. "Now, like I said, we're calling the sheriff. He'll have to figure out how this happened." He nodded at Reb, who stood in a corner with his hat pulled down low and his hands in his pockets. "Who's your friend?"

"My hired hand."

"Hired or not, you treat him like a friend and lean on his shoulder. Go on over to the café and get some decent coffee. Give me another hour to get the boy warmed up. I'll be able to tell you then if we need to transport him."

She waited until she and Reb were seated in a back booth at the Humbolt Station Café before telling him what the doctor had told her. Reb's anger showed in the icy flatness of his eyes and the tension in his forehead. She loved him all the more for his quiet rage.

"You saved Joey's life," she said. "I couldn't have found him without you."

The waitress, a chunky woman in her fifties whom Emily recognized but whose name she couldn't recall, brought coffee to the table. As she set the cups before them, she said, "Sorry to hear about your brother. Is he hurt bad?"

News traveled fast around the valley. Emily figured by nightfall every person within thirty miles would know more about Joey's condition than she did. "Dr. Nelson said he'll be all right."

"The old Double Bar R," the waitress said, shaking her gray head. "I swear the place is cursed. Your dad and mom dying the way they did. Tuff going sour. If it isn't one thing, it's another. Old Garth never had any luck."

Though the woman's words were mild, her tone held disapproval as if Emily were somehow to blame. "We're fine, thank you," she said, staring at her coffee cup.

"Might be a chore staying that way."

Opal, Emily remembered. The woman's name was Opal. "What is that supposed to mean?"

Opal shrugged. "Way I hear it, your own brother is gunning for you. Can't say as I blame him too much. Robbing his birthright the way you did." She chuckled humorlessly. "Yep, you're turning the valley into a regular 'Dallas' TV show. But then, what can you expect? What goes around comes around, I always say. Garth was one old man you shouldn't have messed with."

Emily gasped. "I did not steal the Double Bar R."

"Yeah, right."

Reb slid out of the booth. He reached into his pocket and fished out two dollar bills. He coolly left them on the table, then held out a hand for Emily. "Come on, Emily. Coffee's rotten here."

Wounded and embarrassed, Emily took his hand, allowing him to lead her out of the café.

Opal called to her back, "Go around murdering old men in their sleep, what do you expect? Roses? A round of applause?"

Outside, Emily zipped up her parka. It felt as if every person passing by in a car or truck stared at her. She jerked the hood over her head, down low on her brow. The road was clear of snow, wet and steaming, and water poured off the roofs of buildings. Humbolt was a tiny town, most of the buildings converted from what once had been a minor hub of the Denver–Santa Fe railroad. Narrow-gauge railroad tracks crisscrossed the road. "I hate this place."

"Don't let her get your goat."

"It's not just her, it's everybody." She was grateful for Reb's kindness, but humiliated because he now knew firsthand what some people thought of her. "Plenty of people have accused me of murdering Grandpa. If they don't think I killed him, then they think I tricked him out of the ranch. Maybe I will sell out to Claude. Fifty bucks, and the Double Bar R is his."

Reb wrapped an arm around her shoulders and hugged her just as a sheriff's patrol car pulled into the hospital parking lot. Deputy Tim Patterson got out and looked around. Emily stepped away from Reb and raised a hand in greeting.

"I have to talk to him," she said.

She strode across the street to the hospital. The deputy waited for her at the door. "Hello, Tim. I guess you heard what happened?"

Tim nodded.

"Where's Mickey?"

"Checking the scene," Tim mumbled. He opened the door for Emily and nodded in the direction of the café. "Who's that?"

"A cowboy Joey hired. He drove me into town." She pushed through the doorway. "Dr. Nelson thinks Joey was shot. I think Tuff did it."

Tim took a chair in the corridor. He rested a clipboard on his thigh and held a pen ready to write. "Can you give me your statement?"

Emily disliked talking to Tim Patterson. His face never revealed any emotion, and he rarely made eye contact. He grunted more than he talked, and when he did speak, it was rarely more than a few words. Nevertheless, she told him how Joey had ridden off to search for Tuff and how his horse had come home alone. Tim offered no clue about what he thought of her story.

Dr. Nelson appeared while Tim was finishing writing the statement. "We've got Joey's temperature up, and he's stabilized. He's still unconscious, but he's responding well."

"Can I see him?" Emily asked, ready to go to her brother whether the doctor said it was okay or not.

"Not a problem," the doctor said. "And what about you, Tim? How's your head? As long as you're here, I can take a look for myself."

Joey was the only patient inside the four-bed room. Emily hurried inside, glancing at the nurse who was checking the monitors. Her hair was as red as Dr. Nelson's.

"You must be Emily," the nurse said. Her name tag said Jennifer. She had a cute smile to match her cute, petite figure. "Your brother will be fine. Dr. Nelson is really good." She stroked Joey's shoulder. "Don't worry about his appearance. The swelling in his forehead and eyes is perfectly normal. Had to shave his head, though. Too bad. He has nice hair."

"And he's vain about it, too."

Joey looked worse than awful. His face looked as if he'd gone head-to-head with an angry bull. Rows of stitches closed the wounds on the top of his head and behind his ear.

Jennifer brought a chair to bedside. "He'll be okay, Emily, trust me. The worst part was how cold he was, but he's warmed up nicely. This hospital has great equipment, and Dr. Nelson is the best."

"You're very kind, Jennifer. You're new in town?"

"Not that new. I started working here three months ago. I love it. I grew up in Denver." She smiled. "My dream has always been to live in the mountains so I can have some land and a horse. And ski season is just around the corner. I can't hardly wait. I just love working here in Humbolt. Everybody is so nice and friendly."

"Welcome to the valley."

"Do you ski, Emily?"

"A little. I'm way out of practice."

"We'll have to do something about that. Have you noticed? There's a real shortage of people our age around here. I have to go all the way into Grand Junction for any nightlife."

Emily nodded agreement, uncertain about Jennifer's effusive friendliness, but liking the young woman anyway.

"You and I should make a date for a girls' night out," Jennifer said. "It'll be a blast." She picked up a tray and left the room.

Emily stroked Joey's hand. He had so many blankets on top of him that she couldn't tell whether or not he was breathing. She hoped for his sake it hadn't been Tuff who shot him. That would be a betrayal from which he'd never recover.

"Oh, Joey, I've been so worried about you. You've gone through so much, it just isn't fair. But you'll be all right. I know you will. I don't know if you can hear me, but in case you can, then now is the time for you to listen. Claude offered to buy the ranch. If that's what it takes to keep you safe, then we'll work something out. I feel funny about selling. I can't think of the Double Bar R as my own. I'm just a caretaker—"

Tim Patterson entered the room. He hung back near the door, staring at the clipboard he held up before him.

"He's still unconscious," she said.

"Well, then, I have to stay," Tim murmured.

The last thing she wanted was the deputy hovering over her during her visit. She rose. "I'll be back in a few minutes."

She went in search of Reb, and found him waiting in her car. She rested her forearms on the open driver's window. "He's still unconscious, but he'll be all right."

Reb closed his eyes and heaved a long sigh of unmistakable relief. Her love for him tightened another notch.

"I'm going to stay with Joey," she said. "Go on back to the ranch and find Claude. Have him follow in his truck so you can bring my car into town and leave it for me. Bring my purse, too." She reached through the window opening and touched his face. "Thank you so much. If he'd been out there much longer, he'd have died. I'll always be indebted to you. Always."

"Your dog found Joey, not me."

She smiled wryly. He couldn't accept her gratitude any easier than he could accept her love.

Another patrol car pulled into the parking lot. Emily said, "It's Mickey." She wanted to kiss Reb, but doubted it wise. "Claude probably has a million chores to do, so don't worry about being in a hurry getting my car here. Be careful." Reb drove away just as Mickey stepped out of his car.

As she joined the sheriff, he asked, "Who was that?"

"Hired hand."

Mickey stared in the direction Reb had gone. "At the ranch?"

"Joey hired him. He's good with cattle."

"I'm surprised you'd let Joey hire one of Tuff's buddies."

She cocked her head, unable to grasp his meaning or why he'd say such a thing to her. "He isn't one of Tuff's friends. His previous employer sold out, so he was passing through, looking for work. He's never met Tuff."

"I'm positive he visited the jail a while back. Big boy, black hair, real blue eyes. You know me, I never forget a face." He snorted in disgust. "Darn Tuff tried to turn the jail into a party house. Never again, I'm telling you, honey, never again. From now on no prisoner gets a visit from anybody other than relatives and attorneys. I've got a list of suspects fifteen miles long who could've helped Tuff bust out of jail." He nodded firmly and focused his pale gray gaze on her face. "I ought to check that hired hand out for you."

"It isn't necessary." Doubt crept in, stealthy as a bull snake hunting mice. Reb had dropped into her life as if from thin air, an angel who appeared when she needed him most—not long after Tuff was thrown in jail. He'd helped Joey and Claude with the ranch, and he'd helped her search for the duffel bag, the very bag he swore must contain drugs so she must not involve the police.

Reb had avoided the sheriff, too. And he had deftly turned aside her mild inquiries about his life, hinting that his past contained things better left unsaid. She'd fallen in love with him—spilled out her heart and soul to him, and she trusted him with her life.

And now Mickey, who never forgot a face, was insisting that Reb had visited Tuff at the jail.

"Emily?"

"Joey's going to be fine."

Her non sequitur caused him to peer curiously at her.

Her hand fluttered to her throat. "I'm sorry," she said. "I'm having a conversation in my head. I'm such a mess, I can't think." She turned away, not wanting to reveal to him the confusion plaguing her. On the third floor of the hospital, light gleamed yellow through century-old glass. A person passed by in wavery silhouette.

She remembered seeing two men standing in front of the window in the bunkhouse in the middle of the night. Was it Reb and Tuff?

"It's wet out here." Mickey looked glumly at his boots, their usual dandy shine now dulled by mud. "You already gave your statement to Tim?" He grasped her elbow and led her back to the hospital. On the wide brick veranda, he stopped.

Tell him, she thought, tell him everything. Reb, the duffel bag, the money, the man she thought she saw in the bunkhouse with Reb.

You're so beautiful, Reb's voice purred silkily in her head. *You're too good for me...an amazing woman.* She saw him holding Joey, saw the worry shining in his eyes.

Mickey was telling her something. "...until we pick up Tuff."

She nodded as if she understood what he was saying.

"Looks like Joey waited out the snowstorm in that old cabin on the back of your property. I found blood, but no sign of a fight and not a trace of the perp who shot him. Until I get the situation sorted out, I don't want you staying alone at the ranch. You can bunk in my spare room. Are you hearing what I'm saying, honey?"

Emily pressed a hand over her eyes. "I'm sorry, Mickey. I'm frazzled. I can't seem to concentrate."

"I'm posting Tim to keep an eye out for Joey. I want you in protective custody, too. Like I said, you can stay at my place." He showed an open, empty palm. "No strings. I won't pester you. I promise."

She reached for the door handle. The ornate brass was icy. "I've got to see Joey."

Mickey followed her to Joey's room. Tim sat on a chair by the door, his arms folded over his chest. Jennifer stood next to Joey, taking his pulse while timing it with her wristwatch.

Jennifer set down Joey's wrist and scribbled a note on the chart. She flashed a wide, dimpled smile at Mickey. "Hi, Sheriff. And how are we today?"

Emily caught the gleam of interest in his pale eyes. His shoulders straightened, and his lanky step turned into a strut.

"I'm fine, honey. How about yourself?" He smoothed his thick hair with the flat of a hand. "And how's the boy?"

As Jennifer launched into her perky spiel about how well Joey was doing, Emily got the distinct impression the sheriff and the nurse were both willing to deepen their acquaintance. Tuning them out, she sat beside her brother and covered his hand with her own. In the short time she'd been out of the room, his color had further improved and the swelling around his eyes didn't look so ominous.

Reb had saved his life. Without Reb she'd still be flailing around in the snow, trying to find tracks where her unschooled eyes didn't know to look. If she'd been alone, she never would have been able to get him atop a horse. He'd have frozen to death by the time she reached help.

If Reb had actually visited Tuff at the jail, then it explained why he kept avoiding the sheriff. What other lies had he told her? What truths hadn't he told? Lies by omission were lies all the same.

Or was Mickey lying? Reb had asked her once if she trusted the sheriff. At the time she'd laughed at him. She trusted Mickey as long as she could see his hands and she wasn't confined in too tight a space with him. Mickey had no reason to lie to her about Reb.

She eased hair off her face, enough to see that Mickey was preoccupied, leaning a shoulder against the wall while he flirted with Jennifer.

What about the duffel bag? Emily wondered. Reb didn't want the police knowing about it. She thought of the fears she had mentioned—about drugs and losing the ranch to federal raiders. Reb had played upon them, embellishing them with perfect logic and dire predictions. Mickey wanted to pretend the duffel bag didn't exist. Her every mention of it had brought only dismissal, as if he didn't want her even thinking about it. Did Mickey want the bag for himself?

And how come Joey was the one lying wounded in the hospital?

In the scenarios she'd imagined, Tuff had been the evil monster, and Joey the innocent. Yet he'd visited Tuff in jail every chance he got. He'd brought Reb home. He'd slipped something to Reb on the sly. Condoms, Reb had claimed in a touchingly embarrassing scene, but Reb never mentioned sexual protection when they made love. Why would a man have the foresight to get condoms then forget completely about them later?

Now who could she trust?

Mickey had to leave on a call. He promised Emily he'd return to take her to his place. She managed a wan smile in reply, but thought with her and Joey out of the way, it would be easy for Mickey to search the ranch at his leisure.

After the sheriff left, Jennifer laid a comforting hand on Emily's shoulder. "Would you like something to eat?"

The mere thought of food made her ill. "No, thank you."

"He's going to be all right, honest."

"I can't eat anything right now." She stared miserably at Joey until Jennifer gave up and went away.

She sat alone with her doubts and suspicions and worries. Each time she heard a footstep outside the room, she eyed the door, hoping it was Reb. Mickey had to be wrong about seeing him at the jail. She loved Reb; he couldn't be lying to her. If he came to the hospital, in full view of the deputy, then it meant her fears were ridiculous.

Tim left the room so silently that she didn't realize he was gone until she heard the door close with a soft *whup*.

"Emmy?"

Joey's raspy croak made her jump. Hot tears filled her eyes, and she clasped his hand in both of hers. "Joey, oh, honey, I've been so worried about you."

He peered through swollen eyelids, his eyes glazed and unfocused. "Emmy?"

"It's okay, I'm right here. You're okay now."

"Sorry," he whispered. "Tuff... Tuff..."

"Is he the one who shot you?"

"Dead..." His battered face twisted in a grimace. His fingers tightened around hers. "I killed him, Emmy. I *had* to."

As his words sank in, her horror grew. "Shh, honey, you've got a head injury, and it's a bad one. You're delirious. You don't know what you're saying."

"Money's gone...thinks you got it...sheriff. Don't trust...Reb knows. Tell...you...everything. Sorry, so...sorry." A tear leaked from the corner of his left eye. "Reb knows..."

Tim returned to the room, with a paper cup of coffee. As he approached the foot of the bed, Joey shut his eyes.

"Joey? Joey, talk to me. I know you're awake. Joey? Tim, call the doctor."

Reb knows.

Knows what? she wanted to scream. But Joey wasn't talking. Even when Dr. Nelson declared Joey conscious, he refused to open his eyes or speak. Emily stepped back and kept a surreptitious eye on the deputy. It occurred to her Joey had waited for Tim to leave the room before he spoke.

Had Joey been telling her not to trust the sheriff—or Reb?

"You're awake," Dr. Nelson stated. He lifted Joey's hand and let it drop back on the bed. "Quit playing possum, young man. Do you want me declaring you brain damaged? I'll send you to Denver. They've got so many tests to run you'll look like a pincushion by the time you get out. Now, stop fooling around."

Joey opened one eye. It looked much clearer than it had before.

"I thought so," the doctor said, shooting Emily a triumphant grin. "Now, Emily, my wife is in my office. She brought me some good coffee and a nice chicken pot pie. While I'm poking and prodding your brother, you go get yourself something to eat. Deputy Tim, that's the same prescription for you. Both of you look dog tired."

"I need to take his statement," Tim said.

"It can wait. Go on now. Shoo."

Tim and Emily obeyed the doctor and left the room. At seeing Jennifer entering the ladies' room, Emily formed an idea. She followed the nurse.

"Jennifer?"

"Yes?" she replied from a stall.

"Can I ask you a huge favor? My clothes are damp, I don't have my purse and there's no telling when I'll see my car. I need to get home. Can I borrow your car? I won't be long, I promise."

"Sure."

Dumbfounded by the generosity, Emily widened her eyes. "You don't mind?"

"I can trust you not to wreck it, right?" The toilet flushed, and the young woman appeared, smiling broadly. "That's why I really love small towns. Safe streets, everybody knows everybody else. You can do a favor without worrying about packs of lawyers checking the fine print." She waved a hand in an expansive gesture. "I am more than happy to loan you my car."

"You're a peach, Jennifer. We will definitely have to make a date."

"We'll do that. And you can give me pointers on how to make a date with Mickey Thigpen. I know he's kind of old, but lordy, lordy, what a hunk. Have you noticed how he looks like Sam Elliott? You know, the actor with the cool voice?"

"It's a deal."

Chapter Fifteen

Emily parked Jennifer's little Honda next to the house, then remained inside the car as she looked around the ranch. Joey's truck was parked in its usual spot under the cottonwood tree. Snow had slid off the steep barn roof in sheets. Chickens, feathers fluffed against the cold, pecked listlessly at the sodden ground. The house and bunkhouse were dark, lifeless.

She hadn't the faintest idea about what she was going to say to Reb.

She slowly left the car and used both hands to close the door. She called, "Reb?" Not even Copper answered. When the dog failed to appear, she guessed he was out with Reb.

"Are you looking for Tuff?" she murmured.

Itching with apprehension, she checked the garage. Her car was parked inside. She then peeked inside the old storage shed where Reb had left his Jeep. It sat under a tarpaulin. She looked in the barn next. All the horses were inside their stalls. She petted Jack, silently thanking him for bringing her home. Listening, nerves prickling, half expecting Tuff to leap from the hayloft, she went to the end of the aisle and the last stall.

The bucket where Reb had placed the money Copper had found was empty.

Perhaps Reb was with Claude, she reasoned. She headed for the bunkhouse. The voice of conscience called her a snoop and an idiot—but Reb knew something. What exactly, she had to find out.

The first thing she noticed was how the plank flooring was free of dust and dirt. The iron-frame bed where Reb slept was neatly made. She focused on the army green footlocker on the floor at the foot of the bed. A padlock held the lid fastened.

The enormity of what she meant to do almost caused her to turn around and leave. She didn't trust Reb. She *couldn't* trust him. The pain of impending betrayal, whether his or hers, made her stomach ache. But the padlock drew her. It was a lock to keep his secrets safe—secrets about her and Joey and Tuff. She made herself move. She crouched in front of the footlocker and examined the lock. It was heavy-duty with a reinforced-steel shank.

Spying on Reb was all wrong. She trusted him, she loved him and she owed him for saving Joey's life. He was her friend, her lover, standing by her, helping her, supporting her, offering his strength. Yes, she'd fallen in love with Reb Tremaine, and believed every word he said. She looked around for something with which to break into the footlocker.

Several of the beds were dismantled, the pieces stacked neatly against the wall. She picked up an iron support slat and weighed it in her hands.

Reb would never forgive her for this, she knew. She'd invaded his privacy, and once she broke into the locker, she'd break his trust, too. Except he knew something, and Joey knew he knew.

She worked the end of the slat under the hasp and levered the brads out of the wood. Each piece of splintered wood echoed her splintered heart. She raised the lid.

The locker contained a dark gray felt dress hat and a pair of shiny cowboy boots. At first glimpse, she gasped, knowing her suspicions were wrong. These were merely Reb's personal possessions.

She lifted the hat and realized the bottom board of the locker was removable. After setting the hat and boots carefully aside, she stuck her fingers inside a pair of holes and lifted the false bottom.

She understood how archaeologists must feel after uncovering a layer of dirt and rock to find evidence of another world. Only, she doubted scientists ever felt as sick about their discoveries as she did about hers.

She picked up a round leather case and unsnapped it. She shook a pair of steel handcuffs free. An odd accessory for a cowboy.

The gun was even odder. The make was unfamiliar to her, but she knew it was an automatic small enough to conceal in a pocket or boot top. Its dull black finish made it look like a toy, but its heft proclaimed nothing playful in the least. She kept her fingers well away from the trigger.

The locker also contained a telephone, a little folding job small enough to slip into a shirt pocket. She pressed the on-off button, and the dialing face glowed green, telling her the battery was charged and ready. She pushed her finger through a collection of microcassette tapes and spools of wire. Among the high-tech items was a low-tech plastic bag containing a goodly amount of dried plant matter. Marijuana, she guessed.

"What are you doing, Emily?"

She dropped the phone, fumbled with the gun and spun around on her knees so quickly she lost her balance and sat down hard. She grabbed the gun with both hands and pointed it at Reb.

Backlit by the open doorway, his silhouette loomed, huge and dark and menacing. The shadow under his hat brim masked his expression. He held the shotgun loosely in his right hand, the muzzle pointed at the floor.

"You better put that down before you hurt somebody," he said mildly. He bent gracefully at the knees and laid the shotgun on the floor. He raised his hands so she could see his palms. "I guess it's time we talked."

Keeping the weapon pointed straight at his chest, she awkwardly worked her feet under her and stood.

"So you can tell me more lies?" Fear clamped iron bands around her ribs. Her arms trembled with the effort it took to keep the gun steady. Still, she wanted to believe him, wanted to put the gun down and ask him reasonably for the truth.

"I put mine down, put down yours. I won't hurt you. I promise. You have nothing to fear from me."

"Not a chance. You're a dope dealer, aren't you? You've been stringing me along so you can find Tuff's drugs before he got out of jail."

"No. The bag of dope isn't mine. I found it in your house. It probably belongs to Tuff. I left his paraphernalia in the house. It's in the bottom drawer of his dresser. Scale, sandwich bags, the works. But that's penny-ante stuff. We have a bigger problem right now. Tuff is involved in heavier stuff."

She understood his words, but couldn't grasp his meaning.

"I searched your house the day you went to Grand Junction."

"For what? The duffel bag? That's what you wanted all along, isn't it?"

"Yes."

His simple reply turned her cold inside. Her hands were sweating on the gun, making the metal feel like slippery gelatin. Uncertain what to do, but having to do something, she crouched next to the footlocker and felt around with one hand until she found the handcuffs. She tossed them onto the bed. Backing away from the bed, she jerked her head to the side. "Move slowly, onto the bed. Handcuff yourself to the frame."

He glided across the floor, his boots making no sound. His blue eyes revealed neither fear nor anger. Aware of both his strength and quickness, she backed away, keeping a safe distance between them. He sat on the edge of the bed.

"Do it, Reb. Or—or—or I'll shoot you in the leg! I mean it."

He obeyed, cuffing his left wrist with a swift, expert snap and then attaching the other cuff to the wrought-iron headboard. Her heart pounded, and her mouth filled with an unpleasant metallic taste. Instead of easing her fear, his helplessness heightened it.

The old bed creaked as he shifted on the edge of the mattress. With his free hand he removed his hat and placed it on the bed beside him. Casual as a cat, he raked a hand through his hair, moving it off his face.

He smiled ruefully at her. "Next time you hold a gun on a man, I suggest you release the safety."

She cocked her head, uncomprehending.

"It's an automatic, Emily. The safety is on the side. It won't fire with the safety on."

She examined the gun and noticed the safety button. Floored by the implication, she groped for the lid of the footlocker. It dropped with a bang. She sank onto the locker. A press of the safety made a red dot show. "It was locked, and you knew it."

"That's right." He rattled the short chain on the handcuffs. "Do you feel safer now?"

"What kind of game are you playing?"

"No game. I need you to listen to me. Trust me."

She shook her head, making her hair whip against her cheeks. "Mickey recognized you. That's why you avoided him. You do know Tuff. You visited him at the jail."

"True."

She gestured with the gun. "You better tell me what's going on! Why did you go to the jail?"

"Tuff hired a hit man to kill you."

"Pat Nyles."

"Sort of. He gave Nyles five hundred dollars, but Nyles drank it up. You don't have to worry about him, he's in custody. Before Pat, though, Tuff gave Joey two thousand dollars and told him to hire a hit man. He promised eight thousand more when the job was finished."

She fought a rise of tears. "Joey wants me dead?"

"Uh-uh. Joey thought Tuff was kidding. Tuff had him convinced you were responsible for your grandfather's death and you'd done something shady with the will. Tuff told Joey as long as you were around,

Joey would never get the ranch. Joey's so messed up, he doesn't know what to believe, but he doesn't want you dead."

She saw where this was leading. "Joey hired you." She raised the gun, pointing it once again at Reb's chest. "Oh, God, you came here to kill me." She jumped to her feet, still pointing the gun at his chest. "You low-down, sneaking...give me one good reason why I shouldn't kill you right now."

"Because I'm a cop."

"Right. And I'm a ballerina."

He extended his right hand as if for a friendly shake. "Special Agent John Tremaine, Federal Bureau of Investigation. Sit down, Emily. I'll tell you everything."

She backed up a wary step. How could she have sat across the table from this man for so many meals, kissed him, welcomed him into her bed and never realized the truth? "How do I know you aren't lying now? Do you have any identification?"

"Nope. I work outside the regular agency, always undercover. That's the 'special' tag. The FBI recruited me straight out of college, and I never went to the academy or associated with other agents. I don't carry a badge. I'm not listed on any official roster. My contacts are all outside the agency. It keeps me clean of the cop taint. Crooks can spot a cop a mile away."

His calm, matter-of-fact manner heightened her uncertainty. She sat again on the footlocker. "Does Joey know you're from the FBI?"

"Yes. He knew if he refused to hire someone for Tuff that Tuff would have found a real hitter. Trouble is, Joey is convinced your buddy the sheriff is dirty. Tuff boasted about having a cop in his pocket, fixing things for him. So Joey called the FBI. He's been helping me build a case against Tuff. He doesn't like it. What he wanted was for me to scare Tuff. Slap his hand. But that couldn't happen. So he's been wearing a wire, taping his conversations with Tuff and the sheriff, gathering evidence.''

''Why didn't Joey tell me?''

''He didn't trust you.''

''Does he honestly think I killed Grandpa?''

''He doesn't know what to think. But he saved your life. If he hadn't called the FBI, you'd be dead. Pat Nyles or someone else would have gotten to you. Tuff knew it was only a matter of time before you either found the duffel bag or the body or somebody willing to open an investigation.''

She put down the gun and used her fingertips to massage her aching temples.

''I was involved in an arms deal, posing as a broker buying weapons. I made a buy with three million dollars in marked money. James Mullow was the wheelman for the two dealers I bought weapons from. It was routine. Agents were in place to make the bust. Instead, they found the car and two dead arms dealers. Mullow and the money were missing.''

Seeing where this was going, she said, ''That's the money Copper found.''

''Some of it. As was the two thousand dollars Joey gave me. We had a suspicion Mullow and Tuff were involved in the ambush. But even with the money, we didn't have solid proof Tuff had the three million. They brought me in because I can identify Mullow.'' He drew in a deep breath and exhaled slowly. ''As far as we knew, you were involved, too. The way Tuff talked, you knew too much.''

"You thought I knew about the money. You weren't going to kill me, you were going to arrest me."

He nodded.

"Everything you told me was a lie. You seduced me."

His eyes widened and his forehead tightened. He swallowed hard. "Not that part. That was no lie. It wasn't supposed to happen, but it wasn't a lie."

She wanted to believe him. She wanted it so much she ached.

"I screwed up. I thought I could do my job and protect you, too. I didn't...I never wanted you to know..." He looked away, showing her an anguished profile. "Falling in love with you wasn't part of the plan."

She buried her face against her hands. How she'd longed to hear those words from him. How it hurt to hear them now.

"I was wrong. As soon as I knew you had nothing to do with the money, I should have told you everything." His voice dropped. "I couldn't make myself tell you I lied."

"Why should I believe you now?"

"Good question."

She jumped off the footlocker and paced anxiously. "So where's the money?"

"I don't know." He pulled a face. "I can tell you this much—the call you received warning you to stop searching the forest came from the sheriff's office. It looks like Joey was right about not trusting Mickey."

"Mickey Thigpen is no crook."

"That remains to be seen. He's under investigation. I can't give you the details, but there have been some problems in his office in the past."

She sat and hunched over on the footlocker, her self-confidence shaken. He'd lied to her from the beginning. She lifted her gaze to his face, studying his bright, intelligent eyes. "Joey said he killed Tuff. He wasn't delirious, was he?"

Reb closed his eyes, and his shoulders slumped.

"Why didn't you tell me, Reb? Why did you get my brother involved? He's only a boy."

"Go back to the house. Look up the number for the regional FBI office. It'll be in the phone book. Call and ask for Special Agent John Tremaine. Whoever answers the telephone will tell you that no such person works there. Tell him or her you're sorry, but you were given that number because you've lost your dog. Then hang up."

She wrinkled her nose in a grimace. "Are you kidding?"

"No. My boss will get the message and return your call. You don't have to leave a number."

"And if he doesn't call me?"

He smiled, a slow, seductive pull of his lips that even now teased a response from her heart. "I reckon you can come back and shoot me." He shook the handcuff chain. "I'm not going anywhere."

Emotion rose, and she averted her face so he couldn't see the tremble in her chin.

"I'd give anything to not have hurt you," he said quietly. "As soon as I knew you weren't a suspect, I should have told you everything. I've always had this rule about not caring. A lot of hard cases I've helped bust probably think to this day that I'm their best buddy, but I never cared. I care about you. I was selfish, telling myself I was protecting you when I was actually trying to protect myself. Look at me, Emily."

Tears battled for freedom, and she raised her eyes to the ceiling and swallowed hard to keep them at bay. She knew if she looked at him, she was lost. She grabbed the gun and fled the bunkhouse.

He called to her back, "Tell them you lost your dog."

REB STOOD AND WATCHED through the window. Emily ran onto the porch and fumbled at the door for a moment before letting herself into the house. Heavy-hearted, he dug into his pocket and brought out his keys. He'd told one final lie. When Emily made the coded call, there'd be no return call to confirm his identity. Instead, within minutes backup would arrive. He told himself the lie was for a good cause. She was too upset to trust him enough to call in the cavalry, but once the suits arrived with badges, she'd listen to them.

Copper barked. High-pitched and puppyish, it sounded like a startled yelp.

A heavy tread on the bunkhouse porch told Reb it might be too late for backup. He slipped the keys under the pillow.

Tuff Rifkin shoved open the door. It slammed against the wall. He staggered inside and swayed for a moment before standing tall. With his left hand he clutched his side over his hip. He held a .38 Colt in his right hand.

"Where's my money?" he growled.

His mass of dark curls was matted to his head. Crusted blood streaked his coat, left leg and hands. Several days' growth of beard, pale skin and sunken, feverish eyes made him look like a mad Russian monk.

Reb guessed Joey had popped off a shot before Tuff returned fire. Good for Joey.

Reb's innards drew up tight. One false step, and he'd be eating a .38 round. He nodded at the footlocker. "Looks like you're hurting. Have a seat."

As Tuff staggered to the footlocker and dropped heavily onto the lid, Reb tried to keep his mind off Emily. He imagined if she walked through the door, Tuff would shoot first and consider what he'd done later.

"I've got news for you, buddy," Tuff said. "You're a dead man."

Reb merely shrugged. "How bad are you hurt?"

"The bullet took a chunk out of my side, but it's nothing I can't handle. Don't worry, buddy, I'm not dying anytime soon." He rested his wrist on the foot rail, steadying the gun now aimed at Reb's navel. "You, on the other hand, well, enjoy life while it lasts. Ever notice how you big-city boys always underestimate us goat ropers?"

"You're the one who hired me. You trusted the sheriff."

Emily peered around the doorway, and Reb shook his head. If she got out now, she'd be safe. She slipped into the bunkhouse and silently scooped up the shotgun. Though she held the heavy weapon with sure, strong hands, her wide eyes were terrified.

With smooth animal quickness that jerked the knots tighter inside Reb, Tuff swung around, pointing the revolver at Emily. She froze with the shotgun aimed at Tuff's belly.

"Hey, little sister," Tuff said. "Got the guts to use that gun?"

"You shot Joey."

"He shot me first."

"If you kill her," Reb said, "you'll never see your money. She stashed it."

Emily gasped. "Liar! Shut up!"

Reb forced a chuckle. "He's got the drop on you, babe. You're a thief, not a killer, and he knows it. So give it up and tell him where you hid his stuff. Three million in cash isn't worth it. Take it from one who knows."

She wavered, swinging the shotgun between Reb and Tuff. Reb urged her with his eyes to play along. *Trust me,* he pleaded silently. If she didn't, he was going to watch her die.

"Your sister's one cool cookie, Tuff," Reb said, "but she let slip about seeing you stash the duffel bag. If you'd waited a day or two more, I could have weaseled it out of her. I wasn't going to rip you off."

"You liar! Shut up. I don't know anything about the money except for what Copper found."

Tuff put his left hand on the footlocker lid and pushed, wincing as he stood. He swayed, his eyes narrowed to slits. Sweat poured off his face. He turned so he could see Reb and Emily. "Tell you what, Emmy, give me my stuff and I won't shoot you. How about that, huh?"

Emily met Reb's eyes. Her glance held a flicker of understanding. "Reb is the liar." Holding the shotgun with white-knuckled hands, she backed away until she reached the wall. "I don't have your money. He does. He's been looking for months, and *he* found it. He even stole the drugs you stashed in the house."

Tuff hesitated, looking from one to the other.

"Never trust a woman, Tuff," Reb said. "She tried to buy me off with your money. She's got the rest of it hidden someplace.'' He prayed Emily had made the call so backups arrived before Tuff got his bearings.

"Button, button, who's got the button," Tuff sang softly. He advanced on Emily and grabbed the barrel of the shotgun. Sobbing, she tried to hold on, but even injured, he had a demon's power and he ripped it out of her hands. As she ran for the door, Tuff coolly fired the handgun. It blasted a hole in the wooden floor scant inches in front of her feet. She screamed, stopped in her tracks and clapped both hands over her ears.

Tuff dropped the revolver into his coat pocket. "At least Joey had the guts to pull the trigger. Where's my money, Emily?"

Reb slipped his hand under the pillow and felt for his keys. He was in an awkward position, having to reach over his left side, fearing Tuff would look his way. He understood getting shot hurt like hell, but he worried more about what might happen to Emily if he ended up dead.

Tuff pressed the shotgun under Emily's chin. "Five...four...three—"

Reb closed his fingers around the small, round key. "Shoot her, and the money's gone forever," Reb said. "She's the only one who knows where it is."

Tuff grabbed Emily by the hair, and swung the shotgun around to Reb. "What if I shoot you? Let's make a deal, Emily. How about...you give me my money, and I let him keep his face." He jerked her so hard, she stumbled to one knee.

A vehicle rumbled up the driveway. Tuff hissed a curse and dragged his sister to the door. Reb knew the visitor wasn't FBI, but the noise of the engine and

Tuff's lack of attention gave him cover to unlock the cuff on his wrist.

"Claude," Tuff said in disgust. "Maybe I'll shoot *him*. Will that make you tell me where my money is?" He pushed her through the doorway. As she scrambled to maintain her footing, Tuff smoothly raised the shotgun and fired.

Emily screamed. Reb ran to the door in time to see Paco leap out of the truck bed, slipping over the wall like a flow of black-and-white water. A huge, ragged hole marked the passenger door. Claude was nowhere in sight. Holding Emily as if her struggles affected him not a bit, Tuff aimed at the charging dog.

Reb grabbed the back of Tuff's collar and his right arm. Emily hit the porch floor and rolled. Tuff jammed his elbow backward, catching Reb in the chest, making him see stars. Reb tightened his grip, but holding on to Tuff was like holding a grizzly bear.

Paco flew onto the porch, soundlessly, fearlessly. He bit Tuff's left arm and held on. Tuff collapsed underneath Reb and the dog. With all the power in his forty-pound body, Paco worried and chewed Tuff's coat sleeve.

The world exploded in Reb's face. He knew he had fallen, and yet his entire body was numb. Up and down looked the same, and red mist shrouded his vision. From far, far away he heard Emily scream. Reb struggled through what seemed like a hundred woolen blankets.

He guessed he hadn't been hit with a shotgun round, or he wouldn't have a face left to worry about. But the world was spinning round and round. Six Tuffs rose heavily off the porch. Six Pacos charged the man. Tuff swung the gun like a baseball bat, catching the dog in the ribs, sending him rolling off the porch.

In slow motion Reb rolled to his belly and placed his hands beneath him. Raising the shotgun, Tuff turned, smiling dead-eyed at Reb.

Ah, Emily, I'm sorry...

Tuff grunted, staggered and dropped the shotgun. It hit the porch with a bouncing clatter. Eyes wide, Tuff looked at the dark stain spreading below his shoulder. He stumbled against the wall, and his legs folded. He dropped to his knees, then pitched forward onto his face.

Sitting up, holding Reb's .22 pistol with a thin curl of blue smoke wisping from the bore, Emily met Reb's eyes.

"You're hurt," she said.

"Yes, ma'am," he replied, and a curtain closed over his mind.

Chapter Sixteen

Alone in a private room of the Humbolt hospital, Reb tried to sleep. He wanted to sleep, he craved sleep, Dr. Nelson had ordered him to sleep but anger kept him awake and brooding. He glared at the white walls.

To say the debriefing with his boss hadn't gone well was an understatement. Reb had been accused of acting like a free-lance mercenary, the worst kind of hotshot, and of treating the investigation like a personal vendetta. It was all true—Reb blamed himself for not foreseeing Mullow's intention to rip off the arms dealers in the first place.

The boss had also accused Reb of getting personally involved with possible suspects. Ha! Falling so madly, deeply in love that it skewed his judgment was more serious than mere personal involvement. Even worse, Reb had ignored procedure and endangered civilians. Nevertheless, Reb wouldn't be brought up on charges. After all, nobody had gotten killed, Reb had gathered enough evidence to put Tuff away for life— if Tuff survived the wounds inflicted by his siblings— and they'd recovered the money.

Agents armed with federal warrants had descended on the local sheriff's office. After finding ten thousand dollars locked inside a desk drawer, they'd arrested Deputy Tim Patterson. He'd confessed, leading them to the rest of the money he'd stashed in his garage. Tuff had made the mistake of bribing the deputy when he'd first been arrested. Through bulletins the office had received, which Patterson had never shared with Mickey, Tim had put two and two together and figured out Tuff had been involved with Mullow. He'd allowed Tuff's escape, but after the storm, Tim had looked one more time and found the money.

In spite of how things had turned out, Reb had quit his job.

Without a word the old man had left. Reb supposed his boss meant to give him time to heal, cool his temper and reconsider any hasty career moves. The first two would definitely occur; he wasn't so sure about the third.

A soft knock turned his attention to the door.

Emily entered the room. She wore a dark blue chenille sweater, and her hair was swept up in a twist. It was a different look for her, sophisticated and nice. She was so beautiful, his chest ached. She sat on a chair next to the bed. Her large eyes were solemn and dark with fatigue. Her perfect face seemed carved from pale marble. He mentally urged her to smile.

"How do you feel?" she asked.

From the neck up he felt as if he had a gigantic toothache. He opened his mouth to say he felt okay. Getting slammed in the forehead with the butt of a shotgun wasn't all that bad. But his lies had done her enough damage, and he hadn't the heart for even a little white fib. "Have to get better to die," he said.

Her fingers twitched as if she wanted to touch him, but her hands remained on her lap, holding her purse. "That's what Joey says about his head, too. Dr. Nelson is discharging him. I'm going to take him home now."

"Did my boss talk to you?"

"He told me everything. He said they found the money. Tim Patterson had it. There are still a bunch of agents at the ranch. They're using dogs to search for Mullow's body." She lifted her gaze to the ceiling. "Mickey is really upset. The press is making him look really bad for not believing me. He won't talk to me."

"What about Tuff?"

"They transported him to a hospital in Denver, but he's got an infection in his bloodstream. Nobody thinks he'll make it." She lowered her face and pressed a hand to her eyes. "I still can't believe I shot him. But he was going to kill you. I *had* to."

"I'm so sorry, Emily. I messed up—"

"I'm not blaming you. Tuff has always been dynamite, looking for a fuse. Besides, you saved Joey's life, and that's all that matters anyway."

Despite her reassuring words, she wouldn't look him in the eyes. Her stiff posture rebuffed him.

When he reached for her, her fingers tightened on her purse. He lowered his hand to the bed. "How about you, Emily? Are you okay?"

She gave his question some consideration before slowly shaking her head. "I'll live."

"You're mad at me."

She rose and backed away from the chair, holding her purse to her breast like a shield. "I have to go. Joey's waiting. I'm glad you're okay."

"Don't go. We have to talk."

"Goodbye, Reb." She turned for the door.

"I love you."

She glanced over her shoulder. Tears glazed her eyes. "I don't even know who you are." She walked out of the room, and the door closed gently behind her.

EMILY HELD on to the saddle horn as Strawberry trotted toward the mailbox. It had snowed like crazy for two weeks, dropping three feet of snow in the valley and piling drifts in some places up to eight feet high. Emily felt as if she'd been cooped up in the house for months. Today was gorgeous, picture-postcard perfect without a cloud shadowing the sky, snow-draped mountains and trees cloaked in fluff. The temperature hovered around freezing, but the sunshine was bright and warm.

Head down, his face sporting a frosty beard, Copper followed rabbit tracks. Strawberry pranced through a snowdrift. She hopped friskily and shook her head.

"Hey, hey. Be a good girl, and I'll give you some sugar in your Christmas stocking," Emily promised.

A pretty blue spruce reminded her of the tree she'd put up for Joey. She'd gone whole hog this year, ferreting out every Christmas ornament and light she could find and putting up an eight-foot-tall tree. She'd been baking for weeks. Cookies, fruitcakes, fancy breads, even a chocolate Yule log with marzipan animals. Joey had yet to show the slightest interest.

She was worried about him. He'd recovered from his bullet wound, and they'd finally managed to talk about Grandpa, the ranch and even her marriage to Daniel. Joey agreed to start school in January; she promised to stay until he could manage the business end of ranching. They'd made their peace, but he had yet to make peace with himself. He blamed himself for Tuff's death even though the bullet wounds hadn't killed him directly. If Tuff had received medical care when first shot, he'd have lived.

Strawberry neighed. Emily saw Claude Longo riding down the road. His erect carriage on the saddle made it hard to imagine in less than a month he'd have his seventy-seventh birthday.

She reached the mailbox and raised a hand in greeting.

"Hoping for Christmas cards, girl?" He stopped his horse. Behind him Paco sat in the snow, gazing suspiciously at Emily. Tuff's vicious blow had broken the dog's ribs and punctured one of his lungs. He'd healed completely, and Emily was glad. Paco wasn't nice, but he was a good dog.

She looked around for Copper. He'd disappeared. The coward.

She leaned in the saddle and opened the mailbox. The postal carrier had left a goodly haul of catalogs and brightly colored envelopes. She sorted through them, hoping to find something from Reb.

A pang squeezed her heart. After his release from the hospital, he'd gone away. She didn't know where, and pride wouldn't allow her to ask any of the FBI agents. She kept telling herself she was glad he'd left. He was a liar and he'd hurt her and betrayed her. The only time he'd told the truth was when he said he wasn't good enough for her.

One of these days she'd stop loving him so she could hate him.

She handed over Claude's mail.

"That mare's purebred Appy even if you can't tell by looking," Claude said. "Might be worth the risk taking her to stud. Could get a nice foal out of her."

"Really?" She patted Strawberry's neck. Her winter coat was as thick and soft as wool.

"She comes from good stock. Her granddaddy was a champion." His weathered face darkened and he tugged at his hat brim. "I always say, there's some worthwhile in everything. Just have to open your eyes and look for it."

He was actually being nice to her, she thought, stunned. "You know best."

"You betcha I do. I'm thinking you, me and Joey should put our heads together. I've got some ideas about breeding horses. Might bring in a few extra dollars."

Joey drove up the road. She squinted at his truck. Sunshine reflected off the windshield, hurting her eyes. She expected him to stop and say hello to Claude, but he thundered past, his wheels throwing slush. He carried a large box tied down in the truck bed.

"That's a fine howdy-do," Claude grumbled, stuffing his mail inside his coat. "You need to knock some manners in that boy's head."

"I'm trying. See you." She turned Strawberry for home. "Oh, by the way, I made another gingerbread cake."

Claude's pale eyes lit up with interest. "Lemon sauce?"

"Of course. If you aren't too busy this evening, drop by and have some with us."

"If I find a minute, I just might do that."

By the time she reached the house, Joey had unloaded the box from his truck. Muddy footprints tracked up the porch steps and into the house. She dismounted and tied Strawberry to the porch railing.

"Joey? What are you doing?" She wiped her feet on the mat before she entered the house.

Joey had carried the box into the kitchen and set it near the sink. He used her best paring knife to saw through the cardboard.

"That's my good knife!" She tore at her coat buttons.

He grinned, his eyes sparkling mischievously. Caught off guard, enchanted, unable to remember the last time he'd smiled like this, she drew her head aside. "What are you up to? What is that?"

"Merry Christmas, Emmy. It's for you."

She peeled off her coat as she stared at the box. Blue-and-white printing proclaimed it an automatic, contained-unit dishwasher. Tears rose in her eyes.

"Now don't start blubbering. It's just a dishwasher."

Scarcely daring to believe her eyes, she cautiously approached the box. "A dishwasher. You brought me a dishwasher. Oh, Joey, thank you. This is the best present ever."

Still smiling, he looked past her. "It's not exactly my idea. Only half of it is from me."

She turned around. Reb Tremaine was leaning against the wall behind the door. Time froze as she stared at him. Despite the red scar running horizontally across his forehead, he looked handsome and self-assured. The dark-blue-and-red flannel shirt he wore was open at the collar, revealing the neck of a white T-shirt. His blue, blue eyes regarded her gravely.

"I'll leave you two alone," Joey said, and slipped out of the kitchen.

The old clock ticked loudly, and as the seconds flew by, she grew aware of standing like a dummy with her mouth hanging open. She gave herself a shake. "What are you doing here?"

"Brought you a present."

She stepped away from the box. "You shouldn't have."

"Do you still hate me?"

She wanted to hate him; she should hate him. She even opened her mouth to tell him she did indeed hate him and he should march his lying self right off this ranch. Words refused to form.

"I have something to show you." He held up a large white envelope. He dumped the contents on the table-top. "Will you look?"

She sank onto a chair. She'd missed him with a pain as great as her grief at losing Daniel. Not a day passed when she hadn't longed for him. Not a night passed when his beautiful eyes hadn't filled her dreams. Despite his lies, she loved him with all her heart.

She could no more stop loving him than she'd willingly cut off a hand.

Trusting him, though...

He placed a birth certificate in front of her. "John William Tremaine, born March 29, 1964. That makes me an Aries if you're into that kind of thing. Mom called me Johnny Reb. The 'Reb' handle stuck. No one except schoolteachers ever called me John." He handed over papers and photographs one by one. "Report card from the sixth grade. See, straight A's in the third quarter. Here's my honor-roll certificate. I did well enough in high school to win a scholarship, but that's the only time I pulled straight A's.

"And this is my shot record. I hate needles, they give me the creeps. The first time I ever gave blood, I passed out." He winked at her. "That's my deepest, darkest secret."

He held up a photograph and pointed to the people depicted. "Here's me and Aunt Becky and my cousins Kathy and Virginia. I lived with Aunt Becky for a while." He pulled out a chair and sat. "And this was my high school sweetheart, Yvonne. We were steadies for two years, but she dumped me after the junior-senior prom." He nodded solemnly. "She never returned my letterman's jacket."

"I'm sorry," Emily said.

"That's life. Here's my degree from Arizona State. Agricultural sciences with a minor in business administration."

Emily dropped the papers and photographs on the table. He sat so close she could smell him. He no longer smelled like a cowboy, but she recognized him all the same. Her insides tightened. Every breath caused sweet pain. "What is all this?"

"Me," he said. "Who I am." He picked up the photograph of his aunt and cousins, and his eyebrows knitted together. "I've been undercover so long I forgot who I was, too. So I quit my job. No more lies. No more pretending. No more lowlifes and hard cases and targets. Just me."

Unable to bear his gaze, she idly slid the photographs and papers into a pile.

"All I've thought about is you. How good we were together. It didn't feel like pretending because we weren't pretending. I love you, Emily. Give me a chance to prove it.''

I love you....

"Look at me.''

She lifted her face. He'd cut his hair, so it was shorter on the sides and top. The classy cut suited him. Despite the flannel shirt and blue jeans he wore, he no longer looked like a cowboy. He smiled and her heart melted.

"I never thought about my life before. What it meant, where I wanted it to go. I thought a paycheck was enough. It's not.''

"What is enough, Reb?''

"You.'' He picked up both her hands and brought them to his mouth. He kissed first one then the other. "God, I've missed you. I never knew I had it in me to miss someone so much. Or to love anyone as much as I love you.''

She knew he spoke the truth. Naked truth, his heart laid bare and vulnerable.

She also knew she'd always love him, and what had happened in the past would remain the past and could be forgiven. Something warm burst inside her chest, filling her with joy. All the sadness and grief of the past months fell from her shoulders like sun-warmed snow off a pine tree branch.

"If I give you another chance, what do you intend to do?''

He cupped her chin in his large, strong hand and drew her close. "Whatever you want, ma'am,'' he whispered silkily. He kissed her, a gentle press of lips to lips, a kiss of hope and promises. "Whatever you say.''

REBECCA

43 LIGHT STREET

YORK

FACE TO FACE

Bestselling author Rebecca York returns to "43 Light Street"
for an original story of past secrets, deadly deceptions—and
the most intimate betrayal.

She woke in a hospital—with amnesia...and with child.
According to her rescuer, whose striking face is the last
image she remembers, she's Justine Hollingsworth. But
nothing about her life seems to fit, except for the baby
inside her and Mike Lancer's arms around her. Consumed
by forbidden passion and racked by nameless fear, she
must discover if she is Justine...or the victim of some mind
game. Her life—and her unborn child's—depends on it....

Don't miss *Face To Face*—Available in October, wherever
Harlequin books are sold.

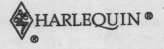

HARLEQUIN ®

®

43FTF

Merry Christmas, Baby!

A romantic collection filled with the magic
of Christmas and the joy of children.

SUSAN WIGGS, Karen Young and
Bobby Hutchinson bring you Christmas wishes,
weddings and romance, in a charming
trio of stories that will warm up your
holiday season.

MERRY CHRISTMAS, BABY! also contains
Harlequin's special gift to you—a set of
FREE GIFT TAGS included in every book.

Brighten up your holiday season with
MERRY CHRISTMAS, BABY!

Available in November at
your favorite retail store.

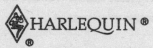

HARLEQUIN ®

A brutal murder.
A notorious case.
Twelve people must decide
the fate of one man.

Jury Duty

an exciting courtroom drama by

Laura Van Wormer

Struggling novelist Libby Winslow has been chosen to sit on the jury of a notorious murder trial dubbed the "Poor Little Rich Boy" case. The man on trial, handsome, wealthy James Bennett Layton, Jr., has been accused of killing a beautiful young model. As Libby and the other jury members sift through the evidence trying to decide the fate of this man, their own lives become jeopardized because someone on the jury has his own agenda....

Find out what the verdict is this October at your favorite retail outlet.

 MIRA The brightest star in women's fiction

MLVWJD

Look us up on-line at:http://www.romance.net